PRAISE FOR *PRETEND I'M DEAD*

A BEST BOOK OF THE YEAR ACCORDING TO *REFINERY29*,
O, THE OPRAH MAGAZINE AND *KIRKUS REVIEWS*

'One of the funniest, most twisted and freshest things I've read in a long time... Beagin combines deep compassion and irreverent humour to create characters with nasty, wonderful, human flaws.'
Observer

'It's Mona's ballsy, kickass voice that makes this novel tick. Unreliable, sharply observant and funny.'
Daily Mail

'Where *Eleanor Oliphant Is Completely Fine* leads, Beagin's offbeat debut follows.'
Sunday Times

'One of the most moving novels I've read all year.'
Elle

'A bright, brittle achievement.'
The Spectator

'Dark and quirky.'
Stylist

'Frank and unflinching... This book invaded my dreams, took over my conversation, and otherwise seduced me totally.'
Joshua Ferris, author of *To Rise Again at a Decent Hour*

'Scathingly funny.'
Entertainment Weekly

'Whip-smart and compassionate.'
Jami Attenberg, author of *The Middlesteins*

'Beagin's work has been compared to Denis Johnson, which is high praise indeed, and totally deserved based on this smart, funny, darkly profound debut.'
Nylon

PRAISE FOR *VACUUM IN THE DARK*

SHORTLISTED FOR THE BOLLINGER EVERYMA[?]
WODEHOUSE PRIZE FOR COMIC FICTION 2019

'Honest (sometimes brutal), compassionate and always able to pick out what's funny in the darkest spot. *Vacuum in the Dark* had me grinning in recognition and laughing even as I winced.'

Sindhu Vee, comedian and Bollinger
Everyman Wodehouse Prize judge

'By turns nutty and forlorn... Brash, deadpan, and achingly troubled, Mona emerges as that problematic friend you're nonetheless always thrilled to see.'
O, the Oprah Magazine

'Beagin's attention to interiors and dialogue is impressive and she manages to capture the intimate portraits of her characters with deft skill... For fans of Jade Sharma and Ottessa Moshfegh.'
Irish Times

'This novel is a joy: truly laugh-out-loud funny, while staying grounded and dignified, even as Mona capsizes again and again.'
New York Times Book Review

'Energetic... These adventures open up into larger questions of Mona's own stalled artistic ambitions and a reckoning with her estranged mother—issues refracted with black humour and a sense of timing that rarely slackens... The escapades are underpinned by a strong voice that seems to have seen everyone's worst, and to have nothing left to conceal.'
The New Yorker

'Sharp and superb...deadpan and savage... Beagin pulls no punches—this novel is viciously smart and morbidly funny.'
Publishers Weekly, starred review

VACUUM IN THE DARK

JEN BEAGIN

ONEWORLD

A Oneworld Book

First published in Great Britain and Australia
by Oneworld Publications, 2019
This paperback edition published 2020

ISBN 978-1-78607-735-6
eBook ISBN 978-1-78607-531-4

Interior design by Alexis Minieri

Printed and bound in Great Britain by Clays Ltd, Elcograf S.p.A.

Oneworld Publications
10 Bloomsbury Street
London WC1B 3SR
England

MIX
Paper from
responsible sources
FSC® C018072

For Maureen and Royce Branch

CONTENTS

VACUUM
IN THE DARK

POOP

IT WAS HARD, MISSHAPEN, PROBABLY HANDMADE. NUT BROWN flecked with beige. Sandalwood soap, it looked like, sitting on a porcelain plate with a peacock painted on its edge. Having just finished scrubbing the toilet, Mona grabbed the soap to wash her hands. Once wet, it fell apart and caked her fingers like clay. The stench, although vaguely sweet, brought instant tears. She blinked the tears away and peered at her hands. The beige flecks, she saw now, were undigested seeds, and something long, wet, and army green had been swirled into the middle. The green thing, whatever it was, had been binding it all together.

"Spinach," Mona gasped. "What the fuck."

"What's happening?" she heard Terry whisper.

Mona leaned against the towel rack, reeling as if she'd been punched in the face. "Someone shit in the soap dish," she said after a while.

Terry didn't say anything. Mona's upper lip was sweating. She made the water as hot as she could bear and rinsed her hands.

"I mistook it for fancy hippie soap, Terry," Mona said, and swallowed. "Like some dumbass."

"Don't panic," Terry said in her most gentle voice.

1

"My mouth feels weird," Mona mumbled.

"You needn't worry," Terry said swiftly. "You're a non-puker, right? Keep breathing through your mouth. Keep rinsing. Look for some real soap under the sink."

"Yeah, no, okay," Mona said.

In the recent past, Mona would've turned to Bob, her nickname for God, but Bob was often a flake in emergency situations. Terry would get her through this. Most days, Terry was simply a sober and inquisitive voice in her head, interviewing her about the day-to-day hassles of being a cleaning lady in Taos, but occasionally she switched roles and became something more: coach, therapist, surrogate parent. At twenty-six, Mona was a little old for imaginary friends, but Terry wasn't just anyone. She wasn't some stranger off the street. She was a real person who lived in Philadelphia. In fact, for well over a decade, on an almost daily basis, Mona had been listening to Terry on NPR.

"From WHYY in Philadelphia, this is *Fresh Air*," Terry said, apropos of nothing.

The jazzy theme song accompanied Mona's search for soap under the sink. Nothing liquid available, but there, in the back, a water-stained box of Yardley's English Lavender. She tore open the box and washed her hands vigorously, surgeon style.

"The air? Not so fresh today, Terr," Mona said.

"Is it human?" Terry asked.

Mona frowned at herself in the mirror. "I believe so."

"Could it be the dog's?" Terry asked.

The clients owned an overweight dachshund named Dinner. Dinner was a dream. This wasn't Dinner's work.

"This was human," Mona said, "and . . . hard-won, if you know what I mean."

"I don't," Terry said.

"Severe constipation," Mona said. "That's what this person suffers from."

"Among other things, obviously," Terry said gamely.

Why hadn't she smelled it right away? Well, because it was old, that's why. Three days old, perhaps four.

"What are you going to do?" Terry asked, sounding worried.

Mona didn't answer. There was still a little shit in the soap dish. Now that his beautiful feathers were soiled, the painted peacock did not look so serene. He looked startled and insecure. Part of her wanted to smear the remaining shit on the mirror. She could draw a heart with it, and then add some wings, and top it with a halo. Feces graffiti. Then she would leave the house and never look back.

Instead, she upended the dish over the toilet and flushed, and then swabbed everything with diluted bleach.

"You just flushed the evidence," Terry said, and sighed. "Nice work."

"This isn't TV, Terry," Mona said patiently. "I can't send it to the lab for testing. I can't dust it for fingerprints."

"Who do you think did this?" Terry asked, bewildered.

"Who knows," Mona said.

Actually, Mona had a couple of theories, but she wasn't ready to share them just yet.

"Someone from the party?" Terry offered.

One of the owners was a therapist and had conducted a group therapy session in the living room the previous evening. Mona hadn't been there, of course, but they'd left pamphlets and pretzels everywhere, and a big white board with a bunch of crap written on it, like "Location/ Occasion" and "Pleasant Childhood Memories" and "Open-Ended Questions."

"Maybe you should write your own note on the whiteboard," Terry suggested. "Such as, 'Whoever shit in the soap dish owes me two hundred fifty dollars.'"

Mona examined the porcelain sink. There was an exciting new rust stain near the drain. From her cleaning bucket she removed a bag of cut lemons and a jar of sea salt. She sprinkled a generous amount of salt onto half a lemon, which she then rubbed over the rust. The stain disappeared in seconds.

"Maybe you don't give a shit," Terry said, and chuckled at her own joke.

Mona shrugged. She didn't want to discuss it any further, as she already knew that she wouldn't bring it up with the owners. No one was home, anyway, and she was almost finished here—she'd saved the guest bath for last. Besides, what was she going to do—wait around? Leave a voicemail?

"I just annihilated a rust stain," Mona said. "Again. I'm telling you, lemon juice and salt are the shit—"

"I don't get why you're not more freaked out," Terry interrupted. "About the . . . actual shit."

"I'm going through a breakup, Terry," Mona said.

Terry was quiet for a few minutes. Mona polished the faucet with Windex and a dry rag.

"I didn't know you were in a relationship," Terry said finally.

"It was short-lived," Mona said. "And disturbing."

"Big surprise," Terry said.

"Anyway, if I say something, they win," Mona said. "So, I'm letting this one go. But it's good to know you're not squeamish about this sort of thing, Terry. You handled that like a trouper. I don't know about you, but I feel like we're even closer now."

Terry made no comment, which was fine. It was after five o'clock and she probably had better things to do. Despite the late hour, Mona went to town on the outside of the toilet, polishing all of its parts with 409, including the often-overlooked bolt covers.

THE FOLLOWING WEEK, THREE SHITS, SAME HOUSE. THE FIRST one was in the kitchen, a small brown frown sitting on a stool.

"A stool on a stool," Mona said out loud. "Wow."

Upon closer inspection, not a frown—a smile. The thing had teeth, or at any rate, here and there something hard and white. She took a photograph of it, and then held her breath as she picked it up with a paper towel. It was a long walk to the toilet.

The second was on a low shelf in the living room. This one resembled a dense, muscular finger with a swollen knuckle. The finger was pointing at a braille edition of *The Old Man and the Sea*. Again, she photographed it, and then tried to think of the significance, if any, as she carried it out of the living room, but she could barely remember the story. An old man. A young boy? The sea. A big fish. He almost dies. The End.

The third was hiding behind a potted palm in one of the guest rooms. This one was sweating. It seemed a little shy. It was as if it had been on-stage and had suffered an attack, and was now recovering in the wings. Up close, however, she saw that it was quite full of itself. It also seemed to have acne. She couldn't bear to carry it anywhere, so she tossed it out the window. Fuck it.

"Let me ask you something," Terry said suddenly. "Have you ever encountered this sort of thing as a cleaning lady?"

Terry was using her on-the-air voice, which happened about once a week. Mona gathered her thoughts as she shut the window and threw away the dirty paper towel. The only thing left to do now was vacuum.

"Well, Terr, I did find a small log in a bathtub once," Mona said, and plugged in the vacuum. "But that guy—the client—was on chemo. This was two years ago, when I first moved to Taos."

"But this is different, wouldn't you agree?" Terry said. "This is deliberate. What's the message here?"

The vacuum whined and then made a screeching noise. Something metal was trapped in the brush roller. She cut the power, flipped it, removed the bottom plate. A nickel and a paper clip fell out.

"This whole situation may be karmic, Terry," Mona said, pocketing the nickel and paper clip. She reassembled the vacuum. "Growing up in Los Angeles, my best friend in grade school was this girl named Penny.

She was an extrovert, a great kisser, and, as I recall, a pretty good gymnast. At recess, she would drag me to the restroom to watch her take a dump right *next* to the toilet. I either gagged and almost puked, or laughed so hard I pissed myself. Afterward, we hid outside and waited. Penny did this sort of thing wherever we went. She pooped on doorsteps, in driveways and gazebos. At parties, she pooped in closets. She pooped in dressing rooms at the mall. I liked to think of it as performance art, and myself as an artist's assistant, but then Penny pooped at summer camp, in the middle of the stream where everyone bathed and drank water, and I realized that Penny was not an artist. She was a terrorist."

"And you were an accomplice," Terry said after a pause.

"I suppose that's right," Mona said.

"Do you know what became of her?"

"Yes," Mona said. "She became Scarlett Johansson."

Terry chuckled softly.

"No, but I wonder about her," Mona said. "I bet she's a Hollywood producer or a lawyer or a plastic surgeon or something."

"Don't be offended," Terry said, "but any way this is all in your head?"

"The shits are real, Terry," Mona said. "They have heft. They engage all the senses."

"Start keeping a record of some kind," Terry suggested, as Mona finished vacuuming. "Indicate the time of day, the location, plus a brief description, and maybe include a drawing."

Not a bad idea. It could be a kind of art project. In a notebook, she might write something like: *Possible suspect: Chloe, daughter, age seventeen, artist. Room: neat as a pin. Keeps diary, decent writer. Favorite movie: Donnie Darko.*

MONA HEADED HOME. SHE LIVED IN ONE HALF OF A HUNDRED-year-old adobe ranch house on the edge of a valley. An older married couple rented the other half. Nigel was a British man in his forties; his wife, Shiori, was Japanese and half his age. They made music with homemade instruments and dressed in matching pajamas. They'd moved to Taos from Indonesia where they'd spent twelve years meditating and gazing into each other's eyes, and had maintained a willful and near-total ignorance of popular culture. They had no idea who Philip Seymour Hoffman was and didn't care, and had never read a book published after 1950. In some ways, they reminded her of John and Yoko, but, as they were both terrible musicians, she called them Yoko and Yoko. They occupied the front of the house, which was all sunshine and flowers, and had a large yard, a paved driveway, and south-facing windows, while Mona lived in the back, in perpetual shade and darkness, and had to sleep with a hair dryer in the winter.

When she pulled into the driveway, they were standing on her porch in their traveling pajamas. They were often waiting for her when she came home, but Nigel was peering into her kitchen window, which was unusual. She cut the engine, opened the truck door, and asked if everything was okay.

"We're on our way to a meditation retreat," Shiori said, "but we thought we heard a dog barking in your living room."

Six months later and they were still bringing up George.

"My dog is dead," Mona said.

"It didn't sound like your dog," Nigel said patiently.

"Big," Shiori said. "It sounded big. Like a wolf."

Mona pulled out her house key. Yoko and Yoko put their arms around each other's shoulders and stepped toward her door.

"Guys, I've had a weird day," Mona said. "Not sure I'm in the mood tonight." She watched them look sideways at each other. "No offense," she added, uselessly. They were never offended by anything she said. She both loved and despised this about them. "But let me get your take on something. I keep finding little shits in this house I'm cleaning. Human shits left around on purpose. It's obviously one of the inhabitants of the house, but what would compel someone to do that? In their own house?"

"Rage," Shiori said, after a pause.

"It's . . . aggressive," Nigel agreed slowly. "I would say this person feels trapped or caged and is very angry about it."

"But one of the shits was on a stool," Mona said. "A stool on a stool—get it? That seems sophisticated and somewhat playful, no? Maybe this person just has a fetish for pooping in weird places."

"Well, then it must be someone who doesn't live in the house," Nigel said. "Your own house is not a weird place, is it?"

Yoko and Yoko smiled smugly.

"Anyway, that's my two cents, as it were," Nigel said nasally.

"I'm going to take your two cents and rub them together," Mona said, "while I watch TV."

They took a step back. Television was kryptonite for Yoko and Yoko. They refused to enter her side of the house unless she covered the entire set with a heavy blanket.

"Would you like us to wait here while you check for the dog?" Shiori asked.

"I don't hear any barking," Mona said. "So, I don't think Cujo's inside."

"Cujo?" Nigel asked.

"Stephen King," Mona sighed. "Never mind."

ALMOST THREE WEEKS LATER, MONA WAS SWEEPING THE KITCHEN floor of the shit house. The shits had vanished. Christmas was around the corner. Dinner was a little fatter; Mona was bloated and about to bleed. Her primary happiness that day was her new broom. Among her favorite sounds in the world: stiff cornstalk bristles on a hard surface. She was in the middle of telling Terry how important it was not to sweep like a gringo. "White people are terrible sweepers," she was saying. "They don't know how to caress the floor with the bristles, how to coax the crumbs from under the—"

"But aren't you a white person?" Terry interrupted.

"Yeah, but I don't sweep like—wait, is that a rum ball?"

There'd been rum balls in the fridge the previous week. Buttery, chocolatey, not too sweet. She'd checked the fridge first thing that morning, hoping for more, but they were gone. Someone must have dropped this one. The Last Rum Ball.

"Should I eat it off the floor?" she asked Terry.

"Why not," Terry said. "You ate all that candy corn off the carpet at the Shaws' last month."

Mona picked it up—slightly deflated, but otherwise perfectly intact—and squished it lightly between her fingers.

"That's not a rum ball," she heard Terry say.

Mona dropped it as if it had bitten her.

"I think you might need glasses," Terry suggested.

"Fuck," Mona said out loud.

She scanned the floor—no other turds. Just this little one at her feet and now some shit on her fingers, which she absentmindedly wiped on her favorite apron.

"'Turd' is perhaps the wrong word," Terry said calmly. "Turds are curved."

"What would you call this?" Mona asked.

"Poop," Terry said.

The poop was upsetting, no question. More upsetting, perhaps, than the previous poops, because, like an all-purpose idiot, she'd mistaken it for something sweet and delicious. Perhaps she should leave it on the floor for some other fool to deal with. She asked herself what a healthy, well-adjusted person would do.

"They would call the owners and complain," Terry answered.

"Hmm," Mona said.

"Where's the dog?" Terry asked. "You might bring him in for questioning."

"Dinner!" Mona shouted. "Come!"

Dinner padded into the kitchen from his nap in the living room. His ears were inside out. She rubbed his head, righted his ears, and then pointed at the poop.

"Din-Din, is this yours?" she asked. "Did you do this?"

He approached it, took a tentative sniff, and sneezed. He made steady eye contact with her and then abruptly left the kitchen.

"Wasn't him," Mona told Terry.

Mona scrubbed her hands at the sink. The bogus rum ball she covered with a paper towel and tossed into the trash. Someone had wanted it to resemble a rum ball and strategically placed it under the cabinets. Was this same someone watching her right now? But where was the hidden camera? In the cabinets, or maybe embedded in the ceiling. She imagined the view from above. There she stood, in her shitty apron, gazing at the trash, lost in her stupid thoughts. Then she pictured herself as a grainy, black-and-white figure on a tiny screen. But who was watching this screen?

"We can rule out the lady of the house," Mona said finally.

"Why's that?" Terry asked.

"She's blind," Mona said.

MONA HAD MET THE HOMEOWNER SIX MONTHS AGO WHEN things weren't going so good. Her only friend, Jesus, had moved hours away and three of her best clients had sold their houses. In her grief, she'd contracted an existential flu. This one had been hard to shake. The blood vessels in her eyes kept bursting, an unbearable scalpy smell lingered in her nostrils, and her insides felt dirty and ravaged. For the first time in her career, she'd canceled her clients for the week, and for three days she didn't see or speak to anyone, not even Yoko and Yoko or Terry Gross.

On the morning of the fourth day, she remembered drinking Pepto Biz from the bottle while reading the quote taped to the refrigerator: "The cure for anything is salt water: sweat, tears, or the sea." Isak Dinesen, author of *Out of Africa*, which she'd never read. The movie, however, was among her favorite period dramas to blubber over. But, as was her custom, only during her period. Still, she decided to take the woman's advice. The sea was off the table, obviously, so she would try tears and sweat, possibly simultaneously.

The tears did not come easily. She gnawed on her hand and produced a few drops of salt water, but, strangely, only out of one eye. The self-pity she felt at having to chew her own flesh made the other eye water. She stuck her head in the closet and cried. It had always been easier to cry in confined spaces. Closets, shower stalls, certain compact cars. She wept silently with her head in the shirt section of her hanging clothes. *You're okay, cookie, you're okay*, she told herself. *There, there, cookie, let it out.*

She'd never called herself cookie before.

Later, seeking salt water from sweat, she'd forced herself to run laps at the high school track. The place was deserted and dimly lit. She ran holding her tits to her chest, as the only bra she owned was an ancient padded thing with loose straps. Someday, and soon, hopefully, she could buy a real sports bra. Cupping her chest was a little like running in handcuffs, but obviously preferable to her tits flopping around.

She wasn't running so much as trudging. Her so-called running shorts were high-waisted, brocade, the wrong shade of pink. Thigh-chafers. She wore her hair in two long braids, one thicker than the other, which tilted her equilibrium. Still, she managed five laps in the middle lane. When her back began to bother her during lap three, she took to skipping. Forward, backward, sideways. It slowed her down but was somehow more satisfying than jogging. In her fantasy, skipping became an Olympic sport for which she'd won the bronze. Twice.

"No gold?" Terry asked.

"If I had a sports bra," Mona said. "Maybe."

She repeated the salt water cure the following day. When she arrived at the track, a woman around Mona's age was running in the outside lane. Then Mona noticed a long white stick tipped with bright red. The woman ran with it held out in front of her. Mona squinted at her face. Those weren't sunglasses, she saw now. The woman's eyes were covered with a kind of blindfold.

"Have you ever seen a blind person run?" she asked Terry cautiously.

Terry didn't answer.

"I'll take your silence as a no," Mona said. "But let me tell you, Terry, it is *really something*. Honestly."

From the bleachers, Mona quietly watched the woman. She was a better runner than Mona, and in better shape overall. She didn't falter once, and her stick barely touched the ground. The fingers of her free hand fluttered as she ran, which Mona found endearing. Her gait was steady and confident, as if she were being pulled along by a large, invisible dog. A dog she adored and trusted completely.

"Or God?" Terry offered.

"God, dog, palindrome," Mona said.

Mona coughed loudly as the woman passed for the third time, but the woman didn't flinch. She was also about three and a half times prettier than Mona.

"Five and a half," Terry corrected her.

Mona was handsome and vaguely ethnic looking. The blind woman was not ethnic looking. Nordic, perhaps, and highly desirable to a certain kind of man. The tall, rugged, Mr. Man type. The Mr. Man type was rarely attracted to the likes of Mona, which was a shame because she was often attracted to Mr. Men.

She began a slow slog in the opposite direction. Her legs felt sluggish and unresponsive, as if she were running in a dream. She and the blind woman were alone on the track. Each time they passed each other, the woman turned toward her slightly and smiled, as if sensing Mona's unease. Her smile was a tad rapturous. It seemed to say, "I am not actually blind. I can see you perfectly. I know you're holding your tits, for example, and I think you're wonderful."

Mona smiled back nervously. She felt this way around some toddlers and dogs: convinced they knew her darkest, most corrupt thoughts. Like the urge to trip the woman and watch her fall on her face. To distract herself, she started skipping.

"There are certain types of people you encounter over and over in life," Mona mused to Terry. "Recurring types. For some people, it's drunks. For others, it's drummers. Or doctors. You know? Or redheads, chefs, amputees. People with herpes—"

"I get it," Terry said impatiently.

"For me, it's the blind," Mona said.

This was a lie. She wasn't sure why she was lying to Terry, of all people, but the concept was intriguing. She closed her eyes and continued skipping. She counted to five and was terrified, but she kept going. Then she felt something strange lapping at her ankles. A warm, knowing tongue. The tongue was doing something incredible to the backs of her knees. Now it rested in the crack of her ass. She felt suddenly and acutely blessed.

"The tongue of God," Mona announced to Terry, "is currently parked in my butt crack."

"It's euphoria," Terry explained. "Triggered by endorphins."

Mona opened her eyes, but only long enough to negotiate the corner. She continued skipping, eyes closed. She felt the woman pass her again. The tongue of God transferred itself to her brain and began licking her cerebral cortex. She laughed for several seconds. Then she found herself crying, which was just as pleasant.

"The cure for anything, it appears, is skipping blind," she told Terry.

"Doesn't sound as, uh, *insightful* as Isak Dinesen's quote," Terry said, and giggled.

It was always good to hear Terry laugh. Mona laughed, too. Then she tripped and fell hard on her right forearm and knee. Her knee was crunchy to begin with and began throbbing. Mona quickly hobbled off the track to the grassy middle. The woman slowed to a stop, ear cocked, listening for something. Coyotes? Mona listened, too. She realized the woman was listening for her. Mona.

"Hello," Mona called out. "Are you looking for me?"

The woman waved and began walking in Mona's direction, tapping her stick.

"I'm on the grass," Mona said uselessly, rubbing her knee.

Now the woman was standing too close with her face pointing the wrong way, as if examining Mona with her left ear. Her earlobe was covered in tiny hairs. Mona checked the woman's legs—same deal, only longer.

"I believe the term is 'peach fuzz,'" Terry said jovially.

It was not unattractive. In fact, it was titillating, the thigh hair in particular. It also made sense. If you're blind, are you really going to bother shaving?

"I heard you stumble," the woman said, turning to face Mona. "You okay?"

"Oh yeah, I'm fine," Mona said. "Thank you! You didn't have to stop—"

"I'm blind," the woman said quietly, and looked toward the ground. "Not deaf."

"I'm shouting!" Mona shouted.

The woman gave her an amused frown. Mona frowned back, and then kept frowning. It felt good not to have to fix her face. The woman wore the sort of blindfold one used for sleeping. An eye mask. Mona envied it for a few seconds. She wanted her own eye mask.

"It's funny," Mona said, clearing her throat. "You kept turning your head toward me when we passed each other, and for a second I thought you were checking me out."

"I was," the woman said. "I was smelling you."

Since the woman couldn't see her, Mona went ahead and sniffed her armpit. Smelled like deodorant.

"How'd you know I wasn't some creepy dude?" Mona asked.

"Dudes don't skip," the woman said. "At least, not around here. And you don't smell like a dude."

"What do I smell like?" Mona asked.

The woman seemed to mull it over while holding her stick against her chest.

"Suicide," she said at last.

Mona gulped. She'd reached a personal high of 7.8 on the Sui-Scale that very morning. The Sui-Scale was a number reflecting her desire to end her life. Like the Richter, a difference of one represented a thirtyfold difference in magnitude. She'd spent over an hour researching suicide methods on LostAllHope.com. She settled on the gas-and-bag method, which had struck her as most affordable and least messy, and which the site warned was not for gestures. Helium was the preferred gas. Mona had imagined breathing in the helium and then talking to Terry in a squeaky helium voice, the bag over her head. They called it an "exit bag," which she'd very much liked the sound of.

"What does suicide smell like?" Mona asked nervously.

For a second she expected the woman to say helium, even though helium was odorless, as were suicidal thoughts about helium. And thoughts in general.

"Strawberries," the woman said, deadpan, as if it were obvious.

Mona heard herself laugh, startled. The woman was fucking with her. As she hadn't been fucked with in forever, she'd forgotten what it felt like. It was . . . arousing.

"I'm kidding," the woman said at last. She stared absently at Mona's tits. "You smell clean," the woman said. "Not like bar soap, but like . . . something else."

"I'm probably sweating Windex," Mona said. "I'm a cleaning lady."

The woman left her mouth open when she smiled. She had the unrestrained, slightly goofy expressions of someone who'd never studied herself in a mirror.

"When I was in high school," the woman said, "my mother shot herself in the kitchen. We got a cleaning lady after that and the whole house reeked of Pine-Sol for years."

Mona glanced at her watch. Five minutes hadn't passed, yet the woman was revealing her most intimate secrets. Often, after Mona copped to cleaning toilets for a living, people took it as a cue to be candid. People probably did that with prostitutes, too. But this might have been a blind thing. Wasn't it easier to be intimate in the dark?

Or maybe this wasn't so intimate. Maybe the woman was simply from California.

"Are you from California?" Mona asked.

"Colorado," the woman said.

Close enough. In any case, there would be no need to censor herself. This was clearly someone to whom you could say pretty much anything, a quality Mona valued highly, after having spent a decade in New England.

"Sorry about your mother," Mona said. "That sounds super shitty."

"You should immerse yourself in nature," the woman advised. "You know? To counteract the cleaning chemicals."

Mona nodded vaguely, even though the woman couldn't see her. It occurred to her that there was probably a lot of talking involved with the blind. "Well, I used to take long walks in the woods. I even collected leaves at one point, but I kept . . . leaving them places."

"What about you? Are you from California?"

"Los Angeles, originally, but I was shipped to Massachusetts when I was thirteen."

"Yikes," the woman said. "Why?"

"Bad behavior," Mona said.

"What brought you here, to the high desert?" the woman asked.

"Love, sort of," Mona said. "I called him Mr. Disgusting. We met at a needle exchange in Massachusetts. He was clean when we met, but of course he relapsed six months later. In his suicide note, he suggested I move to Taos. He said he'd always dreamed of living here, in an Airstream near the Rio Grande. Except his body was never found. So, I followed his suggestion and moved here in the hopes that he was alive and waiting for me. But, he wasn't waiting. Because he's dead."

Summarizing had never been her strong suit.

"Sorry to hear that," the woman said.

Why did she look so radiant and joyful? It was more than just her skin. Was it her chin? No—it was her mouth. The corners of her mouth turned up rather than down. Mona touched her own mouth. Her corners did not turn up.

"Is there a new Mr. Disgusting in your life?" She seemed to relish saying the word "disgusting." "A New Mexican version?"

"I met someone a few months ago," Mona said. "We flirted for fifteen minutes and it felt like a carnival ride, and then he vanished and I never saw him again. I didn't catch his name, so in my mind I just refer to him as Dark."

"Was he black?" the woman asked.

Was she joking? There were no black people in Taos.

"It was more of a personality thing," Mona explained. "He wasn't dark as in dreary, though. His darkness had a spark. It had a charge you could feel on your skin."

"A dark spark," the woman said. "I know the type."

NOT EVEN TERRY KNEW ABOUT DARK. THEIR FIFTEEN MINUTES had taken place at the bookstore in town. It had been more than a few months ago—closer to six or seven. She'd been standing in one of the aisles reading a few pages of *Invitation to a Beheading*, and he'd been sitting on the floor a few feet away. He'd put aside *The Composting Toilet System Book*, finally, in favor of Thoreau, which seemed about right, as he looked like a tax resister who lived alone in the woods, in a cabin he'd built with his own hands, and he had a beard. She could smell him from where she stood. Sweat and sawdust. He kept glancing up from his reading and blinking at her. She blinked back. They did this for several minutes, and then he stood and scanned the carpet as if he'd lost something. He was one long sinew with scissor legs, and his legs scissored toward her.

"Excuse me," he'd said, "but I seem to have lost my contact, and I don't have my glasses." He pointed to his eye, which was the color of wet bark. "Do you mind checking—is it on my face somewhere?"

Searching his face felt somehow more intimate than kissing. She restrained herself from fingering his beard—she wasn't a monkey—and located the contact on the collar of his flannel. She picked it off his shirt, passed it to him like a joint, and then adjusted his collar unnecessarily. He put the contact in his mouth before placing it on his iris, and she realized she wanted to lick his eyeball. She'd never wanted to lick anyone's eyeball before. He asked her if she knew that humans used to have a third eyelid. She said no, she didn't know that.

"That's why we have this little fold in the corner," he said, and rubbed his eye. "One of our vestigial organs."

The word "LOVE," she noticed, was tattooed on the knuckles of his left hand, a letter on each digit. His other hand was in his pocket.

"Love and what," she said, and pointed to the hidden hand.

"Guess," he said.

She guessed rage, pain, sick, and hoped it was none of those.

He took his hand out of his pocket and made a fist, and then held up both fists together.

"MORE LOVE," she read, and felt herself blush.

He lowered his hands and studied her face. "You have a nice voice."

Say more about love, she wanted to say.

"You're reading Nabokov," he observed, "and wearing an apron."

Her face felt hot. She fanned herself with the Nabokov.

"Read me a sentence," he said, and scratched his beard with his MORE hand.

She scanned the open page and selected something short: " 'I suppose the pain of parting will be red and loud.' "

He had a way of smiling and frowning at the same time. "We do need to part," he said, looking at his watch. "I'm on my way to the airport."

She asked him where he was going.

"Alaska," he said, "but I'm going to think about you in your apron."

Then he plucked the Nabokov out of her hands, placed it inside his jacket, and strode out of the store.

"NOT TO PUT YOU ON THE SPOT OR ANYTHING," THE BLIND woman said, "but I'm actually looking for a housekeeper. Are you available, by any chance?"

As usual, it took Mona several seconds to recover from her Dark thoughts.

"Depends," she said at last. "How dirty is your house?"

"Don't be a dick," Terry whispered, directly into Mona's ear.

"Well, it's big," the woman said. "So, I'm always cleaning. Problem is, I'll be vacuuming in one room and then the phone will ring in the other room and so I'll answer it and talk for a while, and then it takes me an hour to find the vacuum again."

"So, you're, like, totally without sight," Mona said.

"I see patterns of light," the woman said. "Always. Total darkness is something I long for. It's what I pray for. I'd give one of my fingers for it, and two of my toes."

"I thought maybe you were an actor preparing for the role of a blind person. You know, like a Method actor," Mona said. "I don't know if anyone's told you this, but you're extremely attractive."

"Are blind people usually unattractive?" the woman asked.

As it could have passed as a rhetorical question, Mona didn't answer. She looked down at her slightly swollen knee, which had finally stopped throbbing.

"I'm a therapist," the woman said.

"Ah," Mona said.

Of course, you had to watch out for therapists. She'd cleaned house for two or three. Not only were they crazier than their patients, they'd all been chronic slobs. Same went for professors. But you couldn't be a slob if you were blind, could you? You'd never find your way out of the house.

"What do you care about?" Mona asked. "In terms of cleaning."

"Well, my old housekeeper always left grit in the bathtub," the woman said, "and a waxy kind of residue on the floors, and the counters never felt quite clean. She had a habit of not putting things back exactly where she found them, and so I would waste all this time searching for the toothpaste, or the cumin, or a dish towel. She was obsessed with bleach. *Obsessed.* So, I had to get rid of her finally."

"Did you kill her?" Mona said.

"No," the woman laughed. "Anyway, it's not about the way things *look* for me, obviously. It's about the way they *feel.*"

Mona felt an overwhelming urge to yawn, which she did, repeatedly, without bothering to cover her mouth. She almost wanted to be friends with this woman.

"What's your name?" Mona said.

"Rose," the woman said, and held out her hand.

"Pretty name," Mona said, grasping the woman's hand.

"Thank you," the woman said. "My real name is Maria, actually."

She didn't look like a Maria.

"What's your middle name?"

Because she didn't have one, asking people their middle name was one of Mona's favorite questions.

"Well, it's funny you ask," the woman said. "My middle name is also Maria."

"So, your birth name is . . . Maria Maria?"

"My parents were drug addicts," Rose explained. "They named me after some Spanish song they were listening to while fucking."

The sexual reference put Mona further at ease. It was the same relief she felt when someone pulled out a cigarette.

"My name is Mona," Mona said.

"Is Mona your real name?"

"Yes," Mona said. "May I ask how you run without a guide? And how'd you get here?"

"I walked," Rose said. "I have maps in my head, and I do a lot of counting. I count the steps around the track, the steps down the street, then the steps to my house." She shrugged as if she'd been bragging.

"Would you like a ride?" Mona asked.

"I prefer to walk," Rose said.

Boundaries, Mona thought. Nice. Maybe she isn't totally nuts.

SHE'D NEVER SET FOOT IN A BLIND LADY'S HOUSE, BUT SHE'D envisioned something dark and dirty. Not crazy dirty, but cobwebby, at least, and dusty. She imagined mustard stains on the couch and wine spills on the rug. And there would be mold, certainly. Mold in the bathroom, obviously, and Rose's golden pubes all over the tub and floor. But what would the place *look* like?

"Fifty bucks says there's a piano," Mona mumbled as she drove up Rose's driveway for the first time.

"Right, because all blind people are piano players," Terry said. "My money is on some other instrument. The cello."

There was neither. In fact, the house was like nothing she'd ever seen in Taos, real or imagined. From the outside, it looked like two very different houses leaning against each other, back-to-back. One big, the other small. The big one was made of brick; the small one was white, weathered wood. A plaque declared it a historic house, over two hundred years old, that was once part of a ranch called Hurt.

Rose answered the door wearing a crisp red sundress. Mona stared hard at her eyes, expecting the empty eyes of a dead person—or, at the very least, cloudy and without spirit. But not only did they seem like seeing eyes, they seemed *all*-seeing, the eyes of a soothsayer or prophet. They were the most curious shade of blue Mona had ever seen. *Your eyes are nearly* purple, she wanted to say. *Are you aware of that?*

"Philip isn't here," Rose informed Mona's forehead. "So, I'll have to show you around. Might take a little longer."

"Is Philip your butler?" Mona asked.

Rose laughed. "Husband," she said. "He's at a conference in Nebraska."

Husband? Mona hadn't thought of that. She'd been looking forward to cleaning a house unseen.

"Any kids?" she asked.

"My daughter," Rose said. "Her name is Chloe. She's seventeen."

Seventeen?

"I had her young," Rose explained, reading her mind. "I was fifteen."

A teenager. Mona didn't despise teenagers, but she preferred that they not be around—ever—while she was cleaning.

The family lived on the brick side of the house. The wood side could stay untouched, as that's where she saw patients. The house had a Spanish vibe. Handmade Mexican Talavera tiles in the kitchen and bathrooms, vaulted ceilings in the hallways, arched doorways. The vast, rectangular living room had an enormous fireplace, exposed and dramatic wooden beams in the ceiling, and wide-planked pine flooring. Rose collected rare Navajo blankets, neatly folded and displayed on long shelves in the hallway. Her only ornaments were three small, identical sculptures: cast-iron crows with human heads. The sculptures seemed to function as landmarks; they were the only objects Rose touched as she made her way through the house.

Hanging over a blue velvet couch was a portrait of Rose floating on her back in a brook. She was gazing skyward and wearing a floral nightgown, her eyes as violet as they were in life.

"What are you seeing?" Rose asked. "Dirt?"

"A painting of you," Mona said.

Rose looked sheepish. "My husband painted it. He said it's not vain to hang a portrait of yourself if you're blind."

"He must really love you," Mona said. Or he might hate you, and painted your last breath before drowning.

On the pine floor lay a large flokati rug and several square pillows. On one of the pillows sat a dog named Dinner.

"He's friendly," Rose said. "You can pet him."

Mona didn't pet him, but only because she saw a loose photograph lying facedown underneath the coffee table. She picked it up. "I just found a picture on the floor," she announced.

"Who is it—Chloe?" Rose asked.

"It's a guy," Mona said. "Your husband? He's holding a hammer."

Rose stopped smiling and cleared her throat. "Could you, uh, describe him for me?" she asked.

"Well," Mona began slowly, "he has small hands. His skin is pockmarked. One of his front teeth is missing. Like I said, he's holding a hammer, but he's also wearing bronzer, along with a woman's blouse, sweatpants, and patent leather pumps."

Rose looked like she might vomit. Mona felt a stab of guilt, as the man in the photograph was obviously dead or important or both. He had soulful brown eyes and a prominent forehead vein that made her think of erections. Standing next to a woodworking bench, he looked both insanely happy and on the verge of tears. She asked who the man was.

"My father," Rose said. "I'm a little freaked out because I keep this photograph tucked away, so I'm not sure how it ended up on the living room floor."

Mona didn't know what to say. She stared at the hair on Rose's legs. So stirring and erotic. *Your leg hair is giving me a boner*, she wanted to say. She recognized in Rose that thing certain men wanted and craved. The blonde thing. The *petite* blonde thing. The delicate blonde hairs. You saw those hairs and you knew what else to expect: pink nipples, blonde pubes, a neat little box.

"What do you see when you think of the color red?" Mona asked.

"Oh, I remember red," Rose said. "I wasn't born blind."

"Oh," Mona said. "Were you . . . in an accident?"

"Sort of," she said, and smiled weakly. "I was having an affair with the man you just described."

Mona silently took a step back. She heard Dinner drink from his bowl in the kitchen.

"Do you mean your father molested you?" Mona asked.

"I thought of it as an affair," Rose said, "which sounds ridiculous and insane, but I was convinced that we were in love. I was thirteen."

"Mayday," Terry whispered. "Bail out."

"Not now," Mona whispered back.

"We never had intercourse," Rose volunteered. "It was more emotional than anything. Which isn't to say it wasn't also sexual. It was that, too."

Mona cleared her throat. "And you went blind?"

"Well, that was partly genetic," Rose said.

Mona looked toward the front door. Closed, but not locked. She imagined herself tiptoeing out of the room and then making a run for it.

"People tell you things," Rose said. "Don't they? They tell you their secrets."

"Sometimes," Mona lied.

People were vampires. Their stories drained the life out of her. Then, half-dead and bloodless, she carried on cleaning their toilets like nothing had ever happened.

"It's your voice," Rose said. "And your energy. It relaxes people so that they open up. You seem so—I don't know—*grounded*. Do you do cleaning full-time?"

Here it comes, Mona thought, the inevitable "other than" question. There was no escaping it, ever. Even a blind person would ask.

"I'm often very tired," Mona said. "Too tired to talk. So, I listen. Also, I'm a writer."

Her new answer to the what-else-do-you-do. She'd only used it three times, so it was still in the testing phase, but so far it seemed easier to tell people you were a writer than an artist. People wanted to see your photographs and paintings. They wanted a look. But they had no interest in reading your writing. None whatsoever. Although, she supposed this wouldn't apply to Rose.

"What do you write?" Rose asked.

"Epic novels," Mona said. "They're kind of plotless and . . . what's the word? *Episodic*."

Actually, clandestine photography was her primary focus. Typically, she'd complete one of her specialized tasks first—removing smudges from walls and light switch plates, crumbs from silverware drawers, wax from candlestick holders, hair from hairbrushes—before searching their closets, and then she dressed in a hurry, not bothering with hair or makeup. She photographed herself wearing ball gowns or cocktail dresses or whatever else caught her eye—a printed silk blouse, a kimono, a mink stole, a Davy Crockett hat. Lingerie and wedding dresses were off-limits. She could already see herself sitting on Rose's blue Chesterfield sofa, wearing Rose's red garments, holding one of the cast-iron crows in her hand. Perhaps Dinner would be on her lap. Or, better, lying on one of the Navajo blankets.

"I've always wanted to write a memoir," Rose said then.

This was the only problem with the new answer. It invited people to tell her why they thought they were fascinating individuals. Though this also didn't apply to Rose, since she was, in fact, fascinating.

"Maybe you can be my ghostwriter," Rose said.

"Oh yeah? Let's talk about it while I clean the kitchen," Mona suggested, and got to her feet.

Outside, a blue truck coasted into the driveway.

"My first client," Rose said, and stood up. "Unfortunately, I have to go. When you're finished, just call me and I'll come over and pay you."

THE NAME GRACE HAD BEEN WRITTEN, PAINTED, AND GOUGED all over the house. She found Grace on the legs of tables, along the seams of lampshades, on the walls behind hanging textiles, on the labels of

Rose's collared shirts, on the edges of pillowcases and picture frames. Grace was etched below the seat of a chair, knifed into a ceiling beam, and scratched into the mirror in the entryway. The tags varied in size, but most were small and difficult to find.

"Might this be the strangest thing you've ever found in a house?" Terry wondered.

"It's definitely up there," Mona said.

Her heart jumped with each new discovery, and the mystery deepened. In the six hours it took to finish the job, she'd found and photographed thirty-eight Graces.

"I have to tell you something," Mona said to Rose as she was getting ready to leave.

"Someone named Grace tagged your entire house. I've never seen anything like it, and I've been doing this a long time."

"Oh yeah," Rose said casually. "Those are from last year."

"You know about it?"

"It's kind of a long story," Rose said, and stifled a yawn. "At first, we thought it was Grace herself, who was a patient of mine for three years. Grace was the daughter of my former cleaning lady—"

"The one obsessed with bleach?" Mona asked.

"Yes," Rose said. "We figured it was Grace because she had her mother's keys, but the funny part is, it turned out to be Chloe."

"Your daughter?"

"I think she was jealous of all the attention I'd been giving Grace. I saw Grace several times a week, and we became very close. Grace and Chloe are the same age and in the same classes at school, and I think it was hard for Chloe, seeing as she's an only child—"

"But did Chloe confess?" Mona asked.

"No," Rose said. "She maintains she had nothing to do with it. But it resembles her handwriting. And Grace just wasn't the type to do something like that, to write her own name all over the place. This was the work of an artist. Like Chloe."

"Hmm," Mona said.

Rose tilted her head. "You sound . . . dubious," she said, and smiled. "You think it was Grace?"

"No," Mona said, and shook her head.

"Philip?"

"I'm pretty sure it was the cleaning lady," Mona said.

Rose laughed. "Speaking of which." She handed Mona a wad of cash. "It smells really great in here. Thank you. Was it very dirty?"

"The dirtiest thing was the inside of the microwave," Mona said. "Which, by the way, is best cleaned by wetting a sponge with lemon juice and water and then microwaving the sponge for two minutes. The acid and steam loosen all the food. You wait for the sponge to cool and then you wipe everything down."

"Wow," Rose said. "Okay."

Mona counted the cash. Rose had overpaid her. A test, perhaps.

"There's sixty bucks extra here, Rose," Mona said.

"It's compensation," Rose said, "for the therapy you gave me earlier. The photograph of my father startled me, and you listened to my story without judgment."

Oh, I was judging you, Mona thought. Don't worry. Rose's mouth hung open. She wanted something. Did she want to touch Mona's face, like blind people did in the movies?

"Do you think we could be friends?" Rose asked instead. "I don't know if you hang out with your clients, but I feel close to you, for some reason."

Before she could answer, Rose asked for a hug. Mona obliged. Rose really got in there, wrapping both her arms around Mona's torso, breathing her in deeply before letting go. Mona had always been a fan of a firm embrace. As a friend, would Rose act like a vampire? Did she want blood? *Here*, Mona imagined saying, offering Rose her wrist. *Drink*. If the blood sucking became too much, Mona could always just walk out the door, unseen, and Rose might never find her.

SHE MET ROSE'S HUSBAND, PHILIP, TWO WEEKS LATER. SHE'D just finished cleaning the house. Rose was out of town. Alone in the kitchen with her eyes closed, Mona ran her hands over all the surfaces.

"Hello," a voice said, as she was feeling the fridge.

She opened her eyes, startled.

"Were you pretending to be blind?" he asked.

A shirtless man stood at the counter. His shoulders red from the sun, he wore dirty white trousers and gum-sole desert boots. This must be Philip, the husband.

"Yes," she admitted.

He opened a cabinet. Out came a bag of coffee and the dreadful coffee grinder. She winced inwardly. He would probably spill grounds on the counter and possibly the floor, and he might even fuck up the stove.

"I do that, too, sometimes," he said. "What would you rather be— blind or deaf?"

That's when she recognized him. And his smell. His hair was shorter, his beard longer, and two bandages were taped to his mostly hairless chest. The bandages were bright white, fresh.

"The way you wear that apron," he said, "makes me want to crush granite with my teeth."

If Rose drained the blood out of her, he put it all back in, and then added more. She felt pregnant, even though they'd never touched. She supposed she'd have to call him Philip now, which was absurd. He was Dark.

"It's a smock," she said.

"I've been looking for you," he said.

"Where?" she asked.

"At the bookstore," he said. "In the same aisle. On the same day of the week. At the same time."

"Which day of the week?" Mona asked.

"Thursday," he said.

"We met on a Monday," Mona said.

He snorted. "We definitely did not meet on a Monday."

"Why don't you wear a wedding band?" she asked.

He paused to scratch his beard. "Rose and I have an open marriage."

"Does she know that?"

"Are you married?" he asked.

"I don't do this with clients," she said.

They stood there, blinking at each other.

"Who do you do?" he asked finally.

"I have someone special I call now and then," she said.

He leaned on the counter. "Will you call him tonight?"

She looked at her watch and shook her head. "It's Tuesday."

"So?"

"Not on a Tuesday," she said.

He laughed. "Can you fuck him on a Friday?"

"Fridays are fine."

"What about Wednesday?"

She pretended to think about it. "Wednesdays are pushing it," she said.

"He wants you all to himself," Dark said. "Is that it? Or you don't want to be tied down."

She didn't answer. The guy tended bar at a tavern one town over, and his schedule varied. He wasn't fat, but he seemed oddly boneless—she couldn't see the bones in his hands—and he had watery eyes and his name was Doug. She could never date a Doug. She could date a Dark, though, easily. There was nothing boneless about Dark, and she suspected she'd have dropped everything for him if he wasn't married to the most interesting vampire in town. And the most beautiful.

"Are you guys swingers or something?" Mona asked.

"No," he said. "It's not like that. In fact, it's probably nothing like you think."

"What are those bandages?" she asked.

"I'd rather tell you about it at your house," he said. "How's eight o'clock?"

The kettle whistled. He snatched it off the stove and doused the grounds. She watched his hands carefully. He'd punched a lot of things in his life, but he wasn't on drugs. She could always tell by a person's hands.

"MORE LOVE," she said.

He raised his eyebrows at her. "Is that what you want?"

"It doesn't match the tone of your other work," she said, referring to the only other tattoo she could see, *A Steady Diet of Nothing*, underneath his collarbone.

"I used to starve myself, in a sense," he said. "Now I'm . . . famished."

"You're a sex addict?" she asked.

He looked confused. "Haven't you thought about me?"

She couldn't answer. She scanned the tiles around her feet. There, near the sink, she'd missed a spot of food or dirt. She would have to leave it. Something else seemed out of place, though, and she realized it was Dinner. Why was he cowering behind the recycling bin?

"I'd rather be deaf than blind," Mona said at last. "And I think about you all the time."

"Me too," he said.

He opened a drawer and took out a pen and a pad of paper. Old-fashioned.

"Write down your address," he said.

BECAUSE HE'D BEEN FORTY MINUTES EARLY, MONA HAD AN-swered the door wearing a full ivory slip beneath a long kimono with a chrysanthemum motif. Her face was masked with green clay.

"I'm slightly early," he said.

"I have clay face," she said. The mask brought out her eyes, and if she could have gotten away with wearing it all the time, she would have. "Since you're so early, help me pick out what to wear for my date."

He looked startled. "You have a date?"

"You," she said. "You're my date."

"Then don't change anything," Dark said.

He was in her living room now, sitting on her orange leather couch. He didn't look around much. She wanted him to admire her stuff: a collection of art by developmentally disabled adults, a collection of framed airline barf bags, and the series of drawings she'd made of vintage Eureka vacuums. Instead, he looked down at his feet and began unlacing his boots.

"Could you bring me a wet washcloth?" he asked.

When she returned with the wet cloth, he was barefoot and flipping through photographs of the Grace graffiti from two weeks ago.

"Cool," he said matter-of-factly.

Didn't he think it was weird, her taking photographs in his house without permission?

"There's a story behind those pictures, but I don't know what it is yet," she said.

She handed him the wet cloth and sat next to him, hoping he'd share his insights about this Grace thing, but he put the photographs aside and wiped his face.

"Thanks," he said. "I really needed this."

She laughed. Emboldened, he straddled her and then calmly and methodically removed her mask. He had a great touch—confident, a little callous—and kept his eyes open as he kissed her, alternately gnashing his teeth against hers on purpose, with just the right amount of pressure, and then sucking her lips and tongue.

"When you do that thing with your teeth," she said, "I forget my name."

"Let's go break the bed," he said.

She hesitated, but only because he would have to return to Rose. She'd never wanted anyone to stay before. She allowed herself a few soul-mate thoughts, which embarrassed her, which made her want a drink.

31

She rolled off the couch, walked to the kitchen, and opened a bottle of red.

"Or we can break . . . bread," he said, as she handed him a glass. "If you prefer. But I'd rather take you to bed."

He took a couple of tentative sips and then chugged the rest. She told him her period had started.

"Bleed on me," he said breezily, and removed his shirt.

His smell charmed her into a trance. She felt she'd do whatever he wanted, even if it was awful, disgusting, or illegal.

"Do you work with wood or something?" she asked. "You smell like a pencil."

"I make coffins," he said.

"I want to hump your armpits," she said. "And maybe your hair."

"Great," he said.

In the bedroom, she saw that his chest was covered in scars—the familiar, self-inflicted kind—but the fresh injury looked more like a puncture wound. She decided to ask later and pulled off his pants. He wasn't wearing underwear.

"Were you raised by animals?" she asked.

"French Canadians," he said.

His cock was the perfect color. So were his balls, strangely. It was like gazing at her favorite vacuum. She put him in her mouth and closed her eyes. She wondered if blind women gave better blow jobs, and were better at sex in general. Like, more sensual, more in their bodies—

"Open your eyes," Dark said suddenly.

They switched positions. He kept pinning her with his LOVE hand and doing things with his MORE hand, things that made her writhe around on the mattress, and then he'd fuck her, and then it was back to MORE LOVE. He repeated this for a long while. He made her feel beautiful and hideous, male and female, dirty and clean. He made her feel old. Not over-the-hill, but ancient and pre-human. He made her feel desperate, horny, and deranged. She betrayed her instinct to be silent.

"You make me feel . . . Spanish," she said.

His eyes smiled at her. For once she didn't laugh or look away. She held his gaze like it was a part of his body and he came thirty seconds later.

"I love your maybe-Spanish eyes," he said, catching his breath, and she wondered if that was because they were seeing eyes. "And your maybe-Spanish skin."

"What happened to your chest?"

He didn't answer at first. He rolled away to face the wall and pulled her arm around him so that she was the outer spoon. "I just got back from Sun Dance."

"The film festival?" she asked.

He laughed. "It's a sacred Lakota ceremony that takes place in Nebraska every summer."

"What sort of ceremony?"

He kissed her hand. "You dance," he said drowsily. "You dance on the open plain for four days and nights, rain or shine, without food or water. You pray, and you have visions, and at the end, you make a sacrifice. It's a four-year commitment."

Like college, she thought. She tried to visualize his dancing. It was hard. "Is it like a mosh pit?"

"You march in a circle to drums," he said. "There are no specific moves. You also spend many hours a day in a sweat lodge."

She touched the strange sores on his chest. "What are these from?"

"On the last day, a medicine man pinches the skin above your nipple—a healthy pinch, one or two inches—and pushes a scalpel through it. The scalpel is replaced with a cherrywood peg, several inches long, the ends of which are looped with rope, and you are tied up to a tree."

"A tree?"

"A young tree," Dark said.

"So, you're just hanging from a tree, twisting in the wind?"

"There's no wind," he said. "And your feet are touching the ground. You dance while attached to the tree, pulling against the ropes, and eventually, after many, many hours, you break free."

"The ropes break?"

"Your skin breaks." He took her hand and squeezed it. "Sometimes people need help breaking free, and someone will get behind them and pull."

"Did you need help?"

"No," he said.

She asked him why he participated and he told her another story. This one was a love story.

Other than Rose, he'd only been in love one other time, with an Inuit woman he'd met in Alaska many years ago. Her name was Lucinda. They met while working at a cannery in Ketchikan. He'd worked in the freezers. He rolled huge beds of salmon into the freezer on casters, and once they were frozen he'd drill a hole into them and take their temperature, and when the temperature was right, the fish would be shipped to Japan or wherever.

Lucinda weighed the salmon, though she rarely needed a scale, he said. Her hands were scales, and so were her eyes. In a glance, she could weigh and measure anything she looked at, including him. Only twenty-two and very cautious, she joined him for a drink after work or visited his boardinghouse. They didn't talk much. In fact, Lucinda often communicated in gestures he either misread or missed altogether. Her touch changed him, and slowly, over a period of many months, he fell in love. Because it was slow, his love seemed more real, and more permanent. Together they rented a cabin outside of town. She read a lot and he painted pictures and they both kept working at the cannery.

"Four months later, she fell out of a tree," he said.

"And?" she said.

"She died," he said. "In my arms."

34

She felt a sudden and familiar pain tugging her nipples from the inside. Her instinct was to cover her breasts with her hands. Instead, she lay still and imagined her chest pierced and tied to a tree. She imagined herself circling on tiptoe while pulling against the ropes, and the pain subsided a little.

"I never talk about Lucinda," he said.

"Why was she in the tree?"

"We were on mushrooms—my idea, not hers," he said. "She went to some dark, faraway place. I tried to get her down when I saw how high up she was. I started climbing. She fell right past me and landed on a jagged rock. There wasn't any blood, but she kept making these gasping noises. I panicked and carried her up a hill to the main trail. I laid her out on the trail, but she was gone by then, and I couldn't get her back."

"Were you alone?"

"I think so," he said. "I don't remember getting help, or the police coming, or the ambulance. I only remember seeing her for the last time. She was lying on a table in the hospital, and I asked everyone to leave the room so that I could be alone with her."

She waited for him to continue, but he didn't say anything. His eyes were closed and he was very still.

"What did you do?" she asked.

"She had a tube in her throat, so I removed it and threw it on the floor," he said. "Then I chewed off some of her hair because I didn't have any scissors."

There it was again, stronger, tugging hard from the inside. She felt the urge to break her skin, to give a little blood, to make her own kind of flesh offering. Ordinarily, she would have waited until he left and then she may have cut herself. But that was too easy, and too familiar, and not as satisfying as it used to be. And besides, she didn't want him to leave. Ever.

"I try to visit the tree once a year," he said. "That's where I was headed when I ran into you at the bookstore."

He kissed her and slipped his hand between her legs. She wanted MORE LOVE, but she also wanted MORE ROSE. Or maybe not MORE, but SOME.

"When did you meet Rose?" she asked.

"Three years ago," he said.

"Is Rose's father Chloe's father?" Mona asked.

He frowned. "Rose's father is in prison," he said. "He's been in prison forever."

"For pedophilia?"

"Transportation of marijuana," Dark said.

"That's it?"

"It was a ton of marijuana," Dark said. "Literally. Two thousand pounds."

"Who's Chloe's father?"

"She doesn't know," he said. "She never saw him. He was a tourist. It was a one-night stand."

"Does Rose know you're here with me?" she asked.

He nodded. "It's part of our agreement."

"Why the open marriage?"

"Rose's idea," he said. "But I'm not opposed. We're like siblings, really."

"So, no sex?" she asked.

He intuitively rested his MORE hand on her stomach, which had been in knots. "I want to hear about you now," he said. "Start at the beginning and tell me everything."

"I can't do that," she said. "It would take another three hours and would feel like the longest year of your life."

He asked for broad strokes. Perhaps he was trying to find out if she was interesting enough for him, or if she'd suffered enough.

"Well, I've never been to prison," she said. "I've never been to Europe. I've never given birth. I've never jumped out of a plane. I've never done quaaludes. I've never read Tolstoy. But I talk to Terry Gross in my head, even while I'm talking to other people, and I've been around the block a couple dozen times."

"Are you talking to Terry Gross right now?"

She shook her head. "Terry doesn't talk when you're around. She only makes noises occasionally."

"Is she making noises now?"

"She just grunted."

"Have you ever killed anyone?" he asked.

"Not yet."

"Have you been arrested?"

"Once."

"Have you been raped?" he asked.

"Twice."

He winced. "Therapy?"

"Many times."

"Have you gone under the knife?"

"Only by my own hand."

"Threesome?"

She smiled and held up one finger.

"Fallen in love?"

Two fingers.

"Pick one," he said. "And tell me the story."

She didn't want to compete with or diminish the stories he'd told, and so she opted for levity.

"Well, it's a little close to home," she said, and pointed at the brick wall in her bedroom. "The couple in question lives on the other side of those bricks. Nigel is a tall, malnourished British man in his forties, and Shiori is Japanese, so who knows how old she is, but they're like twins. I call them Yoko and Yoko."

"You fell in love with your neighbors?" he said.

"Of course not," she said. "This is the threesome story."

"Tell it slowly," he said.

She took a deep breath. "This was a few months ago, when the weather turned warm. They were weeding the garden and arguing. I was observing them from my kitchen window. They have this very deliberate way of speaking that drives me insane, and they were wearing matching linen tunics that looked like cheesecloth. Nigel resembled a large, hard piece of pecorino; Shiori, something smooth and spreadable—Brie, perhaps.

"At one point I heard a single, forlorn fart escape Shiori's square bottom, which touched my heart, and I found myself thinking about her pubic hair. In the Asian porn I sometimes watch nightly, both the men and women have huge bushes, and I wondered about Shiori. At any rate, they must have intuited something, because suddenly they were tapping on my kitchen door and asking if I wanted to join them for some 'guided meditation.' I suggested guided gin martinis instead. Shiori looked confused—she's probably never had a drop of gin in her life—and Nigel inserted a pinkie into his ear and wiggled it, which meant he wasn't in the mood for—"

"Okay," Dark said, and laughed. "Maybe not this slowly."

"Fine, I'll jump ahead," Mona said. "When I entered their side of the house, the shades were drawn and the lights were off. Their furniture had been pushed aside and they were sitting on a Turkish rug. In the center of the rug, a low table topped with a single burning candle. They sat on two pillows and invited me to sit on a third."

"Uh-oh," Dark said.

"Yeah," Mona said. "I was scared. I asked if the meditation would involve a lot of talking or measured breathing or the opening of chakras, and they assured me that it would only involve staring at the open flame, which seemed doable. They instructed me to relax my eyes and to fix my gaze on the candle. Gradually, my peripheral vision fell away, and it was just me and the candle. I had become one with the flame, and it was all I could see. It was peaceful, honestly, and I felt connected in a way I'd never experienced before. I heard Shiori's voice telling me to focus on the blue of the flame and to let the blue into my body. The blue sensation traveled up my spine and out the top of my head, and then I felt this subtle pressure on my shoulder blades and a pair of thin arms circling me. Shiori was hugging me from behind, and I could feel her breasts on my back. Then I became aware that Nigel was missing. I hadn't heard him get up, which was strange, because his bones creak. I saw that he was off in the corner, holding a dreadful bongo between his legs. I looked over my shoulder and saw that Shiori was completely naked. For over a year, I'd been fantasizing about burying my face in her boobs, and here they suddenly were, looking better than I'd ever imagined. 'Where are your clothes?' I whispered loudly. 'Are you on drugs?' Nigel said, 'We'd like to try some tantric meditation with you, if you're ready and amenable.' And I said, 'With both of you?' And Nigel said, in that deliberate way of his, 'I will remain here, in this corner.' "

"So, he just watched," Dark said. "Like a creep."

"I think he was trying to be respectful. He softly played his bongo while Shiori and I messed around on the rug. She did in fact have a tremendous bush. She let me put my face down there for about five minutes, and I swear she tasted like ginger and lychee."

Dark looked away then and closed his eyes.

"Was it racist of me to say ginger and lychee?"

"It's descriptive," he said. "I'm not sure I want to talk about pussy with you, though. I mean, not in any depth."

"Why not?"

"I don't want to be bros with you, Mona," he said.

HER APARTMENT BECAME A LOVE BUNKER ON MONDAY, TUESDAY, and Thursday nights. He brought books, booze, and weed; she supplied food and flowers. They smoked spliffs and drank bourbon in the kitchen. They ate cheese and spilled their guts. Turned out their fathers were both dreamers, drinkers, and amputees. His father had lost his foot on a fishing rig in Alaska. Her father had lost his arm in an explosion at a gas station. His father wore a fake foot. Her father, a hook.

"Did he become a pirate?" Dark asked.

"Plumber," she said.

"A hook is probably a good tool."

"He wore a hat that said, 'Plumbers Have Bigger Tools.'"

"In public?"

"Everywhere," she said. "He was a drunk, so it was often a bumpy ride, and by 'bumpy' I mean violent and vaguely pervy, but he could be good for a laugh once in a while. Before he became a plumber, he drove a truck for Frito-Lay. It didn't have passenger seats, so I had to stand in the well and try to keep my balance while he tore around the neighborhood. Once, when I was about seven, we were stuck in traffic and a cement truck pulled up next to us. The tank was painted with swirling red and white stripes. I asked what was inside the tank. 'Clowns,' he said gravely. 'That's how clowns are made.' Another time I pointed to the fuse box in our garage and asked him what the switches were for. He said they blew up the house, and to never touch them."

"Did you touch them?" Dark asked.

"Twice," she said. "And the cops came both times, and so I thought maybe that's what the switches were actually for. They brought the cops to our house."

"Who was calling the cops?"

"I think it may have been our Korean neighbor, Mr. Hwang. My father beat up my mother in the driveway once, because she was too drunk to get out of her car. It was her birthday. So, he pulled her out of the car with his good arm and kicked her toward the house, and I'm guessing the Hwangs watched the whole thing. I flipped one of the switches that night, and the cops showed up minutes later.

"Anyway, I ate dinner at the Hwangs' five nights out of seven. They got me into kimchi and fish cakes, which I still crave. The first time they served me rice, I asked for butter, salt, and pepper, and they laughed for thirty minutes. I introduced them to Ding Dongs. Their son, who was a teenager, asked me to watch him bathe once and while he was shampooing his hair, he admitted that he liked sticking golf tees up his ass."

"Your stories make my blood dance," Dark said.

"This weed is pretty good," she said.

"Would you stick a golf tee up my ass?"

"I would, actually," she said. "Take off your pants."

He unbuttoned his jeans and let them fall to the kitchen floor.

"You give my boner a boner," he said. "You fill out all the corners and edges."

The sex gave her a peculiar rush, as though his life—not hers—were flashing before her eyes. They liked to do it all over her apartment, but especially in the living room, while watching baking shows on PBS.

"You give me such *an appetite*," she said.

"For coconut cake or my cock?"

"To live," she said.

ON THEIR FOURTH THURSDAY TOGETHER, SHE INDULGED HIS apron fetish and allowed him to film her cleaning her stove in an apron and nothing else. He zoomed in on her tits as she soaked the burner grates and knobs in soapy water, and then pulled back into a wide shot when she got on her knees to wipe down the walls of the oven.

Housekeeping porn, he called it.

"If you put these videos on the Internet, it's over," she said.

He put the camera down. "I wonder how you'll write our story."

"Well," she said slowly, "I probably won't, honestly. Unless our story takes place in your house, which it can't."

His mood seemed to darken later that night. He did a little yoga, which made her uncomfortable, and then stayed in the corpse pose for over an hour, staring at the timbers in the ceiling. She tried to rouse him with fresh mango and peanut butter tacos on homemade corn tortillas, but he remained still and sullen. Not even her hands and mouth would bring him out of it. She got into the corpse pose next to him and asked if she'd done something to piss him off.

"Of course not," he said, startled. "I'm sorry I'm distant. It's the anniversary of Lucinda's death."

The beams in the ceiling—long, rough-hewn, made of fir—seemed to swell slightly.

"What kind of tree was it?" Mona asked.

"Spruce," he said. "A very tall, very rare black spruce. She fell forty feet."

Not the time to ask, obviously, but she wondered where he kept Lucinda's hair. In a wooden box? Maybe she'd look for it the next time she cleaned his house. She wished she possessed a physical piece of Mr. Disgusting. His teeth, perhaps. She imagined a musical jewelry box containing his dentures, along with a tiny, twirling Mr. Disgusting figurine.

"What're you thinking about?" Dark asked.

"Dead boyfriend," Mona said. "Junkie, tough guy, softie."

Crap, it was happening again. The fragments. Always a struggle to talk about Mr. Disgusting in complete sentences.

"How old was he?" Dark asked.

"My father's age," Mona said. "Lived in a residential hotel. Stole flowers for a living. Had a funny way of walking with his hands clasped behind his back. Loved to dance. His signature move: scratching behind his ear like a dog. His favorite food: cottage cheese, which he covered in black pepper and devoured by the quart. We were always on some wild goose chase or treasure hunt. He was a gentleman, but I could never bring him to, say, my cousin's wedding or whatever. He didn't mix well with others. He considered our relationship a grand romance worthy of literature."

"Sounds like you miss him," Dark said.

"I miss his voice," Mona said. "He could say something like, 'I'll stuff your beaver for you, no charge,' and I'd melt."

"Did his dick work?"

"Not really," she said. "Didn't matter to me."

Dark made a noise in the back of his throat. She looked at his face and saw that his cheeks were damp. She pictured him marching around a tree in the sweltering heat, pulling against the ropes, waiting for his skin to break. Perhaps it was time she went out on a limb. Perhaps it was time she offered something new and untouched, something that would work as a salve. Not for her, but for him. The man had suffered as much as she had, and she knew she wasn't likely to meet anyone like him again.

"We haven't known each other long, but I feel like I can be myself around you," Dark said. "My authentic self. I think it's because I've fallen for you—"

"You can put it in my ass, if you want," she said suddenly, and immediately started sweating.

The thought of his ample cock up there terrified her.

He laughed and turned to face her. "That's the strangest reaction I've ever gotten to telling someone I'm in love with them."

Mona felt her face redden. "I wanted to make a flesh offering," she said. "You know, to ease your suffering."

"You don't need to suffer for me," he said. "And you've already offered your flesh."

"I love you," she said. "Which is ridiculous."

"Why?"

"Because you're married?" she said.

They did it on the floor. Afterward, they fell into a pleasant stupor that lasted the rest of the evening. He dozed off at one point and she discovered that he drooled in his sleep. She usually reserved just a tiny bit of disgust for whomever she was dating, especially when she pictured them as a baby or a geriatric, but she couldn't find a thing about him to repulse her. He could have drooled all over her—it would not have mattered.

"Who is he?" Terry asked.

"I'll tell you later," Mona said.

———

HE STAYED AWAY WHEN SHE CLEANED HIS HOUSE, BUT HE LEFT love notes for her. In the first two, he'd plagiarized Tom Waits, Nick Cave, and, strangely, Margaret Atwood. In the third, which he'd boldly taped to the mirror in the master bath, he'd written:

> *My favorite M,*
>
> *I grow increasingly enamored of you with each passing day.*
> *Please stop taking that ridiculous course to reduce your accent—*
> *it drives me wild and is clearly the language of love.*

Of course she didn't have an accent. She smiled and placed the note in the back pocket of her jeans. Then she reached for one of his dirty T-shirts in the hamper. She huffed on the T-shirt as she sprayed the shower walls with Scrubbing Bubbles.

"I love foam cleaners," she mumbled to Terry.

"Whose T-shirt is that?" Terry asked innocently. "And why are you sniffing it?"

"I'm working up to telling you about it," Mona said slowly.

"There you are," Rose said from the doorway.

Rose was wearing head-to-toe white rather than red, huge black sunglasses, and girl shoes. She looked stunning. Mona dropped the T-shirt and felt ashamed, as if she'd been caught with her hand down her pants. She hadn't seen Rose in weeks, not since she started sleeping with her husband.

"I've missed you," Rose said. "I could smell you when I walked into the bedroom and it gave me such a *lift.*" She laughed.

"So, I don't smell like suicide anymore?" Mona asked.

"You smell like you," Rose said. "And like . . . sex, actually."

Mona stepped out of the shower. She watched Rose grope her way toward the toilet, and then lift her skirt and sit down. Mona noted the size of her ass—tiny—and felt like an ape suddenly.

"Are you exhausted?" Rose asked. "You seem subdued."

"My arms are hanging lower to the earth," Mona said.

"The cleaning lady used to put the lid down," Rose said. "I'm glad you don't do that. I hope you don't mind that I'm peeing in front of you."

"Your piss smells like champagne," Mona said.

Rose laughed. "I bet you look pretty today."

Mona glanced at herself in the mirror. Too much eyeliner, as usual, and her hair was falling out of its braid. "I'm okay."

"You're being modest," Rose said. "Philip told me."

Philip. What a ridiculous name. She would never call him Philip.

"He's exaggerating," Mona said. "Or trying to make you jealous."

"I'm not prone to jealousy," Rose said, "which is why we're still together."

Rose finished peeing, dabbed her probably dainty vagina with too much toilet paper, and stood up. She didn't flush. Now she was standing too close, as well as blocking the exit. Mona wondered if this was a Rose thing, or if blind people everywhere were standing in the wrong place.

"Who picks out your clothes?" Mona asked.

"Chloe," Rose said. "And Philip sometimes, when he's in the mood."

"Do you see other people, too?" Mona asked. Was it rude to use the verb "see"?

"Philip and I don't have the same needs," Rose said. "He craves intimacy. And intensity."

"What do you crave?" Mona asked.

Rose removed her sunglasses. Her eyes were puffy, as if she'd been sobbing for two hours. "Solitude, I guess," she said. "And stability."

So, you don't have an open marriage, Mona thought. But your husband does.

"I want him to have the best possible time," Rose said. "We've both suffered a lot, and I want our marriage to last forever, and I'm self-aware enough to know that there are certain things I can't give him."

"You mean, like, sexually?" Mona asked hopefully.

"Oh, no. We have a fulfilling sex life," Rose said, and put her sunglasses back on. "We always connected in that way. He's so intuitive and generous and just, well, *gifted.*"

Why was the bathroom floor moving?

"The room is spinning," Terry whispered. "Hold on."

Mona stepped toward the open window and put her hand on the sill. *There, there, cookie.*

"Philip has a hole in him," Rose said.

Mona focused on the holes in the window screen. "How big of a hole?" she managed to ask.

"The size of Lucinda," she said. "Plus, he hates his mother and calls her a cunt. And he drinks too much."

Outside, a clear plastic bag was blowing across the yard, and Mona thought fondly of the exit bag. Perhaps it was time to rent a helium tank for her "birthday party." Maybe Dark would find her body and chew off some of her hair. She missed him terribly.

"I still love him," Rose said.

"Am I the only other?"

"You're the only one nearby," Rose said. "He has someone he sees in Alaska, and I think he might have a girlfriend in Albuquerque— a waitress—but he may have ended that."

A *waitress*? In *Albuquerque*? She pictured a young woman in a white apron taking his order. Had he used the same line on her? *The way you wear that apron makes me want to crush granite with my teeth.*

"I never got his attraction to her, though," Rose said. "You, I get. You're my all-time favorite. In fact, I'm a little pissed off because I feel like he stole you from me. But I guess he found you first, technically." She smiled.

I am not a dog, Mona thought. I am not Dinner.

"You're not Dinner," Terry repeated.

I'm not dinner, either, Mona thought. I am a side of potatoes.

———

SHE WAITED FOR ROSE TO LEAVE BEFORE SYSTEMATICALLY searching every inch of the master bedroom. Not sure what she was hunting for exactly, or what she hoped to find. Physical evidence of their lovemaking? Love notes for the waitress? Her hands shook as she went through the trash. No used condoms, but so what, and nothing interesting in the nightstand drawers. She pulled the duvet off their mattress and noted grease stains here and there on the sheets. No apparent come. She figured the grease was lube or massage oil, but then she found an empty carton of lo mein on Dark's side of the bed, along with a pair of Rose's underpants.

"Terry," Mona said. "Do you think couples who eat in bed have fulfilling sex lives?"

"Depends," Terry said. "What kind of food?"

"Chinese."

"I'm sorry, but yes," Terry said quietly.

Mona picked up Rose's lacy thong and let it dangle from her pinkie for a few seconds before bringing it toward her face.

"Don't do it," Terry said.

Rose smelled like geraniums and a very specific spice Mona rarely used. Cardamom?

"Jamaican allspice," Terry said.

Mona dropped the underwear and peered under the bed. She pulled out a large hatbox. Inside, half a dozen worn, spiral-bound notebooks. She plucked out a red one and opened it. Judging from the large, looped cursive, the heart doodles, and the abundance of exclamation points, it was the diary of a girl just shy of her eleventh birthday. It seemed to be written in code.

Dear Diary,

I give last night a 3 out of 10. I waited two whole hours for [crown symbol], who came in at eleven o'clock and sat in the chair

———

and read a chapter from The Count of Monte Cristo *& I felt like
I was floating & that thing started happening with [rose symbol].
I wanted [heart symbol] like last week, but it didn't happen. My
chins [shins?] hurt real bad & [crown symbol] rubbed them and I
got tears on my shirt. [Crown symbol] kept touching [rose symbol]
but there was no [ice-cream cone symbol]. Maybe tonight if Mom
goes to the movies with her friend. Anyways, when I woke up this
morning there was a SPIDER IN MY BED!!!*

There was no key or legend, of course, but Mona's own [heart symbol]
felt weak and heavy, because the diary clearly belonged to Rose, and
[crown symbol] was clearly Rose's father, and [ice-cream cone symbol]
was clearly not ice cream. Rose clearly didn't know—had never known—
what was good for her, and probably still didn't, which was why she let
her husband bone the cleaning lady, along with a waitress in Albuquerque,
and who knew how many other women in aprons.

Mona leafed through a second notebook. Rose's handwriting appeared adult sized and she'd dropped most of the code—only the
crown remained. She described her longing for crown's body, particularly his hands and fingers, and the wetness between her legs when she
fantasized about him. Her descriptions were overwrought, romantic,
and, shamefully, a little arousing. In one entry, she'd been grounded for
breaking curfew and was waiting for him in bed. Eventually, he came
in and sat on the chair, and she begged and pleaded and bared herself,
but he refused to touch her, and *that* was her punishment: *not being
molested*.

On the last page of the notebook, there was only this: "Marilyn
Monroe died on a Saturday night. Her, of all people, alone on a Saturday.
Imagine that."

Now Mona had tears on her own shirt. There were more on the way.
She replaced the notebook, climbed into the closet, and cried into the
sleeve of Dark's jacket. She pictured Rose in her childhood bed, waiting

to be crowned, as it were, and then blind, counting her way around town. The counting made Mona cry harder than the crowning.

She canceled her next two dates with Dark. She would've canceled the following week's housekeeping visit, too, but she needed the money and didn't want to disappoint Rose, whom she felt was largely innocent in all of this.

A WEEK LATER, HER FIRST IMPULSE WAS TO DIP INTO THE BOX of notebooks again. As she was lifting the bed's dust ruffle, Dark jumped out of the closet, scaring the shit out of her.

She screamed, which only made him laugh. He opened his arms, apparently expecting an embrace. She swung at his chin and missed. He caught her by the wrists, and she fought and kicked, but when his pencil-shavings smell drifted into her nostrils, she felt her arms weaken. He wrestled her to the floor, where they did some grappling. The next thing she knew he'd ripped her favorite pants and put himself inside her.

The sex felt like an opiate nod. Random, unfamiliar images flickered behind her lids, accompanied by that feeling of forgetting something, and then falling, and falling again. Dark's hand was gripping her apron, using it as leverage, but she was clinging to a large, swinging chandelier, looking down at a roomful of faces. His dry hand squeezed her thigh. Jeremy Irons offered her a cigarette. She looked for a light in her purse and found a barf bag from Japan Airlines. Dark's hand covered her mouth. She fell off some scaffolding and landed on Mr. Disgusting. A man on a sidewalk spoke Spanish to her—not Henry Miller, but the guy that played him in the movie, or maybe it was Sam Elliott—and then she was sitting at a vanity. Dark's hand was around her throat, squeezing. She didn't recognize her face in the mirror. Dark pulled out and let loose on her bunched-up apron.

"You're wheezing," Dark said. "You should quit smoking, babe."

"Go fuck yourself," she said.

He looked startled. "Touchy subject?"

"Waitress," she blurted. "Crown symbol."

"Are you having a stroke?" he asked seriously. "Or an anxiety attack?"

She got to her feet and took a couple of deep breaths. Her teeth were clattering, but she wasn't cold.

"Your poor wife thinks she seduced her own father," she said, rubbing her wrists.

"What? She doesn't think that," he said irritably.

"He turned her on, and then put it all on her," she said.

"You don't know anything about it."

"Doesn't matter. You're married," she said. "I shouldn't have done this with you."

"You're being a dumb twat," he said. "You know that, right?"

"I can't be your mistress *and* your maid," she said quietly. "Ever heard of the women's movement?"

What was she saying? She hated the word "maid," had no interest in being his mistress, and had been setting the women's movement back for years.

Dark looked confused. "I adore you," he said. "I'm not going anywhere. I promise I'll never hurt you."

"You told me you and Rose were like siblings," she said. "And I didn't realize you did this sort of thing in other towns. With . . . waitresses."

"There's only you and Rose," he said. "And it was Rose who wanted to open our marriage—"

"But Rose is fucked up," Mona said. "And two is still too many. And you could have said no—how about that?"

When she saw his eyes well up, she looked at Dinner, who seemed unable to leave the room even though the door was wide open. He sat looking up at her and whining.

"I'd rather be dinner," Mona said.

He blinked at her. "The dog?"

"The main course," she said.

He nodded soberly. "If I wasn't married you wouldn't feel such passion for me, I promise. Passion feeds on this kind of shit."

"Which shit?" she said.

"Obstacles," he said. "Restrictions."

"You're full of it," she said.

He took a step toward her. "I can talk to Rose about spending more time with you. Chloe's away at school—"

"Oh God," she said, and shook her head. "Don't do that. Just be good. Be better to Rose. She's your *wife*, not your *sister*. Don't compare yourself to siblings. You guys have sex, and Rose has incest trauma, and so it's just not accurate. Or helpful. And you know what? Don't be here when I'm here. I don't want to see you for a while. Or . . . ever again."

"Which is it?" he asked.

She didn't answer. She left the house without finishing—a first—and spent the evening shaking. The following day her head turned into a cement mixer, which seemed to give her the shits, and she got her period. Then the longing started. She kept seeing him on the edge of her bed, naked, reading aloud to her and rubbing her shins, his hands inching toward her [rose symbol], over and over. The pain of parting was red and loud, indeed.

By Sunday she was dead eyed and despondent. To distract herself, she watched a little porn. It seemed women were collecting semen in goblets these days. It was a trend. Revolted, she went back to staring at the ceiling and produced hundreds of tears, which she imagined collecting in her own goblet. When it was full, she would march over to the Hurt Ranch and force him to drink her tears. Every drop, motherfucker, she would say, slapping his face. Every drop!

Rose called that night asking to meet over coffee the following morning. Mona said she didn't want coffee. She only wanted to be their cleaning lady for now, and nothing else.

"Philip is a mess," Rose said.

"Whatever," Mona said. "It's not like I fell out of a tree and died."

"He's in love with you," Rose said.

"You know, most of my clients aren't home when I'm there?" Mona said. "They make it a point to stay out of the house?"

Why did she tack question marks to the ends of sentences when she was falling apart? Was she unraveling? Maybe? Would she tear at the seams? Would she wind up in the loony bin? Again?

"I don't hate you, okay?" Mona said. "I'm just not cut out for this?"

"Okay," Rose said after a pause. "I understand."

THE NEXT WEEK NO ONE WAS HOME WHEN SHE ARRIVED. AND then she'd found shit in the soap dish. She figured it was a fluke, but then found shits two, three, and four the very next week, followed by the phony rum ball.

And now, nearly a month later, the final straw: a loaf on the flokati. Bigger, softer, and more pungent than the others, it would have been a twenty-wiper. It took some effort to remove, leaving a buttery stain in the wool. She fussed over the stain for forty minutes.

"Fuck this," she said.

"When oh when are you going to confront these people? Or, better yet, walk out of this place forever?" Terry asked. "Honestly, what will it take?"

"I have a confession, Terry," Mona said, and cleared her throat. "Remember when I told you I was going through a breakup? It was with the blind lady's husband. We Indian wrestled. And regular wrestled. And had sex multiple times. And said I love you—twice."

"Oh," Terry said sadly. "Oh dear."

"But like I said, I ended it," Mona said, "even though I'm pretty sure I'm in love with him. As to our mystery, the pooper is not the daughter. I think it might be Dark. He's now our primary suspect. I suppose he's acting out his emotions, or he might be trying to make it into the story he thinks I'm writing, or he might be trying to get me to—"

A shadow passed by the window. She heard shoes crunching gravel, which was unusual, and then the kitchen door creaked open and clicked shut. Dinner ran into the kitchen but didn't bark. Mona heard footsteps.

"Hello?" Mona called out.

The footsteps stopped.

Mona poked her head into the dining room. A tall, skinny woman with a pretty face and splotchy skin stood next to the table. She wore a pale yellow cashmere sweater with lots of holes in it, dingy gray sweatpants, and blue surgical gloves. Was she a patient? *Rose's office is that way*, Mona almost said. She stopped when she saw the pink plastic bag of poop.

"Can I help you?" Mona asked.

"This isn't for you," the woman said blithely, as if she were talking about a bag of homemade cookies. "It's for her. Rose."

Mona coughed. Judging from the bleach stains on the woman's sweatpants, it was the former cleaning lady. Evidently, she still had keys.

"These people are assholes." The bag swung in her hand as she spoke. "Lunatics. I worked for them for years. Years!"

"Okay," Mona said carefully, as if the woman were holding explosives.

Mona had seen Hispanic women carrying cleaning buckets in and out of houses, but she'd never met another white cleaning lady in Taos. Or anywhere, really. Part of her wanted to talk shop.

"Did you notice Grace written all over this house?" Mona asked, by way of distraction.

The woman winced. "Rose really fucked up my kid . . . and now she's gone."

"Gone?"

"Overdose." She tossed the bag onto the table and covered her eyes briefly with the heels of her hands. "I wrote her name all over the place."

"I'm sorry," Mona said.

"Rose once told me I was *haunted*. She told me I smelled like *incest*. Who says that?"

"An incest survivor," Mona answered. "A blind incest survivor."

The woman grimaced. "Here's how I look at Rose: you made me wear your shit, and now I'm making you wear mine."

"Mona, might this be your future?" Terry said in a loud whisper. "Might this be you in fifteen years?"

"So, it's yours?" Mona asked, nodding at the bag.

"Yep," the woman said.

"You know the expression 'Don't shit where you eat'?" Mona asked, and smiled.

The woman laughed. "Don't give me any more ideas," she said.

Mona thought of Dark's tattoo, *A Steady Diet of Nothing*. It had not been a steady diet, sadly, and yielded nothing. Sooner or later, she would need to stop cleaning his house.

"Where were you going to put it?" Mona asked.

"I don't know," the woman said. "On the crow sculpture?"

"The thing is, I'm the one wearing it," Mona said. "I've been cleaning up after you."

"Oh God," the woman said, and frowned. "Sorry about that. I'm surprised we didn't run into each other sooner."

"I thought it was for me," Mona said. "I thought I was the target."

The woman tilted her head. "Why?"

"I had a thing with Dark." She shook her head. "I mean . . . Philip."

The cleaning lady snorted. "That weirdo?"

Was he that bad? Mona shrugged and fidgeted with the rag hanging out of her back pocket. She felt cemented to the floor, unable to move her feet. The woman hadn't moved, either. It occurred to her that they were locked in a kind of standoff. She knew she would not continue cleaning up the poop. One of them would have to leave.

Mona removed the rag from her back pocket and dropped it on the floor. "I surrender," she said. "I guess I'll go home. And regroup."

The woman smiled. "We should get a drink sometime," she said. "Also, feel free to take something on your way out. I won't look."

"Excuse me?"

"A token," the woman said. "I always either take or leave something when I clean a house for the last time. Don't you?"

"I take photographs," Mona said.

The woman's eyes lit up. "Tell me your name."

"Mona," Mona said. "You?"

"Maria," the woman said.

"What's your middle name, Maria?" Mona asked slowly.

"Funny you ask," the woman said. "My middle name is also Maria. My parents met in Argentina and named me after some Spanish song."

Mona laughed. Then she felt like crying. Not only had Rose stolen Maria Maria's name, she'd stolen the punch line behind it. What else had she stolen? If she was comfortable lying about something as basic as her own name, imagine what other lies she could tell.

Mona took the portrait of Rose hanging over the sofa. She tucked it under her arm and carried it the thirty-seven steps to her truck. As she laid the canvas down in the bed of her truck, she searched for a sign of Grace. She knew it was carved in somewhere, waiting to be discovered.

BARBARIANS

MARIA MARIA LIVED ON THE SOUTH SIDE OF TOWN WITH ALL the Spanish people, Mona on the north side with the fake bohemians, and so they met for drinks in the middle, at a bar attached to a hotel, and ordered cocktails with rye in them.

"Just a couple cleaning ladies out on the town," Mona said as they clinked glasses.

It was cool to bullshit with someone about mops. Mona was all about string mops. Maria Maria preferred the flat, microfiber variety. They weighed the pros and cons of each, and then moved on to vacuums. The best vacuum on the market, hands down, was the Miele Titan canister. Best book-dusting tool? A shoe-polishing brush. To clean grout, Maria Maria liked to flood the tiles with bleach and go at the grout with an electric toothbrush.

"Your obsession with bleach is legendary, by the way," Mona said.

"The white people around here are wimps," Maria Maria said. "I'm sorry, but do you really expect me to clean your bathroom with vinegar and water? It's like, go fuck yourselves."

At one point, as Maria Maria demonstrated her cobweb removal technique, which was indeed advanced, Mona noticed "Grace" tattooed on the inside of her left wrist.

"You know, you should get a poop tattoo," Mona said, "because that shit was *genius*. You're definitely an artist. In fact, you might be the most important artist in this town."

Maria Maria rolled her eyes.

"I'm just glad I took photographs," Mona went on. "When the chips are down in 2033 or whatever, I'll sell them on QVC and make eighty grand."

"How's business?" Maria Maria asked. "Do you have a waiting list?"

Mona laughed. "I wish."

"How many employees do you have?" Maria Maria asked.

"Zero," Mona said.

"How do you make money?"

"I don't," Mona said.

"Come work for me," Maria Maria said. "I'll only take thirty percent."

"No pimps," Mona said. "No offense."

They ordered another round. Mona was slightly tipsy and told Maria Maria a secret: whenever she saw a cleaning lady or janitor, she crossed herself as if she'd seen a saint. Or a ghost.

"It's like this superstitious tic," Mona said. "What's the strangest thing you've ever found in a house?"

"A stainless steel G-spot and prostate stimulator," Maria Maria said. "Which isn't that strange, I know, but it belonged to a woman in her early seventies. Her husband, also in his seventies, had cock rings in his night-stand drawer."

"Wow," Mona said.

"Listen, if you need a new client, I have someone for you," Maria Maria said. "I bid the job already but I don't want them. Too high-maintenance. They're artists from Europe—Hungary, I think. They've got a bunch of cats, which is weird, because they're straight and very wealthy."

"How much?" Mona asked.

"One twenty-five per visit," Maria Maria said. "Once a week. I over-bid because I didn't really want them, but they went for it."

"Well, shit," Mona said. "I'll take 'em."

THE KOSAS WERE IN FACT HUNGARIAN AND OWNED NOT THREE, not four, but five cats. The cats were Turkish, apparently, and mostly white, with apricot-ringed tails and blue or amber eyes. As far as cats went, they were beautiful, yes, but they were just takers. Barbarians. They beat up the Swiss cheese plants and puked on the sheepskin rugs. That morning she'd found a headless wood rat in the foyer. The missing head, it turned out, was under the couch. More carnage near the windows: two small, half-eaten lizards, plus some blood on the floor. Also lizard guts.

She swept the dead bodies into a dustpan, as usual, and flung them off the patio. The bloodstains she wetted with sodium peroxide and scrubbed with a stiff brush. One of the barbarians sidled up to her and made a pass at her thigh. *You can pet my face now*, the cat seemed to say. Mona ignored it and kept scrubbing. *Bitch, rub my face.*

"Beat it," she said.

She nudged the cat away with her foot. The only thing she wanted to pet in this house was the furniture. And the Larry Rivers painting. And the walls. And perhaps the wife.

Although, she wasn't sure what to make of her last interaction with Lena. They'd chatted briefly on Mona's first visit to the house a couple of months ago, and then again a few weeks later, when Lena had come home early to find Mona on her knees, molesting the leg of one of the dining room chairs.

"What's wrong?" Lena had asked. "Is it broken?"

"No," Mona had said, getting to her feet. "It's not broken, it's . . . beautiful. I was just—well, I have a weird habit of, uh, fondling your chairs."

Fondling! Fuck.

Lena was taller than Mona—over six feet—and all angles. She seemed constructed to appeal to the emotions, like a cathedral made of human bones. Her green eyes reminded Mona of old wavy glass.

"So why are you staring at her tits?" Terry whispered loudly.

"Anyway," Mona said, "I don't know what it is about the chairs in this house, but they've cast some sort of spell over me. I usually don't even *notice* chairs." She cleared her throat. "I mean, I don't exactly have, you know, chair awareness."

Stop talking, she ordered herself.

Lena laughed. "Well, it's a very rare chair, actually, which is why I have only one."

They'd stood there, admiring the chair for several seconds.

" 'An Awareness of Rare Chairs,' a new essay by Mona Boyle," Mona inexplicably said.

Lena blinked at her—she was a slow-blinker like her cats—and then nodded. "You're a *writer*," she said. "That makes sense."

"Not of essays," Mona said quickly.

"What, then?"

"Poems."

What did she hate more than poetry? Nothing, except maybe poetry readings.

"Well, Mona, you have excellent taste," Lena sighed. "This chair was designed by Jean Prouvé in 1944. The other chairs in this room are also Prouvé, but this one is special. I bought it off an actress in Los Angeles." She touched the back of the chair with her long fingers. "It was outrageously expensive, but I had to have it."

Mona tried to think of something poetic to say about the chair, seeing as she was now a poet, but then she noticed lint and cat hair sticking to each of the chair's feet. She couldn't stop herself from bending down and plucking it off, and then stuffing the hairy lint balls into the pocket of her jeans—a nasty, lifelong habit of hers. She searched Lena's face for signs of dismay or disgust.

"You know, you have beautiful skin," Lena said instead.

"I do?" Mona said. "Oh. Well."

"Tell me what other chairs you like to . . . what did you say? Fondle."

"Oh, the brown ones in the living room," Mona said. "Although, it seems like those chairs fondle *me*, actually."

"Frits Henningsen," Lena said. "He was a Danish designer. They're beautifully made, very well-structured chairs from the 1930s. I've been collecting them for years."

"I had a feeling they were Danish," Mona said, and nodded. "They're so . . . masculine and gorgeous. Like, uh, Viggo Mortensen. Or Mads Mikkelsen."

"Who?" Lena asked, confused.

"They're Danish . . . actors," Mona said.

Another smile. Of course, Lena had a space between her teeth. A perfect, slender space that Mona wanted to touch, possibly with her tongue. She felt a sudden and intense craving for churros.

"Uh-oh," Terry said in her ear. "Not this shit again. Aren't there rules of ethical conduct for a professional housekeeper?"

"Don't be such a goody-goody," Mona murmured to Terry.

"Do you smoke?" Lena asked.

"Occasionally," Mona lied.

"Feel like taking a break?"

They smoked on the patio. Lena smoked unfiltered Camels; Mona, Marlboro Ultra Light 100s. *I bought these by mistake*, she wanted to tell Lena. *I'm not a candy-ass.*

Mona already knew that Lena owned two galleries—one in Taos, the other in Santa Fe—and that her husband, Paul, was a semifamous painter, but apparently, Lena was a semifamous potter and ceramicist known for her dinnerware. Mona confessed that she owned about eighteen bowls, all mismatched, and only three plates, and that she often thought of bowls as boobs, and spoons as detached nipples. If she couldn't spoon food into her mouth like a baby, she said, she wasn't interested.

"Can I ask you a personal question?" Lena said.

"Sure," Mona said.

"Are you straight or gay?" Lena asked.

Mona blew smoke toward the sky. "Neither. Or both."

"Ah," Lena said.

"Why do you ask?"

"A few years ago, my daughter left her fiancé for a woman," Lena said. "An older woman she met at a coffee shop. They ran away together. I never knew she had it in her to do something like that. She'd always been so boy-crazy."

"There's a place between straight and gay," Mona said, "and it's a very real place, but most people think it's an imaginary place. Some fake, slutty island or amusement park."

Lena smiled. "I don't think that."

"Right," Mona said. "But there's a stigma. I've never liked being labeled bisexual—in fact, I can barely bring myself to say the word."

"Maybe you should give it your own name," Lena said.

"Sometimes I tell people I'm part fruit," Mona said. "I mean, if it comes up. It's like being part Spanish or whatever."

There was a silence.

"Which fruit?" Lena asked, and smiled.

"Lime," Mona said flatly. "I'm part lime."

"You sound bitter," Lena said. "Which I love."

Terry was right: Mona had a small crush on Lena. Was it romantic or platonic? She looked at Lena's boobs again. Were they big enough to suffocate her? Yes. But Mona didn't want to bury her face in Lena's tits. She wanted to *be* Lena's tits. She wanted to be Lena, period.

"Is your daughter still with the woman?" Mona asked.

Lena had stubbed out her cigarette and was now stretching her neck and shoulders. There was something lithe, languid, French, and feline about the way she carried herself, a combination that Mona associated with fame.

"No," Lena said finally. "But I still think about it. I never forget anything."

MONA BEGAN REFERRING TO THE HOUSE AS HER HUNGARIAN lover. She felt as though she were dating the house, especially as it took between four and five hours to clean. The place perfectly reflected her personality and aesthetic, and she felt changed in its presence—more optimistic and imaginative, steady and self-possessed, less bothered by trivialities. Even her skin looked better.

She carried her bucket to the master bath, turned on the light, and checked her face in the mirror. Too much orange lipstick today.

"I don't think it's too much," Terry said warmly.

Mona sprayed the mirror with Windex.

"I heard a rumor that you're in love again," Terry said.

Mona smiled. "You're so corny."

"Well?" Terry asked. "Anyone we know?"

"Actually," Mona said, "it's this house, mostly. And I'm more than in love. I'm . . . *besotted.*"

Terry chuckled. "Must be quite a hunk, this house."

"Hey, the best way to remove soap scum is to lather the tiles with the same soap that produced the scum."

"Really?" Terry said.

"For extra buildup, mix it with Comet or something abrasive," Mona said. She rinsed the tiles and moved to the sink. "Now I'm going to polish the faucet with Windex and a dry rag, which is the only way to get it really shiny and perfect. Always, always use a completely dry rag on reflective surfaces, Terry."

"Dry rags," Terry repeated. "Right. I'll remember that."

"I'll probably remind you again," Mona warned.

"Is it safe to say you're also besotted with the bathroom?" Terry asked.

"The toilet paper in this house is black instead of white, Terry," Mona said. "Which pretty much sums it up for me."

"Gosh," Terry gushed. "Black toilet paper! Where would you even find something like that?"

"France," Mona said, though she had no idea. "Pretty sure it's French."

"Hmm," Terry said.

"Guess what color the toilet is," Mona said.

Terry laughed. "Hot pink?"

"It's the color of black tulips," Mona said. "Which was the color of my childhood bedspread. For me, it's the color of memory itself."

"Interesting," Terry murmured.

"The toilet has a high tank and a long chain flush, at the end of which hangs this terrific black-beaded tassel." Mona pulled on the chain. "I could flush this mother all day long, Terry."

"So, let me ask you," Terry said. "Which famous person, if any, can you envision sitting on this toilet?"

"Fuck, that's a smart question." She wetted a rag with Pine-Sol and cleaned the floor around the toilet. "Don't forget to get *behind* the toilet."

"Have you thought of a person yet?" Terry asked.

"Well, it would have to be someone cool and extremely talented. Right now, I'm picturing the French actress Isabelle Huppert sitting on this toilet, and sitting on her lap is . . . Prince."

"Which prince?" Terry asked.

"Prince," Mona said. "You know, *Purple Rain* Prince."

"But wouldn't Isabelle Huppert be sitting on Prince's lap?"

"I don't think so," Mona said.

Terry seemed to find this highly amusing.

"It's extremely romantic in here," Mona said. "I almost want to light some candles and—I don't know—make out with someone."

"Who would that be?" Terry asked knowingly.

Mona didn't answer.

"You're still missing Dark," Terry declared softly. "Understandably. He had a powerful effect on you."

"I just want to feel Spanish again, Terry," Mona said. "If you know what I mean."

"What about Mr. Disgusting?" Terry asked. "Did he make you feel Spanish?"

"Mr. Disgusting made me feel like a little-known fjord in Greenland," Mona said. "Or the aurora borealis. Unmoored or unknown, a hidden and remote spot not on the tourist map. He said a photograph would never do me justice."

"I'm wondering what makes this house Hungarian," Terry said, changing the subject. "Is there a Hungarian flag on the wall?"

"God, no," Mona said. "It looks like a house you'd find in Los Angeles."

The architecture was refreshingly no-nonsense: a boxy one-story made of steel and concrete, with a flat roof and an open plan. Floor-to-ceiling windows throughout opened onto patios as large as the indoor spaces. A courtyard filled with plants and trees and a reflecting pool centered the house.

"You know, Terry, most of my clients would shit this place up with a bunch of knickknacks and electronics, but they don't even own a television."

"Do you clean that table with regular old Windex?" Terry asked now.

She was referring to the coffee table in the living room, which was a large, square, translucent box supported by short stainless steel legs. Mona wasn't usually a fan of glass and steel furniture, but she made an exception for this table because the clear box was stuffed with thousands of gold leaves.

"Yep," Mona said. "But first I remove all the books and magazines. And this heavy-ass Jean Arp sculpture."

Mona gingerly placed the statue on the floor, and that's when she noticed a pair of shiny black feet standing in the corner near the fireplace. The feet belonged to a statue of a very tall, very naked, very well-hung African man. His cock, however, was dwarfed by the enormous antelope horns coming out of his skull. The horns were real, but the rest of him was carved from dark, solid wood.

"Terry, you'll never guess what I'm seeing right now," Mona said.

Terry sighed. "Not someone's diary, I hope."

"The Kosas' latest acquisition, a life-size statue of a standing naked black dude, staring at me," Mona said. "He has horns!"

She checked her watch: 10:40. Roughly twenty minutes to photograph herself with it safely. She ran out of the house to fetch the tripod.

Her new thing was the photographic sequence. A story told in six to ten shots. Unfortunately, it was the same story over and over.

"Is that unfortunate, though, Mona?" Terry asked. "As part of your overall thesis, I happen to think you're saying something interesting about repetition. And monotony. And perhaps loneliness? Not to mention the tension between the working class and the wealthy. What I also find interesting, Mona, is that you keep repeating your pattern of drifting from house to house, forming intimate and sometimes inappropriate relationships with your clients, and I'm beginning to suspect the photographs are linked to this impulse. They're a bridge, a conduit—"

"Not now, Terry," Mona interrupted.

She tried to have an audience in mind before starting a photo sequence. Someone from her past, a guy she'd dated or been dumped by, or someone like Dark, or her mother, or Yoko and Yoko. Often it was total strangers in a gallery or museum. Today it was Paul and Lena.

1. This is your cleaning lady: sweaty, up close, and blurry;
2. Standing in your beautiful living room;

3. Feather-dusting the long dong of your life-size African statue;
4. Removing her apron;
5. Pretty much naked;
6. Dressed in your favorite clothes;
7. Reclining on your fine Italian leather daybed, pretending to be you.

And . . . cut. Time check: 11:11. Make a wish and wrap it up. She changed clothes and then risked one last shot. Back in her own outfit, she posed behind the statue, feather duster in hand, peeking out from behind its muscular shoulder, gripping its enormous—

"Good morning," Paul said.

Mona froze. Paul was standing roughly twenty feet away, wearing a dirty T-shirt, a pilly cardigan, and paint-splattered pajama bottoms. In his hand, a small piece of cardboard.

She let go of the statue's cock. Paul was staring at her. Thank Christ she wasn't wearing his wife's clothes, but they were right there, sitting in a loose, sloppy pile on the leather daybed. He entered the room. She watched him eyeball her camera before sitting down. The cardboard he held was a piece of dry toast.

"What are you up to?" he asked casually.

She'd been caught doing other things—pretending to be blind, dancing, eating from a bowl of frosting with her fingers—but she'd only been caught taking photographs one other time. She'd fully expected to be fired on the spot, blackballed and run out of town. Instead, her client Henry had handed her a check and told her he had stomach cancer. This was the one who'd undergone chemo and pooped in the tub. Henry was dead now. Paul was very much alive and more muscular than she remembered.

"Well," she said, and took a deep breath. "I guess I'm attempting to . . . make the mundane meaningful."

A borrowed phrase from one of their art books, but it sounded right. True, even.

"What?" he said.

"I'm trying to make . . . *art*," she said, and winced. "Out of the *mundane*."

He bit into his toast and chewed solemnly.

"It makes my life feel less absurd," she explained.

He swallowed. "I thought you were a poet."

"Oh, I do both," she said. "I was just photographing myself with this statue here. I saw it and, uh, fell in love with it, like, immediately."

As if to demonstrate, she rested her hand on its shoulder.

"That's an ancient fertility statue," he said in his usual monotone. "It's from the Ivory Coast. They say just touching it will make you pregnant."

She stepped away from the statue and wiped her hand on her apron like a jerk.

"It appears you're also in love with Lena's shoes," he said.

How to explain that part?

"And her clothes?" He pinched Lena's blouse between his fingers and raised his eyebrows at her.

"I plead the Fifth," she said.

He smiled. "You're not under arrest."

What am I, then? she wondered.

"I'm not angry," he said. "I'm only confused. And curious. Why don't you sit."

She sat across from him. For some reason, he removed his glasses and set them on the gold table. His naked eyes were as dark as the burnished leather they sat on and held a startling amount of despair. The effect struck her as indecent, as if he'd disrobed. *Put your glasses back on*, she wanted to tell him. *For God's sake.*

Unable to meet his eyes, she focused on the familiar black-and-white photograph behind him of a quaint side street in France in the 1960s. It showed a man in a black dress suit leaping off a very high wall toward the pavement below. There was nothing to break his fall, and yet he was suspended, fully horizontal, arms outstretched. He looked happy and insane.

"I take pictures of myself in people's houses," she said. "Wearing their clothes. It's something I've been doing for years." She pointed to the photograph. "It makes me feel like that guy."

Paul glanced at the photograph over his shoulder.

In fact, she had several photographs of her jumping off the daybed with the photograph in the background, her arms outstretched, her face alert and ecstatic. It was her most prized sequence in the Hungarian lover series, as well as the most personal.

She could feel Paul studying her face. Dude, she pleaded inwardly. Glasses. Right there. Pick them up, put them on. So easy.

"This coffee table also feels like an old friend," she said. "I dream about it at least once a week."

"That's funny," Paul said with a straight face.

Mona shrugged. "Is it?"

"The leaping man in that photograph," Paul said, "is the same man who designed this coffee table."

"What?" Mona said.

"His name was Yves Klein," Paul said.

"Shut up," Mona said.

Paul shrugged and laced his fingers behind his head. "Look him up. He's quite famous. You should show me your work. I'm interested to see what . . . you see." He looked around the room, as if trying to see it through her eyes.

"What—like right now?"

"Yes."

Roughly fifty shots were stored on her camera, and she was pretty much naked in about thirty of them. Did she want him to see her tits? The answer was . . . probably not.

"So?" he said. "Show me."

Should she mention the nudity? No. "The whole thing is slightly—" What was the word? "Unethical."

"Good art is never safe," he said. "Or ethical."

"The thing is, the photographs *sound* better than they actually are," she said. "I mean, the idea is good on *paper*, but the *execution*—"

"Don't equivocate," he said.

He stood, walked over to her camera, and began scrolling through pictures. One picture in particular seemed to capture his interest. She hoped it wasn't the one in which she was humping the chartreuse velvet curtains in their bedroom.

"Shit," she said out loud.

He turned the camera off and set it on the coffee table.

"I want to show you something," he said.

Please don't let it be your penis, she thought. He stood up and asked her to follow him down a short hallway. They stopped at a door that was usually locked. Paul opened the door and they entered a long rectangular room with a wall of windows on one side facing a wall of drawings and paintings on the other. The paint-stained herringbone parquet floors led up to a raised wooden platform between two beat-up, red leather chairs.

"This is my studio," he said. He walked over to a drafting table near the windows and began rummaging through some papers. "I spend most of my time here."

The place needed to be power-washed, but she was no longer here as a cleaning lady. She was . . . what, a fellow artist? Unlikely. He wanted something from her.

Praise? Reassurance? A hand job?

The wall of drawings featured a muscular, beautiful woman with long black hair and a big, juicy ass.

She would try praise first.

"You've really captured this woman's behind," she said. "Her butt is very capably and carefully rendered—"

"That's Nadine," Paul interrupted, standing next to her now. "She's supposed to be here." He looked at his watch. "Unfortunately, she's what you call a closet alcoholic."

"Right," Mona said knowingly.

"You are a closet alcoholic, as well?" he asked.

"Living room," she said.

He blinked.

"I'm a living room alcoholic," she explained. "I only drink in my own living room."

He frowned and tugged on his beard.

"You shouldn't be cleaning houses," he said.

Where was this going?

"Am I being fired?" she asked.

"No, no," he said, and shook his head.

She waited for him to continue, but he said nothing. He smiled and looked at his watch again. "I should get back to work," he said. "Carry on with what you were doing." He waved his hand. "In the living room."

"Thank you," she said, relieved. "And thanks for showing me your art."

"And you, as well," he said.

FOUR DAYS LATER, LENA CALLED AND INVITED HER TO FRIDAY dinner but didn't mention a reason or occasion. Mona assumed Paul had told Lena everything, and now Lena wanted to acknowledge that fact and put some boundaries in place. Like: You can take your cute pictures, but stop going through our closets. And please, please keep your paws off my jewelry and the genitalia of my ancient fertility statue.

Strange to be a guest in their house, to see how the mess was made. Paul was at the stove, stirring, and the air smelled like meat and fresh mint. Mona was sitting on the Very Rare Chair, drinking real red wine. The real stuff was dry, apparently, tasted like time itself, and smelled like pipe tobacco and delicious dirt with some blood and dried blackberries mixed in. Lena was talking about how badly she missed rain, a common lament around Taos, and how rain had inspired her most recent outdoor sculpture out on the enormous patio. The base was a rustic wooden rowboat, about ten feet long. Over the boat was a canopy of sorts, a large umbrella-like skeleton of giant glass ornaments, with strings of blue dangling rhinestones. Lena had made the ornaments and rhinestones herself. She'd been blowing glass for fifteen years.

"Did you make the boat, too?"

"No, it's a found object. I use them in all my sculptures."

"You mean you just found that boat?" Mona asked. "In Taos?"

"No, at an antique fair in Connecticut," Lena said.

How can an object be considered found when you bought it? Mona wondered.

"A found object is something that wasn't art before," Lena said, reading her mind.

Mona braced herself for some abstract talk on the function of art, but Lena didn't go there.

"Well, I love it," Mona said.

As Lena refilled their glasses for the third time, her emerald ring winked knowingly at Mona, recalling an early photo shoot, when she'd worn both the ring and the orange lace blouse Lena was now wearing. Mona wondered if Lena had chosen these items on purpose.

"Don't you get lonely cleaning houses?" Lena asked quietly.

"I have people I talk to," Mona said, thinking of Terry. "On the phone."

"Do you have employees?"

Mona shook her head. "I'm more of a lone-wolf type."

"Me too," Lena said. "Although not by choice."

Paul approached the table carrying three plates, waiter-style. The plates were severely lopsided. Lena said she purposely designed them to make it appear as if the food were sliding off. Mona gaped at the plates as if her Hungarian lover had uttered something especially brilliant.

Paul sat and told them to dig in. It was lamb. She hated lamb. She cut the meat into tiny bites, chewed as little as possible, washed it down with wine.

"Paul tells me you're a talented artist," Lena said, and smiled.

Mona blushed and nibbled on a green bean.

"Are your parents artists?" Lena asked.

"No," Mona said. "But my grandfather painted pictures. My father's father. I wouldn't call him an artist, but he painted every day for as long as I knew him."

"What did he paint?" Paul asked.

"Seascapes. Candles burning in darkness. The occasional creepy clown."

He gave her a blank look and continued chewing.

"The last years of his life he painted the same picture over and over. He never seemed to get it right."

"What was it?" Paul asked.

"A bullfight," Mona said, and coughed. "He painted it from memories of his time in Mexico." She wanted to abandon the story, but she was committed now. "After he died my grandmother found dozens of the same exact painting. Now everyone in my family has one hanging in their house."

"Where did you put yours?" Lena asked.

"On the mantel," she lied.

She didn't have a mantel, and the painting was sealed in the original package Mona had received in her late teens, never opened. She kept it under her bed wherever she moved.

"Were you two close?" Lena asked.

"Not really," Mona said.

She hadn't thought of him in years, though she'd practically lived with her grandparents growing up. While her parents were busy ruining their marriage, she'd spent three or four days a week with her paternal grandfather, Woody Boyle, a mild-mannered man, an avid reader and functional alcoholic. But he'd taught her all of life's essentials: how to spit like a man, take a good photograph, drive stick, make a stiff drink, swim butterfly, French-braid, and, perhaps most importantly, how to play dumb.

Something was brushing her leg under the table. One of the barbarians, no doubt. She shifted in her seat and felt something soft under her boot. Poop? She looked down. Not poop: a bloated, half-dead lizard. The cat, still under the table, looked up at her face. *You're welcome*, it seemed to say.

"Your cats remind me of the Manson family," Mona said.

Lena laughed and looked under the table. "Richard brought a little present for our guest," she said. "Didn't you, kitty."

"Oh God," Paul said.

Lena put down her napkin and picked up the dying lizard with her bare hand. She walked to the sliding glass door and chucked the lizard outside. It landed inside the boat.

"Hah!" Lena said, and sat back down. She wiped her hands on her napkin, gulped some of her wine, and then laughed. "It's funny you mention the Manson family," she said. "Do you happen to know that after Charles Manson killed Sharon Tate, who was Roman Polanski's wife—"

"Lena, please," Paul said, and put down his fork.

"Please, what?" Lena said.

"Not that story," Paul said. "Not tonight."

Lena sniffed and poured herself and Mona more wine. "Fine," she said.

They were silent for a minute. Paul's wineglass was covered with greasy fingerprints. In a few days, Mona would be washing these very wineglasses and drying them by hand. And perhaps chucking dead lizards out the window.

"Did you know that whiptail lizards are lesbians?" Mona said.

Paul raised his eyebrows at her.

"They reproduce asexually," Mona said, "but they must mate with a female to ovulate."

Another silence.

"Do you have a girlfriend, Mona?" Lena asked suddenly.

"No," Mona said. "Not since high school. Women don't seem all that into me, actually. The last woman I messed around with lives next door to me. Her name is Shiori. She's short and Japanese, but has these gigantic breasts."

Paul smiled at her.

"Go ahead, Paul," Lena said.

"What?" he said, startled.

"Picture her with the busty Asian neighbor," Lena said.

"Actually, Lena," Mona said, "your rack rivals Shiori's."

Lena grabbed her tits and squeezed. "These?" she said. "These are fake."

Mona swallowed. "What?"

"I know," Lena said. "I don't seem like the type. In fact, I'm not the type. It's a strange story, really. When I was a teenager, I gave birth to—"

"Lena, please," Paul said. "Must you? Tonight?"

She said something in Hungarian that sounded like scolding. Mona watched Paul's jaw tighten. He said something measured and dismissive in return. They glared at each other for a few seconds and then both looked at Mona.

"He thinks I'm as subtle as a flying brick," Lena explained.

"And she drinks like a pelican when we have guests," Paul said.

"You mean fish," Lena said.

"I think we're all a little tipsy," Mona said.

Everyone seemed to be looking at their hands. Mona wished there were more people in the room. People like . . . Terry. She tried to conjure Terry sitting in the chair next to her, but it was impossible—she didn't even know what Terry looked like.

"Time for dessert," Paul announced.

Lena served Mona lemon cake on another of the crooked plates and coffee from a French press. Paul kept staring at her. At least he was wearing his glasses. Presumably, he fucked Lena sans glasses, something she hadn't considered before. They must do it doggy, she thought.

Suspiciously, Paul didn't eat any cake. Lena devoured three pieces with her bare hands. She wondered what they wanted from her. Were they lonely? Bored? Did they miss their daughter?

"So, did you two meet in Budapest?" Mona asked after a minute.

Lena looked at Paul, but he kept his eyes on Mona.

"We met at art school in Los Angeles," Lena said carefully. "Paul was the painter-in-residence. Everyone worshipped him, including me. We had a brief affair and then I didn't see Paul again for several years, until we were both living in New York City—"

"I'm looking for a new model," Paul interrupted.

"*Paul*," Lena said, and rolled her eyes. "Who's the flying prick now?"

"Brick," he said.

He seemed to study Mona's nose, then her neck, then her nose again, and now her wrists and fingers. She nervously chugged the rest of her water.

"Sorry, Mona," Lena said. "We don't mean to make you uncomfortable."

At least now she knew what they wanted.

"Would you be interested in something like this?" Paul asked.

To stand there, naked, for hours? The only thing she was truly comfortable doing naked was scrubbing the tub or having sex with Dark, and Dark was history.

On the other hand, she could already see Paul standing at his easel, asking her to spread her arms so that the sleeves of her brand-new reversible silk crepe kimono with the peony motif fanned open. Lena walked in and almost dropped her cup of tea. *Is that hand-embroidered?* she gasped. *Where on earth did you find it?*

"Maybe you want to think about it for a while," Paul said.

She tried to picture herself naked, completely naked, twitching under the studio lights. No kimono, no hat, no sunglasses, nothing. She slipped her hand under her shirt. Her poor stomach was sweating.

"I'll be there, too," Lena assured her. "In the sessions."

"As a chaperone?" Mona asked.

She laughed. "For myself. I would very much like to draw you."

"Do you still want me to clean your house?" Mona asked.

More importantly, could she still take pictures of herself cleaning their house?

"Yes," Paul said. "Or we could hire another housekeeper, if you prefer."

Another housekeeper? "No," Mona said quickly. "That won't be necessary."

"We'll pay you for the modeling," Lena said.

"Forty dollars per hour," Paul added.

"And you can continue your project," Lena said. "You can bring your portfolio for me to see."

"Oh, it's not like that," Mona said. "I mean, I don't have a portfolio."

"You can show them to me on your computer. Or your camera, like you did with Paul."

"Sure," Mona said. "Okay." She sipped her coffee. "I guess I could give it a try. Modeling, I mean. But, despite what you might think, I'm not exactly the nudist type."

Paul laughed.

"What sort of poses do you have in mind?" Mona asked. "You know, so I can practice at home."

"Nothing difficult," Paul said.

Mona stabbed the cake with her fork. "I better go on a diet."

"This is not for Hollywood," he said.

They stared at her as she ate the rest of her cake.

"Hey look, it's raining," she said with her mouth full.

Pouring was more like it. They looked out the window at Lena's sculpture. The wind plinked the fake dangling jewels and pelted the boat with water. Mona wondered if the boat could float if it had to, or if it was ruined for floating now that it was found.

Lena beamed at her. "Wonderful."

Mona wasn't sure what she was referring to—the rain or their new venture—but she felt apprehensive suddenly, as if she'd agreed to something more intimate, like sexual surrogacy. The feeling quickly passed and was replaced with a kind of yearning. *Such amazing bone structure,* she imagined Lena saying. *Look at her cheekbones.*

SHE PULLED INTO THE DRIVEWAY AND SAW YOKO AND YOKO IN the side yard, sitting on a blanket and staring at nothing. Stargazing, they called it. Somehow, they did this completely sober and without snacks. Tonight, they were wearing orange monk-style pajamas and wool socks with sandals.

"I can't stay," Mona said when she reached their blanket. "I ate half a cake."

"And wine, it appears," Nigel said.

"Am I walking funny?" Mona asked, and yawned.

"Your teeth are purple," Nigel said.

"For the record, I talked about your boobs tonight, Shiori. I almost told these people about our 'guided meditation,' but thankfully, I restrained myself. I did, however, talk about my grandfather, for some lame reason."

"Good," Shiori said softly. "It's good for you to let people in, Mona."

"You are your conversation," Nigel said, for perhaps the eighty thousandth time.

"Except I think I overshared," Mona said. "I'll probably be nursing an oversharing hangover tomorrow. Along with a regular hangover. But the sharing hangover will be much worse. And harder to get rid of."

"They're not thinking about you," Nigel said calmly. "They're thinking about themselves and what they said to you, or perhaps what they said to each other. Or, if they are healthy individuals, they are not thinking at all. They are sleeping."

"We miss you," Shiori said, and reached for Mona's hand. "We never see you anymore."

"What do you think of when you look at the stars, Mona?" Nigel asked.

"Scattered pocket change," Mona said. "Dimes and nickels. Slot machines. Gambling."

"You are bigger than the stars? Or do they make you feel smaller?" Shiori asked.

"I don't have health insurance," Mona said. "My ass isn't covered. Do you know that vultures eat their meals butt-first? They start eating the ass while waiting for the animal to die."

It was a game she liked to play with them sometimes. Not very imaginatively, she called the game Sudden Subject Change. They never wanted to play.

Shiori cleared her throat. "Would you like to learn about the constellations?" she asked. "We'd be happy to teach you."

"God, no," Mona said. "I'm off to bed."

"Stay curious, Mona," Nigel said.

INSIDE, SHE DRAGGED THE UNOPENED PACKAGE CONTAINING her grandfather's painting from under the bed. She stared at her grandmother's name in the return address. Ginger Boyle, dead now five years—Big C. She'd spent most of her career working as a bookkeeper in some mysterious office in Glendale. She'd had bright red hair and long red fingernails, wore white pantsuits and dark sunglasses, and carried herself like a gangster from the forties, pronouncing Los Angeles the old, Anglo way: "Law SANG-lus." She chain-smoked Pall Malls, spiked her coffee with vodka, and drove a black Lincoln Continental with tinted windows. Men she didn't like she called sissy and mister, as in, "Listen, mister, stop being such a sissy and get your shit together." Women she called either broads or gals. "Did you get a load of that broad's getup?" Or "That gal talks a blue streak."

Woody resembled a Mr. Man type—big muscles, suspenders, blurry sailor tattoos—but Ginger made him piss sitting down, and if they took a trip together—to Vegas, usually—she did all the driving. He was older than Ginger by twenty-two years, so it was strange that she had the upper hand, but after retiring from the navy, he essentially became a housewife and personal assistant. He cooked all of Ginger's meals, washed and ironed all her clothes, and ran all her errands. He seemed to enjoy waiting on her, and being ordered around like a dog: Sit down! Stop slouching! Don't wear those pants! Turn down the idiot box! Quit snoring and turn over!

They'd lived in an apartment complex for golden-agers in Palos Verdes. Their apartment was swanky: mustard shag, glossy white walls, clunky black-and-white furniture. They had a wet bar with a minifridge; marbled mirrors and glass shelves for all the booze, which they kept in classy crystal decanters; and a sink with a foot pedal. Ginger invited the neighbors over on Saturday nights and played Glenn Miller records while Mona and Woody worked the bar. Mona knew when to shake, when to stir, when to blend, and the difference between a Tom and an American collins, but Woody wouldn't let her bartend until she turned nine. She'd be tall enough by then, he said. In the meantime, she took care of the garnishes. She cut wedges, wheels, and twists. They all preferred tall drinks: Salty Dogs, Gin Rickeys, Cherry Hookers.

When everyone was good and loaded, Mona sat down at the electric organ and played "Hey Jude" and "Yesterday." She sang, too, and sometimes her eyes leaked. Not that anyone was paying attention to her teary recital—they were all laughing and carrying on with Ginger, the life of the party. Woody was the only one she wanted to impress, anyway. He sat in the green Barcalounger in the corner, applauding and smiling at her between songs.

On weekdays, Woody picked her up after school a couple of days a week. She'd swim laps in the pool and then they'd make French donuts, and then he'd paint for an hour while she practiced the organ. He taught her how to improvise her own little flourishes at the end of songs. At six sharp, Woody fixed dinner and drinks and they'd listen to Ginger talk about her day at the office. "So, I says to him, 'Are you out of your goddamned mind?' And he turns to me and says, 'Sorry, Gin,' so I says, 'Jesus, what are you, some kind of sissy?' And he says sorry again, sorry, sorry, so I says, 'Listen, Lou. Sorry doesn't walk the dog. Sorry doesn't make the bed. Sorry doesn't butter the goddamn biscuits.'"

Later in life, after high school, Mona used to call Ginger in California and complain about her money situation, hoping Ginger would send her a check. Ginger had already lost one of her tits by then, and she kept her cash in the fake one. It was like a magic hat—whenever Ginger put her hand in there, out came a fistful of twenties.

"I'm just barely hanging on," Mona would say whenever Ginger asked how she was.

"You got cigarettes?" Ginger would ask.

"Nope."

"Don't worry," she said. "I'll send you a couple cartons."

Sure enough, two cartons of Marlboros would arrive the following week, with a note from Ginger saying, *Keep these in the freezer. They stay fresher that way. PS: Cigarettes will ruin your face. Take a walk and get some air before it's too late.* Mona searched the package for a card or hidden money, but it was always just the cigarettes.

The last time she'd seen Ginger had been near the end. She was emaciated by then and unable to walk without a walker, and the cancer had spread to her lungs. She couldn't drive her Lincoln anymore, but she wasn't bedridden. When Mona asked if she could do anything for her, like laundry or vacuuming, Ginger said, "Yeah, go down to the market and get me a pack of Benson & Hedges and a bottle of rosé."

"Uh, you're not supposed to smoke," Mona said. "Or drink."

"I haven't pooped in two weeks," Ginger said.

She'd granted Ginger her wish and they'd spent the afternoon drinking and smoking their brains out.

The package had arrived a month or two later. "It's no Van Gogh," Ginger had written in a note. "But it might look okay in your hallway."

Mona dusted it off with a dirty sock, then slid it back under the bed. "Stay curious," she repeated to herself before passing out.

SHE ARRIVED EARLY FOR THE FIRST SESSION. THEY GAVE HER A cup of coffee and one or two reassuring looks, and then Lena asked her to disrobe behind a shoji screen set up in a corner. Mona wished she hadn't overdone it with the trimming down there. More would have been better, in this case. Were her tits lopsided, the little fuckers? She pinched them awake and then covered them with her hair. A cashmere bathrobe hung from one of the hooks. Was she supposed to put it on?

She stepped out from behind the screen. Naked.

"Where do you want me?"

They both looked at her. "Over here." Lena pointed to the wooden platform.

The wood creaked as she stepped onto the platform, which made her feel like a lard ass, and then creaked some more as she walked across it. She stood in the center, facing them, fighting the urge to fold her arms over her chest.

Lena glanced at Mona, smiled, and crossed her legs. Mona felt her face flush and looked at Paul, dressed for bed, as usual, and calmly regarding her from a stool next to his easel. No open signs of disgust. No open signs of anything.

Behind them, the floor-to-ceiling windows. Aspen trees filled the view. Hundreds of white trunks carved with hundreds of lidless black eyes. Dark green leaves with pale undersides. Quaking aspens, they were called, because their leaves fluttered like crazy at the slightest breeze. They were quaking right now, all of them at once, waving maniacally and making a distinct whispering noise.

She scratched her calf with her foot. "So," she said.

"Don't be nervous," Lena said, and opened the sketch pad on her lap. "You look beautiful."

"Hah," Mona said.

"I would kill for your ass," Lena said. "It's so . . . firm looking."

"It's where I hold all my tension," Mona said.

"Do you think you could tie your hair back?" Paul asked.

"A braid might be nice," Lena said.

She gathered her hair at the back of her head and braided it, and Lena handed her a red rubber band, which she fastened to the end. Now what?

They asked her to turn and twist, this way and then that, tilting her head up or down, one arm here, the other there, one leg bent, the other straight, and then hold it, right there, relax your stomach, okay, that's it.

Getting-to-know-you poses, Lena called them.

The aspens had stopped quaking. There was only the sound of pencils scratching paper. *Scratch, pause, scratch, scratch, pause, scratch, scratch, scratch.* If they were getting to know her, they were certainly being quiet about it.

"From WHYY in Philadelphia, this is *Fresh Air*," she heard Terry's voice say.

She waited for Terry to say something.

"Terry?" Mona whispered. "You there?"

"I'm here," Terry said quietly, after several seconds.

"This is what they call a *loud silence*," Mona said. "I wish I were wearing earplugs."

"And an apron?" Terry offered.

"A hazmat suit," Mona said, "with a hood and face mask, and possibly a backpack—"

Paul cleared his throat. "Next pose."

They asked her to sit on a stool and pretend to clip the toenails of her right foot, which was more challenging than it sounded. Tightness in her hips, a sharp twinge near the base of her spine. She was sweating now and could smell herself. A comfort, usually, but there was something off about it. A little too sharp, briny. Her saliva was sticking to her teeth. She swallowed. Swallowed again. Now their pencil scratches were muffled. Her ears felt like they'd been corked with . . . tampons. She swallowed. Swallowed again. No dice. She glanced at Lena's face—her lips were moving.

"Sorry," Mona said. "Did you say something?"

"You have something here," Lena said, and pointed to her chest.

Mona broke the pose and looked down. Her tits were livid red and mottled.

"A little rash," Lena said.

Hives.

"You have allergies?" Paul asked.

"I'm fine," Mona said. "This is just how I manage stress—I break out. I'll probably wake up with acne tomorrow."

"Maybe you'd be more comfortable lying down?" Lena asked.

"I would, actually," Mona said.

The poses were longer now—ten, fifteen, twenty minutes—and were meant to emphasize her curves, but when she looked at herself she saw her grandfather's body—his knees, his toes, his brown skin. Paul had abandoned his easel and was pointing an old Polaroid camera at her. She didn't like the noise it made. A mechanical insect in her ear, buzzing, buzzing. Her limbs felt truncated. He seemed to be dismembering her, chopping off her head, isolating various body parts, arms, legs, feet, wrists. Was there something wrong with her face?

"Of course not," Terry said. "You look incredible."

"I feel weird," Mona told Terry.

"Close your eyes," Terry said. "Breathe. Tell me what you see."

She closed her eyes and saw butterscotch candy in a crystal bowl, scotch sloshing around in a glass, her stockinged feet sliding into a pair of high heels.

"Whose heels?" asked Terry.

"Ginger's," Mona said.

The heels kept snagging on the mustard shag. This was where he wanted her, at the top of the stairs. She was wearing her own bright white bikini, Ginger's long white opera gloves, and four long strands of Ginger's pearls. The stockings on her feet were nude knee-highs. "Put your hand on your hip," Woody said from the bottom of the stairs. He brought the Polaroid to his face. "Smile!"

"Ooh," Lena said. "There it is again."

Bright red splotches on her ankles. These ones were itchy. Mona broke the pose, scratched her right foot. "Sorry, guys," she said, sitting up. "Let me just scratch these for a sec."

Lena placed her sketch pad and pencils on the floor and stood up. She stretched her arms over her head and then untucked her blouse.

"Is something biting you?" Paul asked. He took another Polaroid.

Lena unzipped her skirt and let it drop to the floor, and then peeled off her tights. Not only was she not wearing underwear, she had the biggest bush Mona had seen in years. Dead straight and silky looking. Lena pulled her blouse over her head—hairy pits!—and unclasped her bra. Only her eyeglasses remained, on the beaded chain around her neck.

Mona zeroed in on Lena's boobs. Her tits were two plastic bags stuck in a beautiful tree. The only blot on an otherwise breathtaking landscape.

"You're staring," Lena said. "They look like shit, I know. I'm getting them fixed this summer. Right, Paul?"

Mona laughed and looked at Paul, who was just standing there with his eyes closed.

"Paul, wake up," Lena said.

He opened his eyes and fanned himself with a Polaroid. Lena looked down at herself and frowned. She reached into her bag and retrieved a pair of pointed tweezers. Mona watched them disappear into her bush.

"What's wrong?" Mona asked. "Do you have a tick?"

Lena didn't answer. She held up the tweezers and said, "It's a fucking long white hair." She deposited the hair on the platform—delicately, as if it were a tissue specimen—and then looked down at herself again. "Oh God, there's another one."

"May I ask what it is you're doing, Lena?" Paul asked tiredly.

"Isn't it obvious?" Lena said, and sat in the armchair. "I'm trying to make Mona comfortable by being *myself*."

"I think it's enough for today," Paul said. "Mona, we'll see you next week, I hope. Lena, put some clothes on—I want to talk to you."

"Fuck off, Paul," Lena said. "Mona, let's smoke on the patio."

"Naked?" Mona said, alarmed.

Lena shook her head. "It's a bit chilly."

Mona pulled the peony kimono from her tote bag and held it open for Lena. "Here. Wear this."

"Oh, my," Lena said, and stepped into it. "It's gorgeous. Is it vintage?"

"It belonged to my grandmother," Mona lied. She'd found it on the Internet.

Outside, they chain-smoked next to Lena's boat sculpture. She felt like a head case in her track pants. *I don't usually wear track pants. I don't know what came over me.* Lena, of course, looked like a movie star.

"I hope you're not feeling self-conscious about your looks," Lena said. "You have the kind of beauty that sneaks up on you. It makes you feel like you're discovering something." She picked a piece of tobacco off her tongue. "Something no one else knows about."

"Wow," Mona said.

"Paul will know how to paint you," she continued. "You're in very good hands. He's old and grumpy but extremely talented. You can relax." She brushed a strand of hair out of Mona's face. "You know, I was an artist's model once, about a hundred years ago."

"How old are you?"

"Fifty-one," Lena said.

"You probably know this already, but you don't look fifty-one."

"The insane never age," Lena said.

"I was going to say you look older," Mona said, and smiled.

"You're funny," Lena said, and lit another cigarette. "I was also a hooker for a few years."

"Excuse me?"

"An expensive hooker," she corrected herself. "Not a streetwalker."

Mona tried to picture Lena engaged in an expensive sex act.

"Don't bother," said Terry's gentle voice in her ear. "Pay attention to the way she's scratching her nose."

Mona watched Lena warily. Lena wasn't merely scratching her nose—she was making slow, patient love to it with her fingers.

"What's that remind you of?" Terry whispered.

Mona gulped. "Junkies?"

"Bingo," Terry said.

"Well, it would explain the lithe-languid combo," Mona said. "And her wax-paper eyes."

"Your lips are moving," Lena said now. "Are you praying?"

Mona felt her cheeks redden. "No."

"You do that a lot, I've noticed." Lena smiled. "Move your lips a little bit, like you're saying something under your breath. It's cute."

Mona bristled at the word "cute."

"I'm talking to my imaginary friend," Mona confessed.

"Oh," Lena said. "What's her name? Or is it a man?"

"Terry," Mona said. "Her name is Terry Gross."

Lena opened her mouth and then closed it. "The radio person?"

Mona nodded. "Afraid so."

Lena smiled. "What do you talk about?"

"Killing people," Mona said.

Lena stopped smiling.

"I'm kidding," Mona said. "We talk about everything. And nothing."

"Anyway, I think you should practice at home," Lena said.

"Practice what—being an imaginary friend?"

Lena laughed. "Doing things in the nude," she said. "Not posing, but—I don't know—cooking? Or the crossword? Or yoga, perhaps. Things you enjoy doing."

"Sometimes I enjoy doing drugs," Mona said.

Lena blinked. "Okay."

She could have let it go, but she was unable to stop herself. "In fact, I think I'd like some of what you're on right now," Mona said.

"Pardon?" Lena said.

"I'd do some with you, if you ever wanted company."

Lena looked both stunned and irritated. She recovered quickly, though, and then smiled and squinted. "How do you know I'm . . . *on something*, as you say?" she asked.

"You have a tell," Mona said. "It's the way you scratch your nose."

Lena laughed and shook her head but didn't say anything. Mona watched her take long, careful drags off her cigarette. It was so obvious now.

"Takes one to know one, I guess," Lena said finally.

"Me? I'm not an addict," Mona said. "But I used to volunteer at a needle exchange, way back when. Are you shooting it, or what?"

"Stay put," Lena said, and coughed. "I'll be right back."

"Mona," Terry said. "Painkillers make you cranky, remember? And extremely constipated."

"I know," Mona said.

"So, what's behind that impulse?" Terry asked.

"Hey," Mona said. "This was your idea. Remember?"

"I was only drawing your attention to what you already knew," Terry said.

"I guess I'm looking for a friend," Mona said. "A human friend."

"Am I not human?" Terry asked.

Lena stepped through the sliding glass door, fully dressed. She handed Mona her coat, tote bag, and kimono. "I really like you, Mona," she said soberly.

Fuck. She'd gone too far.

"I really like you, too," Mona said.

"Good," she said. "Open your mouth."

AT HOME, MONA DISROBED AND MADE HERSELF A FRIED-EGG and cheese sandwich with pickled jalapeños. She ate it naked at the kitchen table. She washed the dishes naked, did some naked dancing, and then stood on her head for two minutes, also naked, which supposedly stimulated her pituitary gland, according to Yoko and Yoko. She sat on the couch and scratched her nose, her mind pleasantly blank. She did not think of Dark, not even once, but she felt Mr. Disgusting's presence. She looked around the room, trying to locate him. "Speak to me," she said out loud. "Speak to me, old man with no teeth and baggy underwear!" And then, just like that, he appeared. On the bed. Naked and semi-erect. She'd forgotten about his crooked cock. He gave her his toothless smile and patted the space next to him, and she was overcome with euphoria. "These pills annihilate loneliness," she murmured to Terry. "Holy shit." Then she took a short, naked nap in Mr. Disgusting's arms.

THE MODELING DID IN FACT GET EASIER, PARTLY BECAUSE LENA greeted her at the front door every Saturday and said, "Open your mouth."

Twenty minutes later, after the pill kicked in, baring herself became more bearable. Enjoyable, even. It wasn't being naked that she had reacted to in the beginning, it was being stared at, and she didn't mind their eyes on her now. *Go ahead, guys, drink me in*, she wanted to say. *Drink in my cellulite and man calves, I don't give a fuck.*

There were no hives now, no hearing loss, and no Terry Gross.

Paul handed her a gray mohair blanket. "Could you maybe pretend this blanket is trying to kill you?"

"Sure," she said.

"Don't be afraid to destroy it," Paul said.

"You can bite it," Lena said. "Or rip it. Whatever you feel like."

She went through the motions of grappling with the blanket, and choking it and so on, but it turned out to be difficult to kill a blanket on painkillers. The blanket was nicer than anything she owned, clothes included. For a long while she thought of her childhood blanket, a large, turmeric-colored cotton-acrylic blend with pink satin trim. Mona had sucked on that satin trim for years, rubbing the wet part against her cheek before sleep. When she turned seven, the blanket suddenly acquired a body, the body of a teenage girl named Brenda. Mona continued sucking on Brenda's trim, but she also kissed Brenda's face. She fastened a rubber band to Brenda, giving her a long ponytail. Brenda was submissive, with huge knockers. A cheerleader type. Prom queen, probably. They often rolled around on the floor together and Mona always wound up on top. She'd twist Brenda into a rope and hump her in front of the television while stroking Brenda's ponytail. She made love to Brenda in mixed company—she didn't think anyone knew what she was doing. Eventually, Brenda was taken away from Mona and probably burned, ending their five-year relationship. It was Mona's first breakup and it was a bitch, and Mona wept out of both eyes every night for a week.

LENA CALLED BREAK TIME "INTERMISSION." PAUL STAYED IN the studio while she and Lena smoked cigarettes, drank prosecco, and told stories on the patio. Or, more precisely, Lena told stories—entertaining, highly rehearsed stories that Mona suspected she'd told a hundred times—during which Mona wondered how many other women had sat where she was sitting, and whether Lena had also told them she loved them. She'd said it half a dozen times now, unceremoniously, without the "I."

"Love you," Lena said now, as they clinked glasses.

"More," Mona said.

"More what?" Lena said.

"Love," Mona said. "And war stories, please."

In Budapest, Lena said, she once poisoned a man to death after finding out he was a pedophile. In Los Angeles, a very famous basketball player paid her to poop on him. Also in Los Angeles, a very famous filmmaker tried to sodomize her with a broomstick. In Tanzania, she collected ancient bones, learned to fly a plane, and had a brief affair with a Maasai warrior.

"Wait, was Tanzania before or after you were a hooker?" Mona asked.

"After," Lena said.

"Before or after you were married?"

"Long after," she said. "Open your mouth."

"Again?" Mona said.

"It's only Percocet," she said.

Usually Lena placed the pill on Mona's tongue and then handed Mona a glass of something to wash it down. This time she fed Mona the pill from her own mouth. Their tongues touched briefly and Mona thought she tasted blood. Underneath the blood, a hint of sweet corn, or perhaps cereal. Lena pulled away and smiled.

"Jesus," Mona said. "I wasn't expecting that."

"I just kiss-fed you," Lena said. "I used to do that with my daughter. With food, obviously, not pills."

Mona nodded. "I did that with my dog a few times."

"It's a pretty powerful bonding ritual," Lena said. "It's also where French kissing evolved from."

"I've seen apes do it," Mona said. "On TV. By the way, not to change the subject, but I haven't pooped in like three days."

"That's easy," Lena said, scratching her nose. "Next time you're on the toilet, reach down and slide your thumb into your vagina." To demonstrate, Lena wiggled her thumb into an imaginary vagina. "Press on the back wall," Lena instructed. "You'll feel the shit in there. Massage it like this." As Lena massaged the imaginary back wall, Mona was overcome with tenderness.

"You fascinate me," Mona said.

"I bet you have some war stories of your own," Lena said.

"More than you'd want to know."

"That's not possible," Lena said, and lit a cigarette. "I want to know everything."

Did she? Mona drank the rest of her prosecco and then drained Lena's glass, as well. Lena was looking at her expectantly.

"Tell me something you don't tell other people," Lena said.

"Well, I once knew a guy who murdered his girlfriend," Mona said.

She checked Lena's face to make sure she was listening. Lena seemed to be smoothing Mona's hair with her eyes.

"I met him a couple of summers before he killed that girl, when I was nineteen and he was twenty-two. Earlier that year, he'd chopped off his own finger with a hatchet just to see what it felt like, and tried to burn the tattoo off his forehead with acid. He often threw himself down flights of stairs on purpose and would walk into moving traffic. For whatever reason, I found this guy entertaining. He looked like a psychopath, but I never thought he was an actual crazy person, or even dangerous, because I'd spent a month in a psychiatric hospital with legitimately unstable people, and this guy wasn't like them. He was charming and affectionate. A decent storyteller. A happy drunk.

"One Saturday afternoon in July, he was drinking in my living room while I was getting ready for work. I'd just gotten my own apartment, and he'd stopped by to check it out. I was washing my hair in the kitchen sink, for some reason, and he came up behind me and tried to get under my bathrobe. I turned around and slapped him, which had always stopped him in the past, but this time he dragged me to the bedroom and threw me on the bed. When I tried to get up, he pushed my head down."

She checked Lena's face again. Lena's eyes were now caressing Mona's neck.

"He raped me with a large, round hairbrush. Not with the bristle end, but with the weird rubber handle and only some of the bristles. He was behind me. I was not on all fours, but rather lying flat against the mattress, which felt somehow more revealing, and he had my legs spread. I was in a complete panic, but only internally. From the outside, I looked as though I was playing dead.

"The worst part wasn't the hairbrush, strangely. It was the sunlight. It was streaming in through the room's many windows, and I was fully exposed. He could see everything. My instinct wasn't to scream or fight him off, but rather to find a way to turn around, and I realized that I was ashamed of my cellulite. I was worried about how my butt looked. Part of me wanted to look good for him, which added an extra layer of shame to the whole thing.

"Eventually I managed to convince him that we should be facing each other. He seemed confused by that because we'd talked about sex and I'd mentioned that I liked it from behind. So, he knew that about me. Anyway, he let me turn around to face him and he fucked me for about two minutes, and then—this was another surprise—he pinned me down with his knees and started jerking off. I remember thinking, Is there something wrong with my pussy? Why doesn't he want that?

"Although I despised my body back then, I was on pretty good terms with my face. My face and I were friends. My eyes could have been bigger, perhaps, and more symmetrical, but I liked my cheekbones. My face was the only part of my body that I didn't actively loathe. So, of course that's where he chose to ejaculate. I was like, Fuck—really? No one ever done that to me. I didn't watch porn back then, and so I had no idea that this was something people did, and that it had been given its own category.

"Afterward, he asked me why I was crying and tried to console me.

He had his arm around me like we were old friends. He seemed baffled that I was upset, because I hadn't put up a fight. I had been too distracted, too weakened by my stupid thoughts. I could not speak. My throat was completely closed, and I could barely swallow.

"He said, 'You know, you should work out a little. You don't need much, but you'd feel a lot better about yourself.' He spoke kindly, out of what seemed like genuine concern. My whole body was burning at that point, and the tears kept rolling. They would not stop.

"'Wait, hold on,' he said. 'Here, stand up.'

"I had to be at work in thirty minutes. So why was he kneeling in front of me? For a second I thought he was going to try to give me head, or something stupid like that, but it turned out he was holding an electric razor. Before I understood what was happening, he'd buzzed off most of my pubic hair. I was stunned again and unable to move. 'There,' he said. 'Much better.' He led me over to the only antique I own, a full-length dowel mirror.

"It looked grotesque to me. I felt like a stranger to myself. As I got dressed, I kept telling myself that everything was fine. I even let the guy hug me goodbye. *Okay, yeah, see you later. Uh-huh, yeah, cool, take care*—like that. There was no way I was going to let him know he'd gotten to me. I knew I would tell no one. So, I went to work like it was any other day. I wondered how I was going to explain my missing bush, but my boyfriend was touched and delighted. He said, 'Did you shave your pussy for me?' As if I was a total sweetheart. And I thought, No, the guy who raped me this afternoon shaved my pussy for you. He's the sweetheart.

"Anyway, this is all a long—and perhaps not very interesting—way of saying that if I'd been a normal white nineteen-year-old with healthy self-esteem, I would have called the cops that day, and maybe that girl would still be alive."

Lena let out a puff of air.

"The End," Mona said.

"Does your mother know about that?" Lena asked.

"My mother? No."

Lena's eyes were watering. "Why not?"

"I buried it," Mona said.

Lena stubbed out her cigarette. "Well, at least he's in prison," she said. "Getting raped."

Mona shrugged. Lena went back to staring at the boat. Mona watched her eyes go out of focus and fill up with water again. It was something she did roughly every seven minutes, whenever there was a lull in the conversation, or sometimes even while she was telling a story. Only when her eyes watered did she look away, and then it was usually at Mona's face. The boat seemed to both anchor and unsettle her.

"I do that with your coffee table," Mona said.

"What?" Lena said.

"Stare at it," Mona said. "When I feel lost."

"I'm not lost," Lena said slowly. "I'm praying."

"For what?"

"You," Lena said. "And for rain."

Mona looked up at the sky: uniformly blue, as usual. Not a cloud in sight.

THE FOLLOWING WEEK, MONA WATCHED LENA EAT AN AVO-cado. She cut it in half, removed the pit, and filled the holes with olive oil. She fed herself slowly with a beautiful gold spoon.

"You really know how to live," Mona said.

Lena wiped her mouth with a linen napkin. "Let's look at your photographs."

"Again?" Mona said.

"Yes," Lena said. "We need to figure out your story."

Mona retrieved her camera and handed it over. Lena made appreciative noises as she scrolled through, and then she removed her glasses and looked Mona in the eye.

"Let me send these to some people I know," she said, and crossed her legs.

"People?"

"Curators, gallery owners," she said. "Other artists like yourself."

"I'm not an artist," Mona said. "I'm just a documenter, a record keeper."

Lena rolled her eyes. "You have an exciting career ahead of you, Mona, if you want it," she said, "but you have to want it."

"I'd rather just be you for a few years," Mona said.

"Once we print these out," Lena said, ignoring her, "which we can do very easily on Paul's inkjet, perhaps you'll see what I see."

She did. The sixty or so prints they made were stunning, particularly the photo sequences from Paul and Lena's house. The story many of the sequences told, in Lena's view, was a ghost story in reverse: in the first shots Mona was a pale, nebulous apparition wearing an apron and cleaning; in the final shots, dressed in their clothes, handling their most precious objects, she transformed into a living, breathing, fully fledged badass.

"You start out looking exhausted and—I don't know—anemic? Your power seems very neutered," Lena said. "And then, bit by bit, you come back to life. It's really beautiful to witness, actually."

It was a story Mona hadn't been conscious of telling, and she wasn't sure if it was accurate or even true, but she enjoyed listening to Lena discuss her sensibility as a photographer, how her work was reminiscent of Duane Michals, an American known for his use of the photo sequence, which he coupled with his own handwritten prose, and Sophie Calle, a French artist known for her detective-like ability to document the private lives of strangers. Calle once followed a man she met at a party in Paris all the way to Venice, and then she followed him around Venice, photographing him without his knowledge.

"That's sort of what you're doing with these houses," Lena said. "Don't you think? It's another angle to the story. The detective angle."

"Except these houses aren't strangers to me," Mona said. "I have intimate relationships with them. Especially this house. I feel like I'm fucking this house."

"It's me you're fucking," Lena said. "I mean, in the sense that this house is all me."

"Are you responsible for that coffee table?"

"In more ways than you'll ever know," Lena said sadly.

Mona waited for her to say more, but Lena lit a cigarette instead.

"What about the black violet toilet?"

"Custom-made for me by an old lover," Lena said, exhaling. After a pause she added, in a soft voice, "Do you know that I love you?"

Mona swallowed. She felt lightheaded and weightless, as if she'd fainted and hit her head and was now being carried in someone's arms. Lena was the "I," Mona was the "you," but the arms? The arms were the phrase "do you know." That's what she felt buoyed by: "do you know?" It made Lena's question seem utterly selfless and without need, a question that didn't require an answer. Wasn't that what true love was, according to Stevie Wonder? It asked for nothing. Acceptance was the way you paid.

ON HER NEXT VISIT, LENA WASN'T THERE. ONE OF THEIR CURAtors quit, Paul explained, so Lena needed to spend Saturdays at the gallery in Santa Fe. They would be moving forward without her. Paul gave her a small smile.

"She left this for you," he said.

Allergy Rescue, the label read. The bottle was heavy and contained many days' worth of rescue—weeks, perhaps months. She suspected she wouldn't be seeing Lena for a while, possibly ever again. She'd been ghosted. Was it something she'd said? She should have nixed the rape story, for starters. No one wanted to hear about that. Or perhaps it was what she hadn't said. *I know you love me,* she should've answered. *I love you, too.*

She'd spent all week painstakingly rewriting and editing her house-keeping notes, and then handwriting the best ones and pairing them with the beautiful prints they'd made. She'd placed everything in a fancy leather portfolio she never would have bought otherwise. Pomegranate lambskin, hand-finished and ink stained, with an old-fashioned cord binding. A hundred and fifty bucks. The process of putting it all together had been deeply satisfying and occasionally thrilling, and when she was finished she'd felt immediately attached to it. She'd spent an evening or two snuggled up on the couch with it, petting the cover. That morning, however, she'd felt an overwhelming urge to destroy it, to drown it in the bathtub or set fire to it, and then throw herself off the Gorge Bridge.

"Well, I brought her something, too," Mona said. "Will you give it to her?"

"Of course," Paul said.

She handed him the portfolio and watched him place it on his cluttered desk. Seeing it there made her feel lonely suddenly, and diminished somehow, as if she'd given Paul her pinkie finger.

NEEDLESS TO SAY, THE ATMOSPHERE CHANGED IN LENA'S ABsence. Props began to appear, a different one each week. A dentist's chair, a pink salon chair with a hair dryer, a metal examination table, all dragged out of the huge storage closet at the back of the studio. He always made a few sketches first and then photographed her with a large-format camera.

He asked her to close her eyes in the dentist's chair, to cross her legs and read a magazine under the hair dryer, and to put her feet in the stirrups of the examination table, "but don't worry," he said quickly, "I'm only photographing you from above. I can't see your *punci.*"

"My what?" she asked.

"'*Punci*' is Hungarian for 'vagina,'" he said.

Once she had her feet in the stirrups, he told her she reminded him of Valerie Neuzil, Egon Schiele's model and mistress.

"He's one of my favorites," she said.

"I'm happy you know who he is," Paul said. "He's been a major influence on me."

I can see that, she wanted to say, but stopped herself. Best not to point out that his work was derivative.

"Childbirth is going to be difficult for you," he said.

She blinked at him, thinking he was commenting on her *punci*.

"I don't mean to frighten you, but you have hips like Lena's," he said. "She had a terrible time giving birth. Like pushing a piano through a transom."

"I'm twenty-six," Mona said.

"Can you touch your toes?" he asked. "I think you can't."

"I most certainly can."

"You bend over like an old woman," he said.

"How do you say 'fuck off' in Hungarian?" she asked.

He laughed. "*Baszd meg,*" he said. "*Baszd meg.*"

ONE DAY SHE WALKED IN TO FIND A CLAW-FOOT TUB SITTING IN the middle of the studio. The outside of the tub was painted a rich gunmetal gray, and the inside was filled with mysterious green liquid. She didn't like the looks of it.

"It's just water," he said.

"Why is it green?"

"I wanted it to look like absinthe."

She wondered if that was what he'd been drinking. He looked both tired and manic. His hair was unwashed and standing on end, and there were bread crumbs in his beard. His skin was oddly purple, especially around his eyes.

She undressed and he asked her to climb into the tub. She hesitated.

"I'm not really a fan of water," she said. "That's why I moved to the desert."

She eased herself in while he adjusted the studio lights. The water was warm, but not warm enough. He plucked a red apple from a bowl on one of the worktables. "Would you mind holding this?" He polished it on his T-shirt before handing it to her.

"Hold it how?"

"Bring your knees together, then maybe balance it between them? Rest your arms and hands on the lip of the tub."

She did as he said and watched him climb the ladder.

"Where should I look?" she asked.

"At the apple," he said. "Keep your chin down. Good. Now look up at me with your eyes."

What else would she look at him with—her feet? He took a few pictures and then spent the next thirty minutes moving the ladder around, photographing her from different angles.

AT AGE SEVEN, SHE'D DOGGY-PADDLED ACROSS THE POOL WITH an apple in her mouth to entertain her grandparents, who'd been bickering. She'd even swum four circles around Ginger, who was treading water in the deep end. Woody was standing at the pool's edge, laughing. She still had the apple in her mouth when she got out of the pool and Woody wrapped a towel around her shoulders. He took it from her mouth and bit into it.

"You look like Esther Williams," he said, chewing.

Ginger climbed out of the pool and stood dripping in her red skirted swimsuit and matching bathing cap.

"I made a pork roast," Woody announced to them both. "And homemade applesauce."

"Yum," Mona said.

"You and your pork," Ginger said. "Honest to God."

Woody offered Ginger a towel.

"You're my favorite mermaid," he said to Ginger, but he was looking at Mona.

"You're a piece of work, mister," Ginger said, and snatched the towel out of his hands.

"Let me dry your back, dear," he said.

"Buzz off," she said, and stepped away from him.

Mona watched her walk away, her wet feet slapping the concrete. She looked at Woody's face, expecting to see anger or sadness there, but he was still staring at Mona and smiling. "Well, *you* like pork, don't you?"

She didn't like the way he was looking at her then, which was confusing. His gaze had always been a kind of corrective lens—it brought everything into instant focus. She could even *hear* better when he was watching, and he was always watching—in the pool, in the mirror, at the kitchen counter, at the organ, behind the bar. He even stared at her when she was doing something that wasn't particularly interesting, like reading a book, peeing, sleeping.

But now her ears felt like they had water in them and she fumbled with the towel and then dropped it.

"Let's go inside," Woody said. "You're shivering."

She felt his eyes on her as she picked up the towel and walked toward the apartment, stubbing her toe on a chaise lounge.

"YOU LOOK TIRED," PAUL SUDDENLY SAID FROM THE LADDER.

"I think I just figured out why I hate apples," Mona said.

"Let's eat lunch," Paul said.

Well, this was a first—he never ate lunch with her. She climbed out of the tub and saw that her torso and legs were bottle green.

"Oh," Paul said. "I didn't think of that."

"Is it dye?"

"Food coloring," he said. "It will come out eventually."

———

"Shaving cream will get it off," she said.

Terry would have been extremely impressed with that information, but Paul said nothing. He brought her a towel and held her kimono while she dried herself off. "I like this," he said. It was a new one, hand-painted with a peacock motif. She realized now that she'd bought it for Lena, not herself. He helped her put it on. "I always wonder why you wear this during the breaks. Are you embarrassed?"

"I don't know," Mona said. "Yes?"

"Don't waste your youth hating your body," he said. "You will regret it, believe me."

"What do you want me to do—eat lunch naked?"

"Why not?"

They ate leftover Thai in the dining room. She was happy to see the lopsided plates again. There was an open bottle of wine on the table. She peered at the label, which had a picture of an angry bull on it.

"Bull's Blood," she read out loud.

"It's Hungarian," he said. "From a small town in the north called Eger, where I grew up. My parents were winemakers."

"Is there blood in it?"

He shook his head. "Eger was invaded by the Turks in the fifteen hundreds. The Turks had an army of one hundred fifty thousand, but the people of Eger—the Hungarians—managed to fend them off, even though there were only two thousand of them. The Hungarians drank so much wine that their beards and armor looked bloodstained. They were ferocious fighters. The Turks, who were very superstitious, thought that they must have been drinking the blood of bulls, and retreated like a bunch of wuzzies."

"Wussies," Mona corrected him.

"Or . . . pussies?" Paul offered.

"That works, too," she said, and smiled.

He poured them each a glass and they drank in silence for a few minutes. Then she asked him why he'd left Hungary all those years ago.

"Hitler," he said.

She didn't ask him to elaborate.

"May I ask how old you are?" Mona asked.

"Older than you think," he said, and topped off her glass. "May I ask why you clean houses?"

She sipped her wine and tried to think of something smart to say. Nothing came to mind. "I like how cut-and-dry it is," she finally said. "How black and white."

"You don't make it black and white," he said. "You make it complicated and dangerous."

"Dangerous?" she coughed.

"You're like my wife," he said. "You don't have any boundaries."

"I don't take my work home with me," she said. "That's all I meant."

"Of course you do," he said. "You take photographs."

"But only in secret," she said. "I don't share them with anyone. I live in my own world, trust me. I'm very isolated."

"You like your own company," he said, "but, in your art, you put yourself onstage. You don't want to be invisible. You want to be seen."

He seemed to search her face for a reaction. She felt herself blush and looked at the napkin in her lap.

"It's okay to want those things," he said.

"Did Lena have a chance to look at my book?"

He blinked at her.

"The portfolio I left for her," she said.

"Oh yes," he said after a pause. "In fact, she took it with her to New York."

New York. She pictured Lena wandering around the Village, the portfolio tucked under her arm. Did she appreciate the quality of the leather? Did she smell it? Did she approve of Mona's color choice? Now she thought of Lena sitting in the sunny office of a gallery, meeting with other curators, and Mona's portfolio was on the table. Was it getting warm in the sun?

"Was Lena one of your students? Is that how you met?"

He sipped his wine and looked past her out the window. "She was my model," he said. "I stole her away from a famous painter. I wooed her very heavily. It was a lot of work. And then we had Rain."

"Rain?" Mona said.

"Our daughter," Paul said.

They named their kid after the weather? Her confusion must have shown on her face, because he said, " 'Rain' is short for 'Rainer.' It's a boy's name, but it suited her. We named her after Lena's grandfather, who was German."

"Where is she?" Mona asked. "New York?"

"Not anymore," Paul said. "She drowned herself."

Before she could respond, he stood up and walked into the kitchen. She looked at the boat sculpture out the sliding glass door. Lena had made it because she missed Rain, not rain, and it was Rain she prayed for. Not rain.

Rain.

Not . . . rain, you fucking idiot.

Paul returned carrying a paper sack. "You don't look well," he said. "Did Lena not tell you?"

"Nope," Mona said.

"You remind her very much of Rainer," he said. "Maybe that's why."

"You don't keep any photographs of her," Mona said. "On the walls, I mean."

"She's all over the house," Paul said. "Her drawings and paintings, the photographs she took. We scattered most of her ashes in the sea. The rest are in the coffee table."

"What?" Mona said.

"The table you said you dream about," he said. "We put some of her ashes in with the gold leaves. Lena's idea." He opened the paper sack and handed her a large chocolate truffle. "It's from Budapest. You're going to want to bite it, but don't. Just let it melt in your mouth."

He put one in his mouth, too, and they sat there, not speaking, waiting for the chocolate to melt. It was the kindest way she'd ever been told to shut up.

She got dressed and he walked her to the door—another first—and handed her two hundred-dollar bills and a bottle of Bull's Blood.

SHE STILL COVETED THE COFFEE TABLE, EVEN THOUGH IT WAS essentially a coffin. How strange to place the remains of your only child in an object you rested your feet on. Strange and creepy. She was comfortable with creepy, though, and they knew it. Wasn't that why they'd let her into their lives?

Creepy Woody, that's what they'd called him. She'd overheard two women talking about him by the pool one day. Natalie and Tina, the grown daughters of one of the tenants, staying with their parents for the weekend. They talked at length about his staring problem, and how goddamn creepy it was, and how they avoided contact with him altogether.

"Remember his son?" Tina said. "He was a little creep, too."

"Apple doesn't fall far from the tree," Natalie said.

Mona climbed out of the shallow end and scurried into the apartment dripping wet, where Woody was waiting for her with a butter and sugar sandwich, but she ran past him and into the bathroom, closing the door behind her and locking it. She got out of her wet bathing suit and wrapped a towel around herself and stood there shaking, humiliated, and Woody knocked on the door and asked what the matter was, and why was the door closed?

She couldn't say what was bothering her, but she felt contaminated somehow. "It's not the snake bite that kills you," Woody had told her once, "but the venom." That's what she felt like—full of poison. Her family was creepy. It was something people talked about. Woody had given her father the creepy gene and now she wondered if she was creepy, too.

———

AT HOME, SHE SLATHERED HERSELF WITH SHAVING CREAM AND stepped into the shower. The green stain faded but didn't disappear. She wrapped herself in a towel and then slid Ginger's package out from under the bed and opened it with a box cutter. She saw the back of the canvas first. As usual, he'd written his initials and the date, *W.B. 1983*, but there was also a thick manila envelope wedged into one of the corner braces. She removed it and turned it over in her hands. It was addressed to no one, but she knew before opening it that it was money and that it was meant for her. For the first time in her life, she looked at the ceiling and prayed for thousand-dollar bills.

No such luck. They weren't hundreds, either. Or even twenties, for that matter.

"Christ, Woody, what's the obsession with two-dollar bills?" she remembered Ginger saying. "They're worthless, ding-a-ling!"

"Actually, dear, they're not worthless," he'd said patiently. "They're worth two dollars."

She wondered if it had been Woody or Ginger who'd put the money there. No way of knowing now. She stood up and turned the canvas over, laid it flat on the floor.

There it was, the same composition as always: an exhausted-looking bullfighter on one side of the canvas, the fallen horse with its blood and intestines spilling into the dirt on the other side of the canvas, and the bull, also bleeding, in the middle. It was a gory picture, but it wasn't the blood that made the painting compelling, it was the bull's eyes. They were brown, bloodshot, watchful, and painted to look human. They were her grandfather's eyes.

She rested the painting against the wall and picked up the bundle of money again. The bills were crisp, brand-new, and ordered by serial number. The bull watched her count it. One thousand dollars in two-dollar bills.

———

"What the fuck do you want me to do with this?" she asked the bull.

His eyes followed her to the dresser, where she stuck the money in her sock drawer, and continued watching her as she let the towel fall to the floor. The bull seemed to stare at her ass. She turned the painting to face the wall.

PAUL MET HER AT THE FRONT DOOR ON THE FOLLOWING SATurday. His hair was still wet from the shower, and he'd trimmed his beard. He was also wearing real pants for once. Or apple-green cords, if those counted as real pants.

"I want to show you something," he said.

She followed him to the basement. She'd never been down here before. They came to a closed door and he pulled out a key and opened it.

"I want you to see this," he said.

The room was empty of furniture and lit with track lights. A series of large canvases hung on the walls. She saw the Schiele from the doorway. She'd never seen an original. She walked up to it and took a good look. Paul stayed near the door. It was an erotic painting featuring a bony, black-haired woman in a supine position, holding herself open with both hands. He'd used the same pink for the nipples and the rouge on her cheeks, and the same orangey color for both sets of lips, and the woman's hair and pubes were customarily blurry looking while everything else was in extra-sharp focus. If it had belonged to her it would have been hanging over her bed.

"Well, I can see why you keep this locked up," she said, and looked over her shoulder at him. He was standing a few feet behind her now. "Must be worth millions."

He laughed. "It's worth a lot to me," he said. "I painted it a long time ago."

"Oh," she said, and looked again. So, it was a knockoff. So what. Counterfeit or not, she still loved it and wished it were hers.

"Do you recognize the woman?" he asked.

"Anjelica Huston," she said. "Duh."

He smiled. "Lena," he said. "Thirty years ago."

She looked at the other canvases. Lena was everywhere, doing all kinds of things: bent over, touching herself, wrestling with a scary blonde woman, examining her own nipple, bound, blindfolded, smiling.

Her *punci* was everywhere, too. Sometimes it was small and demure looking; more often it was engorged, exaggerated, the lips rudely parted. It seemed to want to be looked at and admired. Explored.

"A swollen door doesn't close properly," she remembered Woody saying once.

"What makes it swollen?" she'd asked.

"Moisture," he'd said. "It's been humid this summer, so all the doors are warping." He brushed a strand of hair out of her face. "Wood shrinks and swells," he said.

She'd wedged a chair under her doorknob that night, but when she woke up Woody was there, sitting in the chair, staring at her.

So was Paul. "These paintings are older than you are," he said. "They're from another life."

"She's beautiful," Mona said. "Truly. I can see why she inspired you, why you fell so hard for her."

"She was very good in the spotlight, on my stage," he said.

There was a silence.

He cleared his throat. "I've been commissioned to make a painting like one of these," he said. "Would you be . . . interested?"

So, this was why he'd brought her here. Or why he'd hired her in the first place?

"We'd have to start today," he said. "The painting is due in two weeks."

"Oh," she said.

He shook his head. "It's okay if you're not comfortable. I wouldn't want you to do it if you didn't feel . . . good about it."

"Would Nadine have done it?" she asked. "Your previous model?"

"Perhaps," he said. "If she'd had enough to drink."

"What about Lena?" Mona said. "Why not her?"

"Lena doesn't make herself available to me," he said. "Not in this way, not anymore."

HE GAVE HER A PAIR OF LENA'S THIGH-HIGH STOCKINGS, A matching garter she'd never seen before, and a pair of designer stilettos, maroon leather with bright red bottoms, heels she'd worn for her own photographs, as she liked the way they looked with her safari apron. They were half a size too small, however, so she had to stuff her feet into them. She looked at her reflection in the window and decided she looked like a hooker—an expensive hooker.

He wanted her on her back with her legs spread. "Bring your right knee toward your chin. Try and hug it to your chest with your right arm," he said. "Now bring your left arm up and over your head. Like that. Arch your back a little. Look at me."

"How long?" she asked.

He looked at his watch. "Fifty minutes," he said. "Then you can take a break."

Allergy Rescue. The bottle was still in her bag, which was behind the shoji screen, but she was too lazy to make a fuss.

"Can I close my eyes?"

"For now, yes."

She listened to his pencil scratch the canvas, and then his knife. Outside, the aspens were being their usual hypersensitive selves. She heard applause in their leaves and saw herself standing in a gallery in New York City. The walls were lined with her photographs, blown up and framed, and the floor was crowded with people—it was an opening—and there was Tom Waits talking to Jim Jarmusch, and Sophie Calle drinking champagne with Lena, and Laurie Anderson wearing a suit and holding a small dog, and Terry Gross, live and in person, standing next to the self-portrait of her in the Bach home, wearing lederhosen and sitting next to Pork Chop, the family terrier—

She felt Paul's weight on the platform. The wood creaked and she could hear him breathing through his nose. She opened her eyes. He was crouched between her legs, holding the Polaroid. He brought the camera to his face, pushed the button. She heard herself gasp.

"Wait," he said, looking at her crotch. "You have something—"

"What?"

He squinted at it. "Something black."

"Where?"

"On your—" he said. "Wait, don't move." He stepped off the platform and handed her a small mirror.

"It's just your weird toilet paper," she said, and picked it off. She pinched it between her fingers and he took another Polaroid.

"Touch yourself," he said drily. "Like you would if you were alone."

"Like this?" she said.

"Yes," he said.

"This isn't how I touch myself," she said, and took her hand away.

What a fool. The way women touched themselves when they were alone: rarely photogenic. Wasn't he old enough to know that?

AN HOUR LATER, HE ASKED HER TO STAND WITH HER FEET WIDE apart. "Good," he said. "Now, bend over and hug your left knee."

She did as he said, her hair brushing the floor, and grasped the back of her knee with both hands.

"You're choking your knee," he said. "Not hugging it."

Her arms and legs were shaking. "I'm not a contortionist."

"Turn your heels out a little," he said. "Relax your arms."

She forced her chest a little closer to her leg and stared at her trem-

bling knee. Her nose was running. He took pictures with three different cameras and sketched furiously for fifteen minutes. She went back
to her exhibition in New York and walked around the gallery. She was
standing in front of a portrait of her and her vacuum when Dark sidled
up and put an arm around her shoulders. *I'm so proud of you*, he said.
And I miss you like crazy—

Paul mumbled something.

She moved her head slightly so that she could see his face, and
decided she liked the way it looked upside down.

"Did you say something?"

"Your vagina," he said.

She waited for him to continue, but he didn't. "What about it?"

"It's very young."

She studied his face to see if anything might be written there. The
word "weltschmerz" came to mind. That was what she saw in his upside-
down eyes, his upside-down mouth, the way he shuffled his feet. She
hadn't thought of that word since her first date with Mr. Disgusting.

"'WELTSCHMERZ' MEANS 'WORLD-PAIN,'" SHE REMEMBERED
Woody saying in bed. "'World-weariness.'" He lit a cigarette. "You're
only eleven, so you're too young to feel it now, but you are likely to feel it
later, after you've lived in the world a while."

He had the kind of cancer you could see. Black lesions on his head
and face, growing, spreading, morphing. He reminded her of a large, rot-
ting banana. And now there was a new lesion in the iris of his left eye—a
second pupil, it looked like, about to eclipse the real one. Unfortunately,
it hadn't interfered with his vision. He still spent most of his time in bed,
chain-smoking and watching her.

Ginger didn't scream at him anymore. She read him the *Los Angeles Times*, trimmed his fingernails, fed him rainbow sherbet, and

let him smoke with the windows closed. If he asked for scotch, she poured him a triple and didn't water it down. He could watch whatever he wanted on the idiot box, and he could crank it up and leave it on all night, if that's what he felt like doing. She even let him piss standing up.

"Sleep in here with him, Mona," she'd said. "Make sure he doesn't drop his cigarette and burn the place down. That's the last thing we need."

"Where are you going?"

"To your room," she said. "We can't all sleep in the same bed—I'm too fat and you're too big now. If he seems like he's in pain, come wake me up."

Mona sat in the chair next to the bed that night and they watched Johnny Carson. She could tell he was trying to stay awake, but he dozed off when the news came on. She waited until he was snoring before getting into bed.

"FIVE MORE MINUTES," PAUL SAID.

"Then what?"

"You can go." He looked at her face. "Smile," he said, for the first time.

"Say something funny," she said. "I don't smile on cue."

He frowned, scratched his head with his pencil. "Well, then I guess I will have to give you a fake smile."

"Fine," she said.

"Place your left hand on your behind," he said. "Pull your cheek away from your—"

She heard herself shriek. The pain was so sudden and sharp, for a second she thought he'd done something to her. Knifed, or punched her. Then, another spasm. This one felt electric, shooting down the backs of her legs and zapping her feet. She collapsed heavily onto her hands and knees. She was frozen for a second, but then her arms and legs began to quiver, and now her ass was quivering, too. "Fuck," she said.

"What's happening to you?" he asked.

"My back," she said.

"Lie down and rest."

"I can't move." She wanted to kick off Lena's heels, but her feet were swollen and completely numb.

"I have something," he announced. "Downstairs. I will get it for you."

She waited, eyes watering, ass in the air. Wished she had a tail to tuck between her legs, something with which to cover herself. She listened to the aspens quaking outside. The wind called and the leaves answered and it seemed so loud to her suddenly, so inappropriate and out of rhythm.

Her spine whimpered. She fell awkwardly onto her side and then slowly brought her knees toward her chest. A pillow was what she needed, wedged between her legs, something to relieve the pressure. Paul kept a few under the platform. She reached under there and felt around. Her hand touched something soft and smooth. Skin, it felt like. Soft skin.

Lambskin.

Her portfolio.

WOODY HAD TALKED IN HIS SLEEP THAT NIGHT. GIBBERISH mostly, but she could make out a sentence here and there. "Swim over to me," he'd said at 2:18 A.M. "Make a keyhole with your arms."

She'd kept her back to him and stared at the green numbers on the Cartex alarm clock next to the bed. The clock was made to look digital, but the numbers weren't synchronized and only lined up evenly on the hour. This bothered her for a while.

At 3:13 A.M., which happened to be the time she was born, she heard him mumble, "It hurts. It hurts all over the sheets."

She got out of bed, pulled back the covers, and looked for blood or shit or piss. Nothing. He was touching himself through his pajama bottoms. "It hurts," he repeated, and she waited for the rest of the sentence: when your wife doesn't touch it. That's what he'd said before, when she was eight, and she'd felt so sorry for him, because it really did look painful—shiny, angry, the wrong color.

She climbed back into bed and stared at the clock. After a while she closed her eyes and drifted off. When she woke, just after dawn, he was lying on his side, holding his head up with one of his hands and staring at her. His skin looked green and baggy, the lesion on his nose glistening like a piece of tar.

"You sleep like an angel," he whispered.

"Are you in pain?" she asked. "Should I get Grandma?"

"Let her sleep," he said. "Just bring me my medicine and two fingers of scotch."

Fingers. He said two, but he always meant three.

She poured the scotch and went for his medicine in the bathroom. It was in its usual spot on the sink. Oramorph Oral Solution, Morphine Sulfate. She unscrewed the cap, squeezed the nipple-like bulb, and drew a full dose into the dropper. Ginger usually emptied the dose into a glass of water, and that's what Mona did, but it seemed like too little to really do anything, so she added four or five more.

Poor Ginger. When she came into the bedroom that morning Woody's creepy eyes were still open—of course—but he'd been gone for twenty minutes or more. Mona was just sitting there, paralyzed.

"Happy birthday, mister," Ginger said, and kissed his forehead.

"He's not here," Mona said.

Ginger put her face right up to his and shouted, "Woodrow! Wake up!" She looked pissed off when he didn't answer. She turned to Mona and said, "Christ! Why the fuck didn't you come get me?"

She'd never heard Ginger say "fuck" before.

"He said not to wake you," Mona said in a shaky voice.

After they took his body away, Ginger put on her sunglasses and didn't remove them for five weeks. If you hadn't known her, you'd have thought she was legally blind.

PAUL WAS BACK, CARRYING A LARGE TEAK SERVING TRAY, which he set on the platform. A glass of water, a tumbler of amber liquor, two white horse pills. "Muscle relaxers," he said. "One for now, one for later. And some bourbon, if you like. Here, open your mouth." He placed the pill on her tongue and she thought of Lena. He brought the water glass to her mouth. The pill stuck to her tongue and dissolved a little. She made a face.

He smiled and handed her the bourbon. Two burning fingers.

"Do you think you could take these shoes off for me?" she asked.

"Of course," he said. "Roll onto your back."

He crouched at her feet and pried off Lena's heels. His hands were smeared with red and pink paint. She realized he'd never touched her before, not even on the shoulder. He seemed to realize this, too, because he kept his hands on her a little longer than necessary, squeezing and massaging each of her feet. His touch felt reassuring and paternal, but it was edged with something else, something impoverished, deprived.

Allergy Rescue. "Will you bring me my purse, please?" she asked. "And my kimono?"

"Please don't worry," he said, ignoring her. He moved the tray aside and sat next to her on the platform. "It's not the end of the world."

"Yeah, I know," she said.

"Then tell me why you look so sad."

She smiled weakly.

"Is the pill working?"

"I miss Lena," she said.

"What do you miss about her?" he asked.

"Our weird, easy friendship," Mona said.

He got to his feet and walked over to the shoji screen. She thought for a moment that Lena might be hiding there, waiting for her cue. *Surprise!* But he was just fetching her purse. No kimono.

"I wish I had something stronger to give you," he said, handing her the purse. "But I had to throw everything away." He removed his glasses and placed them on the platform. Fuck, she thought, not those naked eyes again. He may as well have presented her with his scrotum.

Christ, Woodrow, turn over, she heard Ginger's voice say.

"I had to empty the house," he said. "It took days. I wandered around with a trash bag. At one point I was convinced she'd hidden pills in the boat. Anyway, what I'm trying to say is that Lena is in the hospital. For drugs. That's where she went last month. That's why she isn't here. She didn't abandon you."

Rehab—right, of course. Her departure had had nothing to do with Mona. Did anything have anything to do with Mona? Probably not. Lena didn't *love* her, not really. She just missed her daughter. As usual, Mona had only been a surrogate, a body double, a substitute for the real thing. It seemed to be her role in life, starting with Woody.

We are all ghosts in each other's stories, she imagined pontificating to Terry.

She thrust her hand in her purse and rummaged around. There it was. She opened the bottle and peered inside.

"You didn't throw everything away," she said. "You gave it to me." She shook out two pills. "See?"

He watched her swallow the pills without water.

"Are you also an addict?" he asked.

"I'm an enabler," she said. "Which is more insidious and perhaps harder to treat."

He grunted. They were silent for a while.

"You two and your secrets," Mona said. "Lena seemed like such an open book, and you seemed so stoic, but you're actually more forthcoming than she is. At least about what matters. She had no problem talking about poop and prostitution and yet she couldn't tell me—"

"Detachment," he said, and rested a hand on her forearm. "It's a question of detachment. Lena is still very attached to her grief. But she loves you. She talks about you all the time."

His hand felt heavy on her arm. She glanced at the paint on his knuckles and closed her eyes. Where would his hand go next? It would find her breast, perhaps, followed by her *punci*. What would she do about it? She was too old to let anything happen. In fact, she felt as ancient as the aspens out the window, as durable and dependable. It was Paul who was quaking, not her. His fingers trembled on her arm. They seemed weak and artless to her now, as if newly born.

"You're so young," he murmured.

She opened her eyes. "You keep saying that," she said. "But I'm not that young."

He removed his hand from her arm. "Have I upset you?"

She felt the pills loosen something in her brain. "It feels like you're about to molest me," she said. "That's the vibe I'm getting."

He looked offended. "No one is molesting you," he said. "You're young, yes, but you're not a child."

"I'm naked," she said. "You're old and wearing clothes."

"You must not assume that every man is out to get you," he said. "My wife is in the hospital. My daughter is dead. I'm old enough to be your father. I am only trying to take care of you now."

"Grandfather," she said.

"I have no interest in you," he said. "It is easy to see that you have buried your shame. It's why you seek intimacy with other people, why you're so desperate for closeness."

He put his glasses back on and left the platform. She listened to his slippers shuffle toward the shoji screen. He returned with her kimono and draped it carefully over her.

"What do I have to be ashamed about?" she asked, bewildered.

"I'm sure you are not without fault," he said. "I'm sure you have made mistakes in your life."

"I'll tell you something I don't tell other people," Mona said. "If you're interested."

"Please," Paul said.

"I used to think I seduced my grandfather," Mona said. "Because I walked around naked and he caught me masturbating a few times."

"How old were you?" Paul asked.

"Seven," Mona said. "He began telling me his secrets as if we were newly in love. He'd killed people in the war. He cheated on his first wife. He cheated on Ginger, his second wife, because she was frigid. That was the word he used. He talked about it as if it had nothing to do with him, like she suffered from hearing loss or low-back pain. According to him, she hadn't touched him in over twenty years. He said it hurt not to be touched, especially down there. I grew up thinking that an erection was like a sprained limb, a twisted ankle, a pulled muscle. My instinct was to untwist the ankle, to massage the muscle. I felt obligated. But, of course, I didn't know how, and he didn't instruct me. So, I just let him ogle me. I let him watch me. And then he got cancer, and I remember thinking that it was because of our secret relationship. But what I'd forgotten, until about ten minutes ago, was that I gave him too much morphine—on purpose—and he died a few minutes later."

"On purpose?"

"Yes," Mona said. "I put him down—you know, like a dog?"

"And you felt shame," he said.

"Relief," she said. "That's what I felt. The only shame I feel is that I've been too passive. I haven't said no to enough in my life. If I had, I'd probably be a different person now. Less tormented, maybe. More . . . successful."

He picked up the bottle of Allergy Rescue and shook it. For a second she thought he might tip his head back and pour the pills down his throat. Instead he stood up and walked into the bathroom. A second later she heard the toilet flush. He returned to the platform and asked if there was anything he could do for her.

"Well, you can give me my portfolio." She tapped the platform with her hand. "I know it's under here."

He blushed and looked away. She waited for him to make some apology, but he said nothing. It was time to leave, and not come back. She rolled onto her stomach, got to her knees, and stood up. The spasm had subsided for now and she was agile enough to step off the platform and get dressed behind the screen. It took her several minutes to step into her pants and pull them up, and she could hear his slippers shuffling across the floor toward his desk. She could also hear Terry breathing in her ear.

"I'm sorry I left you alone with him," Terry whispered.

"Who?" Mona said, pulling her shirt over her head. "Paul?"

"Woody," Terry said breathlessly. "I shouldn't have left you there."

"Jesus, Terry," Mona said. "You don't sound like yourself."

"This isn't Terry," Terry whispered.

"Who is it?" Mona said out loud.

Terry didn't answer.

Mona stepped out from behind the screen, fully dressed. Paul was waiting for her with a check and the portfolio. She handed him her favorite kimono and said, "Give this to Lena, please, and tell her I love her."

"Who were you talking to just now?" Paul asked. "Behind the screen?"

Mona shrugged. "Pablo Picasso."

He smiled sadly and handed her a check, which she glanced at before slipping it into her pocket. She'd expected a Be Quiet Bonus— a hundred bucks, perhaps—but he'd given her five grand. Five zero zero zero. A gift, not a bonus. It was difficult to accept a gift when you didn't know what it was for, but she wasn't about to ask him. She didn't need to know the answer.

The portfolio was heavier than she remembered. Five pounds, six ounces, she guessed. A miscarried baby. She hugged it tightly to her chest and carried it out of the house.

It wasn't until she pulled into her driveway that she noticed the teeth marks. Something had scratched the cover and chewed each of the corners, something with claws and sharp teeth.

Barbarians.

MOMMY

THE MIDDLE FINGER OF HER RIGHT HAND REMAINED IN THE fetal position. The rest of her fingers behaved normally, but the middle one refused, even after three cups of coffee. She tried ice, heat, and aspirin. Her efforts at straightening it reminded her of the times she tried to bend spoons telekinetically as a child. Perhaps her finger felt threatened, subjected as it was to daily chemical baths and vicious scrubbing, and was simply taking a defensive posture. In any case, she stayed in bed, petting it occasionally with her other hand. At least it didn't hurt or smell bad.

The only discomfort she felt was the nearly physical pain of having a word on the tip of her tongue. The sensation had been nagging her for a day and a half. She searched for the word in the novel she was reading, Coetzee's *Waiting for the Barbarians*, but it wasn't there. She found this little gem, though: "I sleep badly and wake up in the mornings with a sullen erection growing like a branch out of my groin." That's what the word felt like, a sullen erection she wasn't able to bring off. Only it wasn't a word, she realized now, but rather someone's name, and it began with the letter M.

Luckily, it was Sunday. But she had two houses tomorrow and, naturally, each required her entire right hand. She decided a visit to the ER was in order, even though she had no insurance.

She drove herself to Holy Cross, shifting gears with her thumb and forefinger, and saw Martin in the waiting room. Not the M name she was hoping to find. She and Martin had met at the Laundromat where she washed her cleaning rags. He'd been reasonably attractive and reading a book by Alice Munro—impressive—and had caught her smiling at him. He jotted his name and number on the cover of *The Beggar Maid* and handed it to her before leaving. Nice touch. On their coffee date, which Terry Gross had talked her into, she discovered that the book hadn't belonged to him. It had been left behind at the Laundromat, possibly by Mona herself. Also, he preferred tea. She detested tea drinkers. In the parking lot afterward he'd said, "If I can guess which car is yours, I get to kiss you." She'd laughed and said, "Don't try to rom-com me, dude. I'm too old." He'd ignored her and pointed to the wrong car, thank goodness. Now Martin was three rows away with his arm in a sling. She kept her head down.

Twenty minutes later, a doctor examined her finger. Old guy in his seventies. White hair and eyebrows, kind eyes, a bit of eczema on his chin and forehead. He introduced himself as Dr. K.

"Trigger finger," he said, after ten seconds.

"What?" she said.

"Trigger finger," he repeated.

She laughed. "You mean like an *itchy* trigger finger?"

"Does it itch?" he asked, smiling.

"No," she said.

" 'Trigger finger' is the medical term," he said. "It just means the tendon is irritated. Are you hard on your hands?"

"I treat my fingers like little barbarians," she said.

"So, you hold things with a firm grip for long periods of time?" he asked.

She nodded. My despair, she thought. And my vacuum. Oh, and my shovel.

That's probably what did it—the shoveling. On Saturday she'd spent several hours digging a grave in her backyard. A baby grave for her portfolio, which she'd placed in a trash bag and then buried. There had been no eulogy.

Dr. K prepared a syringe of cortisone, which he hid behind his back like a magician. She told him she wasn't afraid of needles. He presented the syringe with a flourish and inserted it directly into her finger, which came instantly back to life. He ordered a splint and recommended limited use for three days.

She was ready to leave but Dr. K put his large, pillowy hands on her throat and massaged her glands. Any tenderness? A little, she said. She liked the feel of his hands on her neck. Open your mouth and say ah, he said. He shined a light down her throat and then up her nose. She imagined him finding the elusive M name lodged in her nostril. *Meryl*, he might say. *Malkovich. Marlon. Mia. McDormand.*

"Mother of God," he said instead. "What's going on up here?"

Dreadfully, she knew what he was referring to. Weeks ago, she'd woken up unable to breathe through her nose. She'd cleared the passage before, but the crust kept growing back thicker each time, and she took a keen but relaxed pleasure in hacking at it with trimming scissors. Sometimes her nose bled for a few minutes. The taste of blood had complemented her morning routine for weeks now.

How long had *this* been going on, asked Dr. K. A fair question.

"Couple days," she mumbled.

He abruptly excused himself and left. She inserted an exploratory pinkie into the tiny cave with broken limestone walls. So hot and dry in there! She inserted her other pinkie into the right nostril. The cavity was smaller on that side and in desperate need of excavation. At home she would have been dig, dig, digging, pausing only to tilt back and swallow the blood.

Dr. K returned with two wiry Indian physicians wearing lab coats and mustaches. Drs. Narahjan and Mehta, he said. The ear, nose, and throat specialists at Holy Cross.

Indians from India in New Mexico? They took turns looking up her nose while she tried not to laugh.

"Okay," one of them said.

"Yes," the other one said.

They twitched their mustaches at each other.

"You have a serious staph infection," the first one announced.

"If you had let this go much longer, the infection would have entered your bloodstream," the second one said.

"Do you know what that means?" said the first.

"Trouble?" she offered.

"It means you would have died," Dr. K interjected.

How close was I to death, she wanted to ask, but the Indians were looking at her funny. Not at her face, but at her feet. She was wearing old Vans high-tops held together with black electrical tape.

"What did you think was happening?" Dr. K asked.

She shrugged. "To be honest, I blamed it on the climate. It's so dry here, my face is falling off. And it's wind season so I'm dealing with a lot of dust."

They seemed to mull this over.

"If it doesn't start to clear up in forty-eight hours you must come back," Dr. K said. "Understood?"

"Yes, sir," she said.

He splinted her finger and prescribed something called Levaquin, which she filled at the hospital pharmacy. She swallowed the first pill in her truck in the parking lot, followed by a few stale Oreos. As she turned the ignition, she felt immediate, palpable relief. The name that had been eluding her was suddenly there, right in her goddamn mouth. The name—God help her—was Mommy.

Not Mom. Not Mother.

Mommy.

Not a name that typically escaped a person. Neither obscure nor hard to pronounce. She felt so basic and ordinary. She also felt the sudden urge to eat something out of a bowl—cereal, yogurt, ice cream, anything—and swerved into the parking lot of a Smith's grocery.

Unearthed, the name infected her vision. Mountain High Mommy Yogurt. Chunky Mommy. Sweet Mommy and Cream. She left quickly. Back on the road, it inserted itself into bumper stickers:

I'd Rather Be Mommy
One Mommy at a Time
This Car Climbed Mt. Mommy
Practice Random Acts of Mommy
Mommy Loves You

At home watching television, she ate an entire pint of Chunky Mommy left-handed, which took forever.

"Like masturbating with your nondominant hand," she told Terry.

Terry didn't laugh.

"Whose mommy?" Mona asked Terry. "Any ideas?"

No answer.

Not her mother, she decided. Not for a very long time had she heard the word "Mommy" or "Mom" and thought of her mother. She repeated Mommy, Mommy, Mommy out loud, testing for buried thoughts and feelings. Nope. All it seemed to give her was the munchies.

Perhaps it was time she followed the advice of that drip Eckhart Tolle, author of a self-help book she liked to call *The Power of Poo*, a book for which several of her clients had had a total boner a few years back. She'd reluctantly read a few pages while sitting on their toilets. His basic advice was that she spend less time in her head, identifying with her stupid, ego-driven thoughts, and more time in the rest of her body, and to take in the goddamn surroundings as much as possible, blah, blah, and to just live in the Now. If she were fully present and unattached to her "pain body," she wouldn't feel the need to devour an entire pint of Chunky Mommy. According to *The Power of Poo*, everything she needed was already there, inside her.

Back in bed, she listened to the wind tearing through town. Right now, it was groping her pink linen curtains. It blew the curtains into the room and then sucked them against the screen, over and over. It occurred to her that the words "wind" and "window" were probably related, something she'd never considered before. She fetched her laptop and looked up the etymology of "window" (from an old Norse word meaning "wind-eye"), which in her mind earned her a short visit to Pornhub.com.

Now she was in the Czech countryside, watching some lady with sad tits get banged by strangers on the highway. Dogging, it was called. The strangers stood in line with their pants unzipped, waiting their turn, and they were all grubby and potbellied and could barely see their own dicks. The man dogging her wore a business suit and a black mask over his face. The woman—early fifties, maybe older—was bent over the open trunk of a sedan, which was parked next to a cornfield, of all things, bracing herself against the spare tire. She had wet, dirty blonde hair and splotches of mud on the backs of her dimpled thighs. Mona had expected hooker boots, but the woman wore bright yellow rubber rain boots, also splattered with mud. That's someone's mother, Mona thought. And that's someone's corn growing in the field. Is that someone's phone ringing?

She muted the volume. The ringing phone, buried under the comforter, was her landline, which meant it was a business call. She brushed the hair from her face and cleared her throat.

"Bee's Knees," she said. "Mona speaking."

"Do you clean crime scenes?" a woman asked nervously.

Mona sat up and put her feet on the floor. Crime scenes, she repeated to herself. Did she clean crime scenes?

"You there?" the woman said.

"Are you with the, uh, police department or something?"

"No," the woman said slowly. "I've just committed a crime."

Mona pictured the woman from the video, her yellow rubber boots splattered with blood rather than mud. In the trunk, where the spare tire was, the man in the business suit and face mask lay bleeding from the throat.

"Hellooo," the woman said again.

"Is this a joke?"

"No," the woman said, and let out a quiet sob.

"I'm sorry, but may I ask where you're calling from?"

"My house," the woman said. "I just killed someone. With a hammer. Boy, is there a lot of blood—"

Mona sighed loudly. "Hi, Mom."

"I get a 'Mom' for once," Clare said, amused. "Hallelujah."

Mona had been calling her mother Clare for years, which everyone thought was weird. Especially since her mother's real name was Darlene.

"I've been thinking about you lately," Mona said, closing the lid of her laptop. "Sort of."

"How do you sort of think about someone?" asked Clare.

"I didn't recognize your voice at first," Mona said. "You sound . . . different."

"I found the Lord," said Clare calmly.

Fuck, Mona thought, another goner. It was a goddamn epidemic.

Clare laughed. "Relax," she said. "I sound different because I'm sober. For the first time in sixteen years. I went to rehab, finally, for a whole month."

Fuck, Mona thought again.

"Say something," Clare said.

Mona sighed. Clare sighed back. Sighing had always been their secret language.

"You got my letter, I guess," Mona said.

About a year ago, she'd sent Clare a letter explaining that Sheila, the woman who'd adopted Mona as a teenager, had retired and moved to

Florida, and that Mona had fallen in love with Mr. Disgusting, who had died, and that she'd pulled a geographic to start over.

"Look, I'm sorry I haven't been in touch," Clare said. "I realize you probably hate me."

You want me to hate you, Mona felt like saying. You're a masochist, and my hatred would give you something with which to sodomize yourself, over and over and over.

"I don't hate you, Clare," Mona said softly.

"You're still calling me that," Clare said. "God help me."

Mona smiled. "It's my pet name for you."

"Pet names are supposed to be cute," Clare said. "What's cute about 'Clare'?"

"It rhymes with 'teddy bear,' " Mona said dryly.

And "electric chair," she thought. And "warfare." And "despair," of course—don't forget that. She walked into the bathroom, where the wind was rattling the window.

"Listen," Mona said. "The wind keeps sucking my pink curtains out the window and then blowing them back in, but the window is screened, so the curtains don't fly out the window. They cling to the screen." She looked at her face in the mirror over the sink. "What does that remind you of?"

"Are you stoned?" Clare asked.

"Maybe," Mona said.

"I kept my eyes closed when I pushed you out," Clare said. "Took me four and a half hours. When I finally opened my eyes, you weren't there. You were off in a corner getting cleaned up, and the doctor was still between my legs, wiping blood off his glasses. The nurse standing next to him had blood on her blonde ponytail, and there was blood on the overhead light, and I was terrified to see your face. I was worried you'd have my birthmark."

"But you love your birthmark," Mona said.

"Love-hate," Clare corrected her.

Clare had an oddly beautiful port wine stain on her face. The stain was heaviest on her left cheek, but it spilled down her neck and trickled over her collarbone. As far as Mona remembered, Clare had always embraced the stain. She wore lipstick and nail polish the exact same shade of red, along with belts and shoes, and made the stain seem like the perfect accessory for any occasion.

"Listen, Frank and I are renewing our vows," Clare said, "and we both want you to be there."

Mona was startled to see her eyes water in the mirror.

"Also, I'm getting rid of my apartment and you have some stuff in the closet."

Clare and Frank had eloped over a decade ago, but they'd always kept separate apartments on the same block. In practice Clare didn't really *live* in her apartment. She used it as a storage space and psychic refuge. It was the one place she could truly relax and be herself. Strangely, she only needed to reside in this authentic state for an hour or so every couple of weeks. The rest of the time she spent at Frank's, cooking his meals, watching his television, and sleeping in his ancient waterbed.

"Why get rid of the place now?" Mona asked. "After all these years?"

"Every time I set foot in there I want to weep," Clare said. "Also, Frank's hours have been cut. Seems silly to pay rent on two places."

Clare made a very good living as a technical writer but spent most of her money on Frank's expensive hobbies: medium-stakes poker and motorcycle racing.

"Your stuff won't fit at Frank's," Clare said. "Do you want to come get it, or should I toss it, or what?"

Her stuff, as far as she remembered, was all in one box. Photo albums, drawings, paintings, diaries, some other odds and ends she couldn't recall just now. Clothing, maybe. Some jewelry.

"How about you send it to me," Mona suggested. "In the mail."

"How about I give it to Bill," Clare said. "Your homeless friend."

"You mean Billlll?"

Clare was referring to the handsome schizophrenic who lived in the alley behind Frank's apartment. "My name is Billlll," he'd said when they'd first met. "With five Ls." He liked to wear wetsuits on dry land, but as far as she knew, he was petrified of the ocean. He told Mona that her name translated to "white wave" in some language she couldn't remember, and that she would die in a tsunami when she was in her late fifties.

"He's still alive?" Mona asked.

"Disappeared," Clare said. "About a year ago."

"Bummer," Mona said.

"Look, I'll buy your plane ticket," Clare said. "Okay?"

"I can't leave town, Clare," Mona said. "I'm self-employed."

Wait a minute, Mona thought, for the first time ever. I'm the boss. I can leave town whenever I want.

"The ceremony's in three weeks," Clare said.

"I have trigger finger," Mona said.

"Does that mean you're suicidal?"

"It means the tendon in my finger is inflamed," Mona said. "I just got back from the ER. I also have a staph infection that almost killed me."

"When you were little you used to splatter yourself with ketchup and tomato sauce and then lie in the bathtub until I walked in," Clare said. "Sometimes you waited hours alone in there until I got home from work. I wonder what a psychologist would call that."

"Neglect?" Mona said.

"I just hope you can get here," Clare said softly. "And I'd love it if you said a few words at the reception. You know, like a toast? But casual."

"How's Frank?"

"He's fine," Clare said. "He's laying out on the lawn."

Sunbathing was Frank's other passion. Rather than go to the beach half a block away, he preferred laying out on the yellow lawn that belonged to the apartment building. When Clare got off the phone, she'd probably slather his back with baby oil and then water his feet with the hose for ten minutes. Mona heard water running and wondered if Clare already had the hose in her hand.

"Where are you?" Mona said.

"In the kitchen, feeding Takoda and Wahkan breakfast."

Takoda and Wahkan. Mona's vicious stepbrothers. They were hand-fed Malt-O-Meal for breakfast and took their morning dumps in the kitchen sink. They were a pair of treasured African gray parrots. Takoda, whose name was Sioux for "Friend to Everyone," was friend to Frank alone. Wahkan's name was Sioux for "Sacred," but, again, the bird was sacred only to Frank. No one else could stand the little fucker. Although African grays were gifted talkers, Wahkan had a heavy lisp, so much of what he said was unintelligible. Takoda's specialties were electronic and nonhuman noises—car alarms, ringing telephones, microwaves, coffee percolators, dripping water, barking dogs, etc. Takoda's only human impersonation was the sound of Clare sobbing. It was pitch-perfect but conveyed a deep, soulful pathos and sense of penitence missing from the real thing.

"I miss Howard," Clare said. "He's on vacation for two weeks. He really helped me in the hospital. In fact, I don't know how I would've survived without him. He got me through the worst of it."

"Who's Howard?" Mona asked. "Your shrink?"

"*Howard*," Clare repeated, as if Mona had mispronounced the name.

"Oh God," Mona said. "I forgot about him."

Clare was referring to . . . Howard Stern. He'd been her steadfast companion for over twenty years. They'd never met in person, of course, or even over the phone, but Clare had been listening to Howard religiously since 1986. She talked about Howard and the other cast members of his show as if they'd all grown up together.

"I'm worried about Artie," Clare said. "Apparently, he tried to kill himself again, poor baby."

"How's Robin?" Mona asked.

"The same," Clare said.

"As Artie?"

"No—she's the same as always," Clare said.

"Hey, let me ask you something. Do you talk to Howard when he's not around?"

"What do you mean?"

"Like, in your head," Mona said.

"Of course not," Clare said, and laughed. "I'm not nuts."

TWO WEEKS LATER, ON A DRIZZLY SEPTEMBER MORNING, MONA wrapped her suitcase in a trash bag and loaded it in the bed of her truck. She heard footsteps on the gravel and saw Yoko and Yoko approaching. They were wearing knitted ponchos over their pajamas and their eyes and noses were red.

"You're not moving, I hope," Nigel said nasally.

"Nope," she said, and smiled. "I'm catching a flight to LA for a few days. My mother called—finally. She's downsizing, and I have a couple boxes in her apartment—you know, from when I was little—so I'm going to fetch them before they end up in the garbage."

"Boxes," Shiori repeated.

"Yeah," Mona said. "My stuff. From childhood."

They looked apprehensive suddenly, as if she'd said the boxes contained a deadly virus or meth.

Nigel licked his lips. "Have you read Homer yet?"

"You gotta stop asking me that," Mona said.

He'd given her a beautiful edition of *The Odyssey* two years ago. She'd read a few pages here and there but could never fully commit.

"Don't open the boxes while you're there," Nigel warned.

Shiori nodded. "Wait until you're back here. Safe."

Mona rolled her eyes. "What's the big deal?"

"Beware of Aeolus, master of the winds," Nigel said with a straight face. "He gave Odysseus a leather pouch containing all the winds—"

"Except the west wind," Shiori reminded him.

"Right," Nigel said. "But Odysseus's men opened the leather pouch thinking it was gold, and all the winds escaped and blew the ship back the way it had come."

Mona nodded gravely.

"Do you understand what I'm saying?" Nigel asked.

"These boxes definitely don't have gold in them," Mona said. "Or wind."

"You'd be surprised," Nigel said, and sniffed.

"PS, my mother and her husband are renewing their vows and want me to make a toast," Mona said. "Apparently, they know nothing of my lifelong fear of public speaking. But I wrote the speech and it's quite touching. It's all about how I worshipped my mother as a child, how she was the center of my universe, Jesus reincarnated, et cetera. Then I hired an Indian man to read my speech in a Hindi accent."

"Pardon?" Nigel said.

"An Indian man," Mona repeated. "From India. I found him on the Internet. He's a grad student in Minnesota."

"I'm confused," Shiori said. "You hired an Indian man to accompany you to the wedding? In Los Angeles?"

"No, no, no," Mona said patiently. "I paid the man seventy dollars to make a recording of himself reading my toast in an Indian accent, which I will play over a loudspeaker at the reception."

Nigel frowned. Shiori fiddled with a hole in her poncho.

"It's supposed to be funny," Mona said, and shrugged. "Do you want to hear it? His voice breaks beautifully at the end, like a little boy's, and I love the way he says 'Mommy.' Gives me goose bumps."

Nigel ran a hand over his buzzed head. "It's a strange choice you will come to regret," he said finally.

NO ONE WAS WAITING FOR HER AT LAX. BUT, A BREATHLESS voicemail from Clare: "Mona, this morning I realized that I haven't

---

driven on the freeway sober in twenty years. I don't think I can do it, honey. If I take surface streets, it'll take me forever to get there, so—I don't know—can you get a cab? I'll pay you back as soon as you get here. Is that okay?"

It was fine. She rolled her suitcase over to the taxi stand. "Where you go?" said an older Asian man. She told him Hermosa. "I take you," he said, and flung her suitcase into his open trunk.

She looked out the window. The sky was a bland baby blue and not saturated enough. The streets were all too wide. It was strangely comforting to see palm trees again, but, as usual, their leaves weren't close enough to the ground for her taste, and there was too much vertical space between the tops of the palms and the tops of the buildings, which were all too short. She felt a sudden fondness for stucco, for some reason. Fuck adobe.

"For a culture obsessed with being thin, there's a startling number of donut shops in Los Angeles," Terry pointed out suddenly.

"Tell me about it, Terry," Mona said. "I've counted eleven since El Segundo. It's like, who the fuck's eating all these donuts?"

"Your mama," Terry said, and laughed.

As a kid, most of Mona's weekends had started with a maple bar binge. She and Clare split half a dozen in the car, a rich brown Buick Riviera with cream leather interior. It was like eating a maple bar inside a maple bar. Between bites, Clare complained bitterly about how fat she was, and called herself Lard Ass every five seconds. She even slapped herself across the face a couple of times, and then asked Mona to verify that she was indeed a worthless lard ass. Clare had a demon in her that fed on outside confirmation, needed it in order to survive, and the demon was hungriest on weekends.

"My thighs look like cottage cheese . . . don't they?" Clare would ask slowly.

Mona usually gave the demon what it wanted. "Not cottage cheese," she'd answer. "Creamed corn."

Fueled with donuts, they'd head to the gym for the second, equally enjoyable part of the routine: a prolonged fit of exercise bulimia. The gym was posh and near the beach. Their routine consisted of two aerobics classes back-to-back, a round of weights, laps in the pool, and finally the sauna.

"I could deadlift a hundred sixty pounds at age eleven," Mona bragged to Terry.

"That seems strange to me," Terry said.

"I did it to impress Clare," Mona said. "Also, there was a French model I was trying to seduce. I can't remember her name, but she starred in several music videos for ZZ Top."

"Who was your mother trying to seduce?" Terry asked.

"Frank," Mona said. "Frank was a major gym rat. That's how they met."

Frank was extremely tall and broad-shouldered with a mustache and big muscles, but he wasn't gay. He was divorced, unattached, and infatuated with Clare. Clare, on the other hand, was still married to Mona's father. Mona's father did not have a mustache. Or big muscles. He had two legs but only one arm, and he didn't work out because he was a plumber. And he liked to drink a little.

THE AIRPORT TAXI PULLED UP TO VISTA DEL MAR, A THREE-story pink stucco building just a block and a half from the beach, one of the few left over from the 1930s. Mona still liked how starkly it stood out among the cookie-cutter condos lining the street. She tipped the driver five dollars and he popped the trunk. As soon as she pulled out her suitcase, he peeled away as if being chased.

Clare lived on the second floor. She knocked but no one answered. She opened the unlocked door.

"Hello?" she called out.

Everything was a sad, muted mauve. Clare hadn't started packing yet. Dozens of books were stacked haphazardly on floating shelves, most with their spines facing the wall. Literary novels, mostly, one or two Oprah books, some National Book Award winners, nothing to be ashamed of. A lot of the covers were torn or missing, the pages cockled and chocolate stained. Clare loved chocolate, especially while reading.

The apartment was a scary mess. The silverware drawer held three butter knives, tangled jewelry, and a pile of utility bills. Where were the spoons and forks? In the nightstand drawer with the linty gummy bears. She kept an iron, of all things, in her underwear drawer. Old tax returns, her birth certificate, hospital bills, and other important paperwork—all of which were splattered with beige liquid foundation—filled the sock drawer. In what should have been the pants drawer lay six empty cans of feminine deodorant spray.

As a young girl, all Mona wanted was to live here. This was back when Clare and Frank first started dating. Clare picked this place for its proximity to Frank's. The plan had been to sleep at Frank's one or two nights a week, but to live here full-time. Instead, they ate dinner at Frank's every single night. Mona ate every bite of his terrible beef stew, endured hours of cop shows on TV and lame Neapolitan ice cream. They never went home to their own apartment. At night, Mona was stuffed into a sleeping bag, alternating between the thin, bumpy carpet and the slick Naugahyde couch. Why not let her sleep in the empty apartment, she'd wanted to know. It was only a block away!

"You're only eleven," Clare had said.

"I feel like I'm a hundred and eleven," Mona had said. "My back is killing me."

"Do some sit-ups," Clare had said.

So, Mona invented Wendy, her new best friend at her new school. Wendy was a fraternal twin, she told Clare, and a straight-A student, and a pretty good cellist. She lived in this really cool condo—you know those condos on The Strand?—and her parents thought Mona was great, so was it okay if she slept at Wendy's this Friday and Saturday?

The charade worked flawlessly. Part of her wished Wendy were real, but despite her loneliness, she was happy to have the place to herself. She kept the curtains drawn and stayed up watching late movies on cable, ate whatever she wanted, taught herself to dance to *Soul Train* reruns, and slept diagonally in her mother's big bed. When bored or lonely she sometimes spent the afternoon in one of her neighbors' apartments. In time, she'd ventured beyond and visited fancier apartments right on the water.

She'd been confused by the term "breaking and entering" because she never broke anything. It was just entering, in her case. People either left their doors unlocked or they hid a key. Inevitably, she'd tripped a silent alarm in one of the fancy apartments and the cops showed up. They seemed disappointed by what they found in her bag: antique scissors, a pair of underwear with unicorns on them, an embroidered pillowcase. "Look, I don't even like unicorns," she explained. "I'm not here to take things." Then what are you doing here, they wanted to know. She couldn't articulate it at the time, but she felt it must be some variation of the Goldilocks Principle: she was searching for a place that felt "just right." Except, unlike Goldilocks, she never cared for the middle one, or the one between opposites. Rather, she was searching for a place that felt "not quite right" or "just weird enough," and it didn't seem to be in Hermosa Beach.

When she gave Frank's address, the patrolmen laughed and removed the handcuffs. Frank's father had been a decorated detective, so these officers were friends. They escorted her to Frank's and he entertained them in the living room for a while. After they left he turned to her. "Never use my name again," he said. "Next time you get caught don't give them this address."

She was back in the sleeping bag after that. And there were rules, lots of rules, and she just didn't have what it took. No discipline. No self-restraint. She couldn't get her act together, as her mother kept saying. And then a few weeks later, that thing happened with the neighbor, and soon after she was on a plane to Massachusetts.

THE BATHROOM SMELLED LIKE OPIUM, CLARE'S SIGNATURE SCENT. A green-and-white G-string hung from the doorknob. The first panties Mona ever sniffed had belonged to Clare. The effect had been immediate: bracing, restorative, unforgettable. She remembered the underwear (peach-colored nylon with bright orange trim), where she was standing (in her parents' creepy walk-in closet), and what she was looking at (a heavy, industrial-looking iron with a turquoise cloth cord). Daughters were supposed to have a thing for their fathers, but Mona's thing had always been for Clare, and Clare alone.

A bottle of Xanax was in the medicine cabinet. Only two left, but Clare's pills were like cockroaches—if there were two, there were twenty. She placed one under her tongue and pushed aside the shower curtain. Mold in the grout near the window. She hit it with Tilex from under the sink and went back to the living room.

She waited ten minutes and then walked over to Frank's. He lived five buildings down, in a two-story contemporary called the Fountain-bleu. The eponymous fountain wasn't bleu, however, but beige and filled with dirt and dead leaves. The building had four units, a small front yard and a bigger backyard. Frank lived on the bottom floor facing the street. The shades were drawn. She rang the doorbell, twice. No answer.

Then she heard a vacuum running. She tried the knob—unlocked—and let herself in. The place smelled like fake citrus. Clare was wearing workout gear—red leotard, shiny black leggings—and vacuuming the dining area. As usual, Takoda was perched on Clare's head. He looked handsome from a distance, his wings purplish gray, his tail as red as Clare's birthmark and leotard. He seemed aware of Mona's presence and she expected him to make his usual big-rig-backing-up noise, but he was too preoccupied with keeping his balance.

Clare was vacuuming with a vintage upright Eureka 1428. Mona loved the color combination: the motor was encased in hard pink plastic, the bag in perforated red-and-orange plaid vinyl. Almost as beautiful as Clare herself.

"Clare!" she shouted.

Clare turned, startled, and tripped over the cord. "You're here!" she said, and smiled. She was lightly sweating and looked stunning, but why was her hair blonde? She gave Mona a stiff, one-armed hug, and then backed away when Takoda started barking.

"Shh!" Clare said, and stomped her foot. He abruptly stopped. She crossed her arms over her chest and smiled again.

"You weren't at your apartment," Mona said. "So, I came here."

"You wouldn't believe what a pigsty this place was three hours ago," Clare said. "I wanted it to look nice for you."

But I'm not staying here anymore, Mona wanted to remind her. *Remember?*

"What on earth did you do to your hair?" Mona asked.

"Highlights," Clare said.

"You're like, fully blonde," Mona said. Like every other bitch around here.

Clare shrugged. Takoda trained a baleful yellow eye on Mona's face. When he fluttered his wings, she saw patches of missing feathers. He was a chronic self-plucker. If Mona had had feathers she'd probably have plucked them out, too.

"He's been mutilating himself again," Mona said, and, to her surprise, he started weeping, a low, broken moan just like Clare's, followed by some sniffling. Clare reached up, brought him to her face, and kissed his beak.

"I had a feeling he'd start crying," she said between smooches. "Does Takoda want a Pop-Tart?"

"You should feed him some of your Zoloft," Mona said.

"I'm not on that stuff anymore," Clare said. "He's crying because I hugged you. Still jealous after all these years." She gave his beak another peck. "Aren't you, Sugar Bear? Yes, you are. Mommy loves you."

Mommy Loves You. One Mommy at a Time. I'd Rather Be Mommy.

"He's really boo-hooing," Mona said.

"He'll calm down in a minute."

"Looks like he needs a back rub," Mona said. "He carries a lot of tension in his neck and shoulders."

She was joking, of course, but Clare massaged his neck with one of her fingers. "He's been really exhausted lately," she said.

"I'm just thankful he hasn't punctured my face."

Clare laughed. "Don't worry—I clipped his wings yesterday."

His last "love bite" had made her lower lip bleed for hours.

She was just about to compliment his good behavior when he flung himself at her. He landed on her right hand, which she'd instinctively brought to her chest, and sank his beak into the tender meat between thumb and forefinger. He loved pressure points. Mona screamed and shook her hand around, throwing him to the floor, where he skidded on his side before getting to his feet. He looked dazed but quickly regained his bearings and scuttled under an end table. He was quiet for a second before the fake sighing started.

"Phew!" he said.

Mona gaped at the hole in her hand. It was star shaped and bleeding steadily.

"Phew!" Takoda said again.

"You're okay, you're okay," Clare said, looking from Mona to the bird and back.

Who was she talking to? Clare glanced at Mona's wound and picked up Takoda carefully, with both hands, and cradled him like an infant.

"He hates this," she said.

It didn't look that way. His eyes were closed and he seemed completely at ease. Mona hoped she'd given him a concussion. She hoped his little brain was swelling.

"Have a seat, honey," Clare said. She put Takoda in his cage next to Wahkan's and motioned to Frank's hideous orange and purple love seat with its printed Southwestern-style coyotes and cacti. On the wall loomed a huge longhorn skull with polished horns. If someone hadn't airbrushed a fake desert landscape across the forehead, it would have looked semicool.

Frank identified as Native American, but he was mostly white and Hispanic. Francisco was his real name. He was an ex-marine and used to be a professional bodyguard; now he worked as a detective for the Carson school district. He never left home without his Glock. He wore triple-starched Ben Davis shirts, Wranglers with a heavy crease, and engineer boots. To be fair, he did have a drop or two of Navajo on his mother's side, but he hadn't embraced it until after he'd met Clare. It started with a painting, a tasteless double portrait of a wolf and a windblown Native American princess, with a full moon in the background. The painting seemed to revive an atavistic American Indian aesthetic. He soon adorned the walls with five lifelike human masks marked with face paint and wearing elaborate headdresses made of real fur, antlers, and feathers. His collection grew: sand paintings of wolves, eagles, and buffalo; vision seekers and warriors on horseback; ceremonial peace pipes; bows, arrows, knives, and other weapons; kachina dolls by the dozen; humongous dream catchers—or dust catchers, as Mona called them; and granite rocks painted with desert landscapes. His apartment looked like a Native American gift shop off Interstate 40. Some people find Jesus, others find the Universe or their inner child, but Frank had found his inner chief.

His inner chief had always wanted a son. Mona faked an interest in cars, memorized parts of a V8 engine, did pull-ups, challenged him to arm-wrestle, accompanied him to the shooting range, and accepted his dare to eat a habanero chili without drinking water. She ate two, just to show him who was boss, and then stifled her fear when he said she'd need a seat belt for the toilet the next day. In the end, her efforts were futile. She was too emotional to pass for Frank's son, and too attached to wearing burned-on eyeliner and fishnet, and to masturbating to pictures of Prince from the seventies.

He'd grown up with the nickname Pancho, which Mona had discovered by accident, the one time she'd made the mistake of answering his phone.

"Could you please pass the peas, Pancho," Mona remembered asking at the dinner table later that week. His face had turned crimson, as if she'd just called him Cholo or Beaner.

"My name's Frank. How would you like it if I called you Moron, Mona?"

"I'd love it," Mona said.

His revenge was having noisy sex with Clare on his waterbed that night. The walls were paper-thin. Mona could hear them looking at each other. She could hear them thinking about it.

Should we do it?

Do you feel like it?

Of course.

She had listened carefully, holding an unnecessary glass to the wall. As usual, their lovemaking birthed huge swells, both in the waterbed and inside herself. She felt seasick and out of control, yet unable to stop listening. When it got to be too much (three minutes), she pounded on the door with both fists. Apparently, she had a demon in her, too.

"Get a room!" she screamed.

But they had a room.

She should have screamed, "Get me a room!"

When she heard Clare roll off the waterbed, she tiptoed into the bathroom and hid in the tub. She sat hugging her knees to her chest, something she'd seen women do in the movies when they were upset, usually after they'd been raped or cheated on.

Clare flipped on the light. "Why are you in the tub?"

"I'm a twat waffle in a douche canoe," Mona said, repeating something she'd heard on the bus.

"No, you're not," Clare said, and tugged her bathrobe closed.

"What's with the getup?" Mona asked.

Clare was usually either fully nude or fully clothed. Mona had only seen mothers in bathrobes on television.

"Frank's modest." Clare smiled as if modesty was suddenly this super-adorable quality. "He doesn't believe in walking around naked," she added.

"I know what 'modest' means," Mona said. "You moan whenever he touches you, even if it's on the arm."

"You'll moan someday, too," Clare said. "Trust me."

"Gross," Mona said.

"WHERE'S FRANK?" MONA ASKED NOW. SHE PICKED UP A PEACE pipe and dropped it when she saw that it was fashioned from the limb of a hoofed animal.

"He's at the race track, but he'll be back in a bit and then we'll have dinner."

"Can't we go out alone? I haven't seen you in over *three years*."

Clare blinked expressively. "You haven't seen *him*, either," she said. "He'll be hurt if we eat without him. He's pretty sensitive, you know."

"You have bird shit in your hair," Mona pointed out.

Clare shrugged. "Why are you wearing all black? I thought you'd grown out of that."

"I'm regressing," Mona said. "Do you have any beer?"

"Aren't you hot wearing those tights?"

"I'm chubby," Mona said.

"Well, what are you eating?" Clare asked seriously.

"It's baby weight," Mona said.

Clare grimaced. "Is it your time of the month?"

It wasn't. Embarrassingly, she'd spent much of the plane ride imagining the two of them locked in a bear hug, Clare smoothing the back of her hair and whispering, *Welcome home, my little nutcase. I've missed the shit out of you. Your face is prettier than I remember, and that shirt looks perfect with your hair. And I love how your hair looks.*

"I'm sweating," Clare said. She picked up an issue of *Bird Talk* magazine and fanned herself. She seemed nervous suddenly. "You're going to make a toast at the reception, right? It would mean a lot to me."

"Where is it?" Mona asked.

"At our favorite Mexican restaurant," Clare said.

Mona's stomach dropped. How would she play the Indian man's recording at a Mexican restaurant?

"Will there be a DJ?" Mona asked. "My toast requires a loudspeaker."

"Mariachi band," Clare said.

"Fuck," Mona said.

"What's the big deal?" Clare stopped fanning herself. "God, I wish you lived closer. I don't understand why you chose New Mexico, of all places. Seems so . . . random."

"It's the Land of Enchantment," Mona said. "And I was very disenchanted in Massachusetts."

"I know," Clare said.

Did she?

The guy who'd raped her in Lowell had been covered in ink, but the most vivid tattoo in her memory was on his abdomen, a dick eye-fucking a skull draped in a banner reading "HOME OF THE WHOPPER" in wild-style graffiti. She thought of Mr. Disgusting, whose chest tattoo had been an ancient wooden ship with a banner that read, "Homeward Bound." She remembered Dark ravaging her with MORE LOVE, which had felt like its own kind of homecoming. Perhaps her preoccupation with home led her to terrible things—rape, murder, addiction, suicide. If homesickness really was a sickness in and of itself, then perhaps she needed a separate and very specific course of treatment.

Or maybe she just needed to get over it already. She gazed at the Eureka, still parked in the dining area.

"Where'd you find that vacuum?"

"It's Frank's," Clare said. "Probably older than you are."

"How's the suction?"

"Good." Clare placed the magazine on the coffee table. "How's your love life?"

"Speaking of *suction*," Mona said. "I fell in love with a married man— a client—but it's over now. His wife was blind . . . like, literally."

She considered herself over and done with Dark, and yet, when asked to create a new password, she always chose "SPANISH."

"Are you still in touch with Sheila?" Clare asked tentatively.

Clare never knew how to talk about Sheila, the woman who'd unofficially adopted Mona as a teenager. The takeover had been arranged by Ginger. Sheila was single, sexually repressed, and sober. She'd made Mona the center of her universe for six years, introducing her to therapy, psychiatry, the twelve steps, the cleaning business, and Chinese food, among other things.

But Clare and Sheila barely knew each other and never spoke, so Mona never discussed Clare with Sheila, or vice versa. When Mona tried to imagine the three of them in the same room together, she felt like she was trapped in a salad spinner.

"We talk once or twice a year," Mona said, examining her wound. Still bleeding a little. "I should wash my hand. I don't want to get bird disease."

Mona walked down the short hallway toward the bathroom, pausing at the doorway to their bedroom. The waterbed was still there, neatly made as usual.

She washed her wound. You're here, she told herself. You're home. You got your wish.

The wish was stale. A decade too old. It was as if she'd finally gotten that cashmere sweater she'd wished for at fourteen, but now the sleeves were too short and it was some weird New England colonial pumpkin color.

Six days, she told herself. Go to the wedding, get your stuff, and then get back to the desert.

HER SUSPICION HAD ALWAYS BEEN THAT CLARE AND FRANK used the birds to avoid intimacy with her, but now it seemed they used the birds to avoid intimacy in general. This she discovered later that day. It was six o'clock—their dessert time, strangely—and Mona expected the usual: Frank and Clare tangled together on the love seat, watching television and feeding each other ice cream from the same bowl, pausing occasionally to make out.

Instead they were sitting in separate recliners, each with a bird on their shoulder and a bowl of ice cream on their lap, pausing occasionally to . . . feed the birds out of their open mouths.

"You guys used to make out with each other," Mona said from the love seat. "Now you make out with your birds."

"Oh, we still make out," Clare said quickly, and glanced at Frank for confirmation.

But Frank was too busy narrowing his eyes at Mona. He was wearing a Hawaiian shirt with palm leaves on it and jewelry made of melted-together gold nuggets.

"Are you in a cult?" he asked suddenly.

"I beg your pardon?" she asked.

"That thing around your neck," he said.

He was referring to the ankh pendant she'd bought many years ago after seeing *The Hunger*. In the film, Catherine Deneuve and David Bowie are vampires and they wear ankh necklaces that pull out into little knives, which they use to slash people's throats. Mona wished her ankh pulled out into a knife, but alas, it did not. It was still beautiful, though, and very old.

"It's Egyptian," Mona said. "Symbol of life."

"It looks satanic," Frank said.

"I think you're thinking of the pentagram, maybe."

"We have some devil worshippers at Carson High right now, so."

Frank was essentially a narc, though he also dealt with teenage gangs. And devil worshippers, apparently, which struck Mona as a little quaint. She was about to ask how many devil worshippers there were but was distracted by Wahkan, who kept poking Frank's cheek with his dry, black tongue.

"Your bird's tongue looks satanic," Mona said. "Like a satanic . . . phallus. But just a phallus *symbol*, not like an actual evil mini-penis."

Clare smiled, but Frank looked disgusted.

"A parrot's tongue contains bones," Frank explained for the five hundredth time. "And has the dexterity of three human fingers."

Frank passed the bird a nut from a nearby bowl. The bird rolled the nut around on his tongue for a few seconds, then dropped it and bit Frank's earlobe.

"Ow!" Frank yelled.

"Honey!" Clare said. "Are you okay?"

Frank winced. "I'm fine," he said after a few seconds.

"His ridiculous bird bit him," Mona whispered to Terry. "He's bleeding. From the ear."

"Maybe his bird is your inner child," Terry suggested.

"My inner child isn't a biter," Mona told Terry.

Frank blotted his ear with a napkin. "He's never done that to me before," he said. "Never ever."

"Need a washcloth, hon?" Clare asked.

Frank waved his hand. The bird had climbed off Frank's shoulder and was hanging off the front of Frank's shirt. Frank seemed fully recovered. He placed the bird back on his shoulder and went back to eating ice cream like nothing had happened. The bird did some fake coughing and sneezing.

"How do you know these high schoolers worship Satan?" Mona asked.

"They come out and say it," Frank said, and shook his head. "They're proud of it."

"What else do they do?"

"One of them has been asking people—strangers—for locks of hair, so."

"Paintbrushes," Mona said, nodding. "They make paintbrushes with human hair and then paint their walls with the blood of Christians."

He was silent for a minute.

"You think you know everything," he said.

Clare sighed, stood up, and walked into the kitchen. Mona listened to her unload the dishwasher.

Frank cleared his throat. "I actually end up saving some of these kids, you know."

From what? Mona wondered. Making art?

When she was twelve, she'd written *I will not sniff Liquid Paper* exactly one thousand times in a notebook and then presented it to Frank in private as a gift, thinking he'd be pleased and impressed. This was after he'd caught her rolling around on the floor, not two feet from where they were sitting now, a sock saturated with Liquid Paper wrapped around her face, the empty bottle dripping in her hand, her eyes still watering from laughing. She'd even wetted her pants a little without realizing it. He'd pulled off the sock, sniffed. His head snapped back in surprise and disgust.

"What the hell is this?" he asked.

"Wipeout," she said, and laughed. "I mean Wite-Out."

She could tell he wanted to slap her, but he did nothing. He didn't even mention it to Clare. A girl she knew at school had been made to write *Stop repeating what others say* five hundred times by her parents, so Mona took it upon herself to do the same, only double.

"What is this?" he asked, when she handed him the notebook.

"My punishment," she said.

She wanted him to look at each page. She wanted him to marvel at her penmanship. She hadn't merely scribbled her penance pell-mell—she'd printed carefully, perfectly, with a set of high-quality colored pens. And she'd made doodles in the margins—good ones. She'd sketched in pencil before tracing the final doodle in pen, and then erased the underlying pencil lines. It had taken forever. The doodles were tiny masterpieces as inspiring as the illustrated scrolls of medieval monks. A significant work of art, in her opinion.

He glanced at a page or two before closing the notebook. He looked scared, confused, and suspicious all at once.

"I never asked you to do this."

"I know," she said. "But isn't it cool?"

He shrugged and handed her the notebook, and they never discussed it again.

But maybe the whole thing had gotten under his skin, she thought now, which was why he became a school cop. Was it narcissistic of her to think that? Terry?

"Don't ask me," Terry said. "Ask him."

In the kitchen, Clare kept dropping silverware—deliberately, willfully, as if tapping out a code. It took Mona a few seconds to decipher the message. *Would it kill you to just be nice?* Frank scraped his ice-cream bowl with his spoon. The sound grated on her. She could feel it in her teeth. She focused on the pink handle of the Eureka standing in the hallway.

"Frank, I have a confession," she said.

He stopped scraping and gave her a startled look.

"I'm in love with your vacuum," she said quickly.

He spooned the last of the ice cream into his mouth. "What?"

"Your vacuum," she said. "I love it. Where'd you get it?"

He opened his mouth, allowed Wahkan to drill his teeth for a second, and then wiped his face with a fresh napkin. Wahkan wolf-whistled from his shoulder.

"You're so weird," he said.

"How much you want for it, chief?"

He snorted and looked at her like she was crazy. "Not for sale."

"Fair enough," she said.

He drummed the armrest with his fingers and then picked up the remote and flipped through the channels.

"How many years you been working for the Carson school district?" she asked pleasantly.

"Too many," he said, and belched softly. "Nine and a half."

"Were you assigned that job or did you have to apply for it?"

"I applied, but," Frank said.

"Does it pay the same as being a bodyguard?"

"I took a cut, but, well, the hours are better, so. And I wanted to work with kids."

He settled on a Charles Bronson movie. *Death Wish III*. A group of gangsters were sitting around, repeating, "They killed the Giggler! They killed the Giggler!" Frank watched the screen with a placid, satisfied look on his face. Wahkan made a kissing noise and polished his beak on Frank's shirt.

"I'm pretty good with them, you know," he said without looking at her. "The kids, I mean. Most of them, anyway. Some are too far gone— you know—beyond help—but."

He had a new habit of ending his sentences with "but," "and," or "so." A verbal tic. Sometimes he strung them all together. "Well, yeah, so, but, and."

"But what," she said.

"What?"

"Some of them are beyond help, but . . . what," she prompted.

He looked over at her and shrugged. "You can't save everyone."

MONA DUCKED INTO THE LIQUOR STORE FOR WINE, A CORK-screw, and her favorite West Coast candy bar, Abba-Zaba, which she ate on Clare's couch. Terry wanted to know if she was more in love with the candy (white taffy, creamy peanut butter filling) or the wrapper (yellow and black checkerboard taxi pattern). Or was it equal?

"Who the fuck cares?" Mona asked.

"Emotions are stored in the body," Terry said. "If they're not released, they cause illness. Boredom, for example, is a lower-frequency emotion—"

"Boredom is stored in my butthole," Mona said.

Terry sighed. "Any old friends here?" she asked. "From grade school?"

Mona didn't answer, but it wasn't a bad idea. And it would kill time. If she hurried she could make it to the house before dark. She put her boots back on.

"What just happened?" Terry asked. "Where are you going?"

"You'll see," Mona said.

It was a pleasant twenty-minute walk. Mona was the only pedestrian, unless you counted zombies waiting for the bus. She walked along two avenues, one wide boulevard, and finally a lane, at the end of which stood the house. The house itself looked the same, a sprawling one-story stucco with a red-tiled roof, but they'd ditched the water-wasting lawn and replaced it with desert grasses, shrubs, and ice plants. A white car sat in the driveway.

"I made it," Mona told Terry. "I've arrived at the residence of Penny the Pooper."

"What?" Terry said.

"You heard me," Mona said.

"But she pooped in the stream at summer camp," Terry said. "You called her a terrorist."

"She pooped all over town, Terry," Mona said. "I still want to peek in her window."

Penny's bedroom was at the front of the house, just to the right of the entrance. Unfortunately, her bedroom window wasn't street-facing.

Rather, it faced the walkway to the front door, which didn't make for easy peeping. But at least the curtains were open. Still, she would be seen by anyone standing in the kitchen. Not for the first time, she wished she were wearing a UPS uniform and carrying a package.

"I would say UPS driver is my sixth-most frequent fantasy," Mona told Terry. "For the record."

"Shit or get off the pot," Terry said.

Mona walked past the house and then backtracked across the yard. She got on her hands and knees and crawled alongside the front of the house. When she reached Penny's bedroom, she stood on her knees and cupped her hands at the window. Penny's room was exactly as Mona remembered—lavender walls, white furniture, a double bed with canopy. The only difference was the shit on the walls.

"There's shit on the walls?" Terry asked, alarmed.

"Photographs," Mona said. "And posters. From high school and college. It seems Penny was very popular. Extremely blonde. Lots of friends, proms, parties. Looks like she went to UC Santa Barbara. She's got, like, zero edge, but she's a babe."

"So, the total opposite of you," Terry observed.

"Pretty much," Mona agreed.

"It's funny," Terry mused. "Seems like you'd be the pooper, not her."

"Yeah? Why's that?" Mona asked, though she already knew.

"Because you were vaguely goth?" Terry said. "And in a mental hospital? And on meds. And you dated a junkie—"

"Hang on," Mona said. "I think I hear footsteps."

The front door swung open. There stood Penny's mother. Barbara. Or Babs, as they'd called her. She was dressed like a golfer. Her face looked strangely bland and frozen.

"Babs loves Botox," Terry whispered.

"May I help you?" Babs asked.

Mona got to her feet and brushed wood chips off her pants. "It's me, Mona."

Babs's face held no expression, but she had to be feeling something. Anger? Surprise? Delight?

"I don't think it's delight," Terry said.

"I don't know if you remember me, but I was best friends with your daughter," Mona said, and swallowed. "In grade school."

Tight, tight smile. So tight!

"Focus on her eyeballs," Terry advised.

"I was just visiting my mother," Mona went on. "And I got to thinking about Penny, and I wondered if she still lived here. We haven't spoken since seventh grade."

"She's at nursing school," Babs said. "In Oakland. She's getting married next year."

"That's wonderful," Mona said.

Babs nodded in agreement. Now would've been the time for Babs to ask about Mona's career and marital status, but she said nothing. Her daughter had taken dumps in dressing rooms all over the city, and yet Babs was giving Mona the *Caddyshack* treatment. *We have a pool and a pond*, her eyeballs seemed to say. *The pond would be good for you.*

"Well," Mona said finally. "Give Penny my best."

"Will do," Babs said.

On the walk back, the taffy in Mona's stomach arranged itself into a giant knot. She stopped walking several times and clutched her stomach. In Clare's bathroom at last, Mona discovered that she'd started her period. She'd been free-bleeding for a couple of hours, if not longer, and she had what looked like blood on her cheek. What the fuck.

SHE SPENT THE FOLLOWING DAY ALONE AND STARVING IN Clare's apartment. Her food choices: Diet Cherry Vanilla Dr. Pepper and root beer Popsicles, Clare's staples. Thirteen years ago, she would have crept upstairs to the third floor and jiggled some doorknobs. The apartment directly above her had always been unlocked, she remembered, and always smelled like bacon and Budweiser. The tenant, a lonely alcoholic named Brian, had named his two cats Bacon and Bud. She remembered wolfing down bologna from his fridge and looking at his *Playboys*.

The two old banana boxes in Clare's utility closet were the only things she planned on breaking and entering today. She placed them on the coffee table in the living room. The cardboard was shiny, vaguely greasy, and each box was marked "MONA'S BULLSHIT" in red Sharpie (her own handwriting).

She sat on the couch. Box #1 held a jumble of construction paper art, homework from elementary school, magazine clippings, and other junk. The only thing worth saving: a snapshot of Spoon and Fork, her Jack Russells. When her parents divorced, Spoon and Fork were given to a "farm in Idaho." In this picture, they were hunting in a field of carpet weeds. Fork had his head in a hole, ass in the air, tail blurred midwag. Spoon was on his back, probably rolling around in something vile. She stared at the picture and let her eyes go out of focus. Tears welled but didn't spill over.

Hours later, Clare was gently shaking her shoulder. She opened her eyes and lifted her head. She'd drooled all over the mauve corduroy cushion.

"You were having a bad dream, sweetie pie," Clare said.

She had been in the backseat of a car parked next to a nodding donkey in a scrubby oil field. Dark sat in the driver's seat with Spoon on his lap, Fork and Mr. Disgusting in the passenger seat. They both looked at her over their shoulders. *We're here*, Dark said, *waiting for you. Why aren't you looking for us?*

Clare sat on the arm of the couch. "You found your stuff." She peered into the open box. "Anything good?"

Mona cleared her throat. "Just a lot of wind, mostly."

Clare yawned. "Ready for dinner, baby?"

She looked past Clare, out the dirty window. The sun was glinting off the windows of the condominium across the street. "What time is it?"

"Five," Clare said. "You know Frank likes to eat at five thirty."

She had the sudden urge to snatch the ballpoint pen from the coffee table and stab Clare in the arm with it, a physical urge she felt in her fingers. The impulse startled her, made her wonder if she was a terrible daughter. Then again, she had a history of doing violence to Clare with her fingers. As a kid, part of her morning routine had been to wait for her father to get in the shower before climbing onto Clare's bed, straddling her, and massaging her neck and back with vitamin E oil. *Harder*, Clare would say. Mona pressed down with all her weight. She dug in under the shoulder blades. She tried to cleave the muscles from the bones. *Ouch*, Clare would say. *Are you trying to kill me?*

"Frank's waiting," Clare said. "I better get over there before he eats without me. We're having tacos. We'll probably play cards after. I'll put a plate aside for you, okay?"

Play cards—a euphemism, she assumed. They probably played cards loudly, with no regard for the neighbors.

ALONE NOW AND WIDE AWAKE, SHE EMPTIED THE REMAINING box onto the floor and reclaimed the gold: photo albums, diaries, the Liquid Paper project, good drawings. The only genuine gold was a locket from Clare's mother. The locket, large and pear shaped, was suspended from a beaded chain the color of gunmetal. Inside, her grandmother had placed a picture of Clare as a teenager. "That way, she's always with you," she'd said as she fastened the locket around Mona's neck. "Making sure you don't do anything stupid."

The last time she'd worn the locket had been a month or so after her thirteenth birthday. Frank and Clare had had tickets to an Emmylou Harris concert, but they didn't know what to do with Mona. This was shortly after her "arrest," and so she was grounded. They refused to leave her alone. Clare must have called Luisa, the Brazilian lady next door, because that's where Mona ended up.

They were having a party over there. Luisa greeted her at the back door and led her through the kitchen, past an old woman stirring a pot, and into the dining room. A large, gap-toothed woman chopped strawberries on a flimsy card table. Here Luisa stopped and handed Mona a plate full of rice and plastic silverware. Mona followed her into the large, sunny backyard of the apartment building, where the music was louder and people were dancing. Shirtless men stood leaning against the fence, smoking and watching women, and she heard Brutus, the German shepherd next door, barking his head off.

Luisa beckoned her to the corner of the yard, where eight or nine men were gathered around something on the ground, yelling and laughing and jostling one another. Mona thought they must be playing a game, but as she got closer she saw that it was a barbecue pit, and the spectacle they all seemed so fascinated by was meat roasting on thick metal spikes. There were seven spikes in all, and impaled upon each one was a different kind of meat—steak, ribs, sausages, pork chops, whole baby birds. The spikes rotated and dripped over the hot coals.

Luisa deposited her next to her husband, Sergio; said something to him in Portuguese; and then disappeared. Sergio wore a bright green apron over his massive belly and held a long, serrated knife. He smiled at her with his silver teeth and offered her the plastic cup from which he was drinking. She took a sip and it tasted like strawberries and he gestured for her to finish it. Then he shouted at the men to stand back and he leaned over the pit, picked up one of the spikes, and sliced beef onto her plate with his big knife. The meat was too pink for her, but she didn't say anything.

Mona picked at her food and watched the women dance. They rolled their hips and whipped their long hair in circles and made their arms look like snakes. Three of the men at the fence began dancing with the women, and then a man was talking to her in Portuguese. He peeked inside her empty cup and refilled it from his own. She pretended to understand him as she drank. Suddenly Luisa was scolding the man and pulling her inside.

Luisa gently removed the cup from her hand and said, "Go to my bedroom and watch TV. You can bring your plate in there and eat on my bed."

But Luisa's room was occupied by kissing people, so Mona closed the door and sat in the living room. Now that Luisa was gone, she slipped out front and let herself into Frank's apartment with the hidden key.

The birds were screeching at her. She tossed some meat into their cages. Wahkan hissed and wouldn't go near it, but Takoda pecked at it and then started screaming again. She covered their cages with towels and then went into the bedroom to snoop and to try on Frank's cowboy boots. There, on the floor next to the bed, lay one of the dresses Clare had chosen not to wear to the concert. A sundress printed with brown and orange paisleys, backless with a plunging neckline. Mona stepped into the dress and paired it with cork wedges. Then she dipped into Clare's makeup, since it was sitting right there. Brown eyeliner, gold eye shadow, mascara, bright red lipstick. She dusted her breastbone with bronzer, just like Clare, and took her hair out of a ponytail and brushed it until it was shiny.

Next door, they'd dimmed the lights and turned up the music, and there were twenty people in the living room alone, and thirty more in the yard. She walked right past Luisa, helped herself to strawberry punch, and watched the writhing knot of dancers in the living room. She felt overdressed. Some women seemed to be wearing the Brazilian flag and nothing else.

As guests squeezed past her, she stumbled and knocked over a tall plant in a bright pink pot. It was a freckle face plant—Frank had one in his kitchen—but this one was fake, which made her laugh.

A young man helped her pick up the plant. At first, she didn't recognize Chaz without his uniform. Chaz parked cars at the Velvet Turtle, an upscale restaurant in Redondo, and lived here with his aunt Luisa and uncle Sergio. He usually kept his long hair in a ponytail, but now it was down around his shoulders—dirty blond, uncombed—and he wore a yellow T-shirt and tight, faded jeans.

He only knew eleven words in English. This she'd discovered a few days earlier, when he'd gotten locked out. It was raining, so Clare invited him in. His name tag said Charles, which he pronounced Chaz, and he said he was twenty-five but he looked older, and he listed the words he knew in English: "keys," "door," "car," "house," "beach," "ocean," "yes," "please," "thank you."

Now Chaz was pulling her toward the dancers but didn't seem to recognize her from next door. She was certain he thought she was someone else. Someone named Linda. He whispered *Leenda* in her ear while they danced. *Leenda, Leenda, Leenda.* She told him, "My name is Mona. I live next door, remember?" But he just smiled and put his hot hands on her hips. They conversed through body language, though he did most of the communicating. *Here, drink this. See my necklace? It's a pot leaf. I smoke pot. Do you? You don't? You should try it. Take off your shoes—you're too tall. Are you hot? Here, have some of my ice. Wait—let me pass it from my mouth to yours. Now give it back. Oooh, do that again. Loosen your hips. Like this. Don't move your feet too much. There you go. Turn around. Now lean back into me.* And then more *Leenda Leenda* in her ear.

Two hours later, Frank suddenly materialized, sitting on the couch with Sergio, looking her up and down. Something was awry—very awry—because he smiled winsomely at her even though Chaz was essentially dry-humping her buttocks. Between songs Frank told her it was time to leave.

She didn't realize Frank was drunk until she saw him walk. He lost his footing on one of the steps and caught himself, and then stumbled in the courtyard and almost landed in the fountain.

Clare was passed out on the couch but Frank had no trouble picking her up and carrying her to his waterbed. She felt envious. Other than Spoon and Fork, being carried was the only thing she missed from childhood.

Frank came back into the living room while she was changing into her pajamas.

"What's the matter?" he said. "You look sad."

He put a blanket over her, and then he staggered into the bathroom, where he did some very efficient, no-nonsense puking. "Don't stay up too late," he yelled down the hall on his way to bed.

She heard the door click shut and waited, anticipating the sounds of their fucking, but she only heard shallow breathing and then snoring.

She was sleeping when the pounding started. BOOM-BOOM-BOOM, pause, BOOM-BOOM-BOOM, pause. Must be a stranger, she thought, because no one came to their front door. An emergency of some kind. But the pounding didn't sound desperate. It was confident and entitled, a cop's knock, and she thought it might be one of Frank's friends.

It was Chaz. She turned on the lights and opened the door, thinking maybe he was locked out again, but he walked in like it was his own apartment and embraced her. He smelled like a campfire and immediately started fumbling with her nightgown. And she thought, Okay, but would you carry me first? She would have asked, had he spoken English. Would you carry me out the door and around the block a few times?

He nudged her toward the couch. He seemed to be telling her a story, and presented her with a condom. She turned it over a couple of times, wondering what it was. She gave it back. He took this as a cue and ground against her. She'd had a man's hand in her underpants before, but he didn't do that. He just rubbed himself roughly against her, and she followed her instincts and pretended to be dead.

The birds' cages were covered, but they were awake. Wahkan mimicked the noise of a door creaking open—Frank's door—and Takoda made strange little gasping noises as he shredded newspaper for another useless nest.

Chaz's eyes were closed in concentration. Did he still think she was Linda? She stared at the blond hair on his brawny forearm, and then out the window. She imagined that this was her apartment now, and she was pitching Frank's shit into a Dumpster on the lawn. A stack of *Bird Talk* magazines went first, followed by dream catchers, peace pipes, and the creepy face masks. She yanked the bronze sun face off the wall and threw it like a Frisbee into the Dumpster. Same with the portrait of Sitting Bull. She gathered all the weaponry together—the tomahawks, lances, war clubs, bows and arrows—and tossed those, too. The knives with stone blades would stay—she liked those—and so would the kachina dolls. Well, not all of them. She would get rid of the foxes, wolves, and roadrunners, but she would save the clowns, rain priests, badgers, and morning singers for a—

Chaz stopped moving and collapsed on top of her. He murmured in her ear and rested his dry lips on her neck for several seconds. He climbed off her and went into the kitchen and drank from the faucet. She pulled down her nightgown, covered herself with the blanket, and then closed her eyes as he passed through on his way out the door.

The next morning, in the kitchen with Clare, Mona tried to pretend everything was normal by making her favorite breakfast, a fried-egg and jalapeño Cheez Whiz sandwich on white Wonder bread. Her hands were shaking and she was nauseated. That's when Clare found the condom, still in its package. Clare gasped as if it were a piece of human feces.

"Oh my God," she said.

Mona's stomach churned.

"Where'd this come from?"

"Chaz," Mona said.

Clare looked stricken. She couldn't understand.

"The Brazilian guy? Next door?" Mona said. "He came over last night. You guys were asleep." She left her plate and retched into the sink.

Clare covered her mouth and left the kitchen, and Mona heard the bedroom door open and close. She turned on the faucet and closed her eyes. She wished herself back into the house she grew up in, and imagined she was rubbing Forky's little belly, and Spoon was licking her entire face. When she opened her eyes, hot tears rolled down her cheeks.

Clare called her into the living room, where she and Frank were sitting on the couch. Frank's hair was messed up and he looked lost.

"Tell us what happened," Frank said. "The whole truth."

"Well, I was asleep and then I heard someone pounding on the door and it was him, Chaz. So, I let him in and . . ." She shrugged. "He was drunk. I don't think he knew what he was doing. I think he thought I was someone else. Someone named Linda."

Frank looked at her with interest. "Why do you think that?"

"That's what he kept calling me. Linda. *Leenda*."

" '*Linda*' means 'pretty,' knucklehead."

"Oh," she said. "Well, okay, but I still don't think he knew who I was."

"Oh, he knew," Clare said with a shaky voice. "He knew."

"Did you, uh, say no?" Frank asked. "I mean, did he force himself on you?"

"I felt bad for him. He wasn't mean about it or anything. He just humped me like a dog and then left."

They were all silent for a minute. She remembered asking if she could go visit her dogs. In Idaho.

"No, honey, you can't," Clare said miserably.

MONA SNAPPED THE LOCKET SHUT AND PUT IT IN WITH THE other items, forcing herself not to look at anything too closely. As a reward, she took herself to the liquor store and dropped twenty dollars on a bottle of red and a can of Pringles. On the way back, she peeked into Frank's living room window. What she saw surprised her: there they were, sitting across from each other at the dining room table with actual cards in their hands.

She slunk away, gripped by a weird sadness that it took three glasses of wine to shake. Now she was tipsy. She felt the urge to snoop—not in Clare's apartment, but perhaps upstairs. It seemed urgent that she know whether Brian, Bacon, and Bud were still alive. The tenants were each assigned their own parking space so it was easy to see who was home. She looked out the window. The space for the apartment above was empty.

She crept up the stairs on all fours, tried the knob, and then entered using her old technique, by flinging the door open. Confidence was key. If someone happened to be sitting on the couch, she'd play dingbat. *Oh God, wrong floor! These apartments all look the same!*

But no one was home and she was alone. Brian was long gone, but a guy still lived here—she could tell by the size of the television. Other giveaways: bad overhead lighting, not enough lamps, no full-length mirror. He owned a compass.

He used his bed as a desk, so they had that in common. She liked a man who slept with books. His journal was waiting patiently for her on his nightstand. Please don't be a dream journal, she thought. She opened it to the middle and looked at the dates. The journal was ten years old, but she didn't care.

Phnom Penh, Cambodia

Last night I got drunk in the tourist section of town, at a bar called the Friendly Lounge. The place was filled with douchebags from every nation. I sat on one of the couches and sucked down three gin and tonics. The jet lag was extreme. A woman squeezed in next to me on the couch. She was sitting on my bad side, but I could see her shoes, and was happy to see they weren't Birkenstocks.

"They should rename this bar Shithead International," I said after a minute.

She gave me a blank look. I asked if she spoke English and she said of course. She was half French, half something else. Her first and last names rhymed, so I was worried she had shit for brains, but she turned out to be smart and high on MDMA.

"Your eye reminds me of a Magritte painting," she said. "Is it a birthmark?"

I told her I was stabbed with a steak knife.

"Who stabbed you?" she asked, with a bored expression on her face.

"My pet hamster," I said.

She didn't like that. I told her she shouldn't ask such personal questions of a stranger.

"I thought we were getting to know each other," she said, and shrugged.

We kept talking and our knees touched. An hour or so later, she invited herself back to my hotel. She spent what seemed like a very long time with my balls in her mouth. I wasn't completely into it, but I didn't know what to say, or how to stop her. I was reminded again that I'm not cut out for casual sex. I figured the French thing to do would be to light a cigarette and act nonchalant, which is what I did. But, as I don't smoke, I doubt I looked French. She made a big show of wetting one of her fingers and inserting it in my ass.

"Tickle, tickle," she said.

"How old are you?" I asked.

"You really are regressing," Terry said suddenly. "You weren't kidding about that."

"Jesus, Terry," Mona said. "Where have you been for the last twelve hours?"

"Close the journal," Terry said firmly.

"It's pretty good actually," Mona said. "Shockingly."

"Don't push it," Terry snapped. "Get out of there right now or I'm calling the cops."

Terry hated Mona's snooping, which was strange considering how nosy she had to be for a living.

"How old are you?" I asked.

"Twenty-six," she said.

She didn't ask me how old I was. She was too busy treating my dick like a ballet barre.

"It's attached, you know," I said. "To the rest of me."

"You're pretty drunk," she said.

I told her I wasn't into strange pussy.

"What really happened to your eye?" she asked.

"I warned you," Terry said. "I'm on the phone with the police right now. 'Yes, hello, I'd like to report a break-in—'"

"Fine," Mona said, and closed the journal.

She went back downstairs and killed the bottle of red in Clare's bed. It occurred to her that part of her had wanted to be caught. Perhaps this desire was what motivated her to snoop in the first place. On the surface, snooping was about discovering the truth about others, but perhaps it was also about being discovered?

Clare's landline rang. Mona, convinced it was the police, answered on the fourth ring.

"Hello?" she said tentatively.

"Aren't you hungry?" Clare asked.

"Do you know the guy upstairs?"

"He's too old for you, honey," Clare said. "What are you doing?"

"Contemplating."

Silence. "What are you, uh, contemplating?" Clare asked nervously.

"What to do with my life."

"Well, what are you good at, hon?"

"Vacuuming," she said truthfully.

She listened for background noise—Frank's voice, the television, the birds. For the first time in years she heard nothing.

"What else you good at, hon?"

Mona stared at the glitter on the textured ceiling. "Listening, I guess. People seem to tell me things about themselves. You don't know how many times I've heard the phrase 'I've never told anyone this, but . . .'"

"Maybe you should become a therapist," Clare suggested.

"I cleaned house for one recently," Mona said.

"And slept with her husband," Terry reminded her.

"I'm definitely fucked up enough to be a therapist," Mona said to both Clare and Terry.

"But is there something that brings you joy, that makes you feel really alive and good about yourself?" Clare asked.

"I've always wanted to be an artist," Mona said. "But I suffer from imposter syndrome."

"What's that?" Clare asked.

"A fear of being exposed as a fraud."

Clare didn't say anything. Neither did Terry.

"Ideally, I'd like to remain an outsider artist—self-taught, I mean. I've been working on a photography project for many years now. I even put a portfolio together."

"It's a shame you buried it in your backyard," Terry said.

"Anyway," Mona said, "I'm secretly hoping it's a masterpiece, but I'll probably be dead by the time—"

"Come over, Mona," Clare interrupted. "We'll teach you rummy. It'll be fun."

"Honestly, I'd rather go to the movies," Mona said after a few seconds.

Clare groaned. "Frank can't sit in those seats. Hurts his back."

"Well, he doesn't have to come."

Clare sighed, twice.

"It's a movie, Clare, not bungee jumping," Mona said. "I promise you won't get hurt."

"He—he'll feel left out," she stammered. "Besides, he made your favorite dessert of all time and it came out perfect."

THEY ATE RICE PUDDING WITH RAISINS IN FRONT OF THE TELE-vision. "I don't care what anyone says," Clare announced at one point. "I love pudding."

"No one's arguing with you," Frank said.

Later, while Mona was rinsing dishes in the kitchen, she heard a choking sound coming from the next room. She turned off the faucet and tiptoed a few steps into the dining area, thinking one of the birds was having an episode, but their cages were covered and they were quiet. Clare was in the bathroom and Frank was alone on the couch, watching television. His cheeks and neck were glistening with what she thought must be sweat—he never opened the windows—but then his face crumpled and he let out a little sob. That's when she knew he hadn't seen her. His eyes were riveted to the television. She glanced at the screen, expecting to see a dog bleeding all over the place, or someone wasting away on their deathbed. But it was only Whoopi Goldberg dressed as a nun and leading a choir of black teenagers. The final scene of *Sister Act 2*. The choir was clapping and singing "Oh Happy Day" and Whoopi was beaming with pride, and then one of the kids belted out a solo and brought the house down, and the camera panned to the uptight white people in the audience, and they were all bowled over and misty eyed. And so was Frank, apparently.

She quietly backed away into the kitchen, waiting for the movie to end. A few minutes later, he blew his nose and changed the channel.

"HE ALWAYS CRIES DURING SAPPY MOVIES," CLARE SAID THE next morning. "But if you say anything about it, he just says he has dirt in his eye."

It was eight A.M. Clare had shown up an hour ago and asked Mona if she wanted to go to the swap meet in Gardena with her and Frank. Mona declined. Now Clare was fresh out of the shower and resting her foot on the edge of the bed, aggressively applying Good-bye Cellulite cream to the back of her thigh. The cream was dense, lardlike. Clare practically beat it into her skin. When she switched thighs, Mona caught a glimpse of her nether region: completely shaved but for that hard-to-reach place at the top of the wishbone. A wild little tuft. It reminded Mona of the hair inside an old man's ear.

"Or a spider?" Terry offered.

"Why not ear hair?" Mona asked.

"A spider is kinder," Terry said.

"Both are disturbing," Mona said.

"What's that look on your face?" Clare suddenly asked.

"What look," Mona said. "I have a look?"

"You look . . . repulsed," Clare said.

"I'm constipated," Mona said.

"You were staring at my you-know-what." She removed the towel from her head and wrapped it around her body. "I saw you." She began opening dresser drawers and slamming them shut, pretending to look for something.

"What's happening?" Terry whispered.

"The demon's back," Mona murmured to Terry, "demanding food."

"But you told me you liked feeding the demon," Terry said.

"It was different back then," Mona said. "I was a kid and there were donuts involved. I'm actually terrified of the demon."

"Your lips are moving," Clare said. "What are you saying?"

"Nothing," Mona said quickly.

"You're like a drunk trying to act sober," Clare said. "If you have something to say, just say it."

"Why do you shave it like that?"

"Like what?" Clare asked.

"Backpedal," Terry advised.

"At your age, I mean," Mona said.

"I'm only fifty-one," Clare said in a shaky voice.

Mona thought of Takoda. How jarring it was when he lifted his wings. Birds were supposed to have feathers. Mothers were supposed to have . . . bushes.

"You're saying it looks stupid, right?" Clare sniffed. "You think I'm disgusting."

"Smooth it over," Terry said. "Right now. She's going to start crying in five, four, three—"

"Smooth it over how?" Mona asked.

"Show her your own fucked-up bush," Terry suggested.

Mona's bush resembled a defective martini glass. She flashed it at Clare and smiled. "Cheers!" Mona said.

Clare laughed and let the towel drop.

"Phew," Terry said.

Clare removed a dark purple blouse from her closet and then stood in front of the mirror and buttoned it. She slipped into a denim skirt and pulled on a pair of calf-high suede boots with multiple layers of beaded trim.

"Hey," Mona said. "Let's go get donuts like old times."

"Donuts?" Clare snorted. "I haven't eaten a donut in thirteen years. Do I look okay? Frank bought me these boots for Christmas."

"You look like you're going to a pow-wow," Mona said. "And you forgot to put on underwear."

"I didn't forget," Clare said, and smiled. She tossed her hair forward, mussed it with her fingers, and then flipped it back. After putting on lipstick, she sprayed herself with Opium while checking her backside in the mirror.

"You've been married for over a decade, but you act like it's your third date."

"I still get butterflies." She sat on the edge of the bed and crossed her legs, absentmindedly fingered a bead on her boot. "How did that guy die? The one you were with in Massachusetts. You mentioned him in your letter."

Mona thought of the leather jacket she'd splurged on just before she met Mr. Disgusting. After wearing it for a week, she decided to take it back—too big, too brown. The saleswoman turned the pockets inside out and a bunch of cookie crumbs fell onto the counter. "You've worn this jacket," the woman said with a bitchy look on her face. "You can't return it." Mona remembered feeling like a degenerate. She also remembered feeling affection for the crumbs.

Now Clare wanted Mona to empty her pockets, but Mona didn't want Mr. Disgusting to fall out. Her favorite crumb.

"Freak accident," Mona said, and cleared her throat. "Involving some machinery. At a job site. He was a carpenter."

Clare covered her mouth with her hand. "Jesus, Mona," she said through her fingers. "Why didn't you say something?"

"It was over two years ago," Mona said, and stared at the dust on the lampshade.

"Did you go to the funeral?"

"Of course." She closed her eyes and invented it: Heavy casket, light drizzle, muddy grass, a procession of sodden crackheads and junkies without umbrellas. Music at the grave site. Bagpipes? No. Someone playing guitar and singing. What? A Leonard Cohen song, she supposed. "It was really depressing."

"I don't know if I ever told you this, but my first boyfriend died in a freak accident. His name was Mahmud. He was Arab and spoke eight languages—that was part of his appeal. He was also a fifth-degree black belt in judo. Anyway, I was so naïve, I believed him when he said butt sex was normal after you were married."

"You have told me that story, actually," Mona said. "More than once."

"But your dad turned out to be the bigger pervert. I think it was genetic in his case. He seemed pretty normal when we first met, but then he lost his arm, and so I think the trauma triggered it." She frowned. "You know, like schizophrenia."

Trauma. In the loony bin, she'd talked at length about her parents' trauma, because her shrink had been a psychotherapist and because Freud, Elektra, repression, etc., but her shrink had only wanted to hear about Mona, weirdly. Mona told the shrink a few incest stories, and mentioned Chaz, and the time one of her father's friends put his hand in her underpants. As it turned out, according to the shrink, Mona's real trauma was feeling unwanted and passed over. Abandoned. Given up on. That's why she razored geometric patterns on her arms and legs. "That's all?" Mona had asked, disappointed. And her shrink had said, "Isn't that enough?"

"Did I ever tell you that your dad ate an entire cupcake covered in ants?" Clare asked.

"Only about nine hundred times."

"This was after he'd taken Thorazine," Clare said. "For fun."

Clare thought this anecdote explained everything about Mona's father.

"Did he have phantom limb syndrome, by any chance?" Mona asked.

"Is that when you feel the arm that isn't there?"

"Yeah, but it's usually really painful. The phantom limb feels shorter than the real one and like it's in a painful position—bent backward, or something. The pain can go on for years and years, long after the limb is gone."

"Well, if your father had it, he probably didn't even know," Clare said. "He snorted a lot of cocaine."

"You know, I felt like I had a phantom limb in high school," Mona mused.

Clare tilted her head slightly. "But you never lost a limb, honey."

You, Mona thought. You were my limb.

LATER THAT AFTERNOON, SHE WAS SITTING NEXT TO CLARE IN the ER waiting room at Kindred Hospital. Apparently, Frank had suffered some kind of attack at El Pollo Loco. Severe chest pain, profuse sweating, nausea. The paramedics came and everything. Now he was in with the doctor. They were giving him an EKG.

"If he dies, I might kill myself," Clare said. "Just warning you."

"It's probably just gas," Mona said.

Mona had expected an air of urgency here, but the ER was calm. They were sitting on a pink vinyl bench against the wall. Across from them sat an Asian woman and her son. The boy, who looked old enough to tell time, was sobbing quietly. The woman suddenly lifted her blouse and offered the boy her breast. She was braless and her breast was small and covered in stretch marks. The boy immediately stopped crying and fastened his mouth to her nipple. He was far too big to be cradled and merely stood between her legs, his arms wrapped around her torso. The woman closed her eyes and Mona felt lonely on her behalf, which was ridiculous—the woman didn't look lonely at all, but as if all was right in the world. Mona stared, unable to stop herself, and looked around to see if anyone else was having the same problem. The few people waiting were in their own trance, watching CNN on the television. Clare was sniffling and gazing at her lap. Whenever her skirt rode up she lifted her ass a little and tugged it toward her knees.

"Frank loves you," Clare said suddenly.

Mona shifted uncomfortably on the bench.

"We both do," Clare said. "Frank did something special for you. I never told you about it, but I think you should know." She took a minute to adjust her skirt and crossed her legs. "You remember Chad—"

"Chaz."

"You remember how he wound up in the hospital afterward?"

"Yeah," she said. "He fell off a roof."

Clare shook her head. "Frank and his friends beat the crap out of him."

"What?"

"He didn't come out and say it, and I knew not to ask him, but I could tell by the way he was acting that he was involved somehow, and his knuckles were all torn up, so I put two and two together."

She remembered seeing Chaz after he got out of the hospital. He'd had his *face rearranged*—that was the phrase she thought of. Bandaged head, eyes blackened and lopsided, nose broken, jaw wired shut, the whole nine yards.

"Then Frank must have had him deported. That's why he disappeared so suddenly."

"Wow."

Clare looked pleased.

"That must have felt . . . cathartic," Mona said.

"It does feel good," Clare said. "I don't know why I kept it from you for so long."

"Not for you," Mona said, and rolled her eyes. "For Frank. And his friends. It's rare to feel justified in hurting someone like that."

Clare looked confused. "Why not be grateful?" she said. "He made the guy suffer for you and taught him a lesson."

"You can't beat that out of a person, Clare. He's probably alive and well and raping chicks in Brazil."

"I really wish you'd stop calling me Clare," she said quietly. "That's what I wish."

"What would you rather be called?"

She blew her nose with the balled-up Kleenex on her lap. "Mommy would be nice," she said finally.

"Really?"

She shrugged. "When you call me Clare I feel like a stranger. You know? Like I'm nothing to you. Like that wrapper on the floor." She pointed to a silver candy wrapper pinned under a chair leg. The Asian woman and her son were gone. Mona didn't remember seeing them leave.

"Why not just plain Mom?"

"That's what you used to call me—Mommy. Back when you were little. You loved everything and everyone, except grass. You hated grass, wouldn't go near it." She chewed on her thumbnail and looked sideways at Mona's face. "You look like you're being tortured or something. It's not like I'm asking you to call me Cooter. Or Gary, or something disgusting."

"I'm just wondering why now," Mona said. "I'm twenty-six. I can't go around calling you Mommy. Can I?"

"I'm not asking you to say it in the supermarket. Just sometimes when we're alone." She looked around the room. "Like right now."

"Okay."

"Okay, what?"

Mona smiled. "Okay . . . *Mommy*."

"Why are you whispering?" Clare whispered.

"Mommy!" Mona shouted. "Mommy!"

The nurse at the front desk looked in their direction. Mona smiled and waved.

"Can't you make it a natural part of your speech?" Clare asked.

Mona cleared her throat. "Well, *Mommy*"—she took a sip of water from Clare's bottle—"I've been meaning to tell you something, actually. That guy I was dating who died? He was a junkie, not a carpenter, and he killed himself. His body was never found, but he would've been buried in a pauper's grave, and the only person who would have shown up is me. And a few hookers."

Clare picked up an issue of *Newsweek* and began fanning herself. "Sorry," she said. "Hot flash. I'm going through the Change."

"You've been Changing for ten years," Mona said. "Anyway, a few weeks before he disappeared, we got high together. He shot me up with heroin and cocaine, and I overdosed, or had some kind of allergic reaction. This is going to sound crazy, but while I was unconscious I had some minor convulsions, during which I remembered being born. I remembered coming out of you. The passage through the canal, crowning, being delivered, the whole thing. Except it wasn't a warm and fuzzy feeling—it was the most sickening thing I've ever felt or experienced. It was just . . . *vile*."

"My heart's racing." Clare stopped fanning herself and touched her chest. "I can feel it beating in my neck."

"It was worse than being raped . . . Mommy," Mona said. "Anyway, my point is, I don't feel any animosity toward Chaz. What I resent, actually, is being born."

Clare reached into her purse and frantically rummaged around. For a second Mona thought she was looking for a weapon. Something with which to stab herself—or Mona.

"What are you looking for?" Mona asked.

"Pills," Clare said. "I don't have any, but I keep looking. Old habit."

Mona felt sorry for her. Truth-telling: a ridiculous idea. Too late for that, just as it was too late to call Clare anything other than . . . Darlene? No—she would call her Mom. She should've just written Clare a letter, and then added it to the large file she kept in a drawer: Letters I'll Never Send.

"You all right, Mom? Want me to get the nurse?"

"You were born with teeth, you know," Clare said. "Nursing you was extremely painful. My nipples bled."

Mona yawned.

"You also secreted breast milk when you were an infant," Clare said.

This was new. "What?"

"The doctor called it neonatal milk," Clare said. "But the nurses called it Witches' Milk."

"I had milk coming out of my baby nipples?" Mona asked.

Clare smiled wistfully. "Yes."

"Did I breastfeed anyone?" Mona asked.

"Only the dog," Clare said.

Mona laughed. "We didn't have a dog yet."

"The neighbor's dog," Clare said.

"How many teeth was I born with?" Mona asked.

"Two," Clare said. "And you had hair on your forehead, and I was never more in love with anyone. I suppose it doesn't count, though, because you don't remember."

"Well, I remember Woody," Mona said. "The guy eye-raped me at least once a week."

Clare frowned. "I'm sorry about that. He eye-raped me, too. I never should have left you alone with him."

They were silent for a minute.

"You okay?" Clare asked.

"Just waiting for the déjà vu to pass," Mona said.

Clare brought a shaky hand to her face and touched her cheekbone with the tips of her fingers. "I barely knew where my own vagina was until I met your father, and then he tortured it, and the rest of me, for fourteen years," Clare said. "I've had a number of concussions."

Concussions were reserved for holidays. The most vivid in Mona's memory: Halloween, the year she went as a giant, individually wrapped roll of toilet paper. Scott tissue. An elaborate and delicate costume, the result of a weeks-long collaboration between herself and her art teacher at school. They'd hand-painted the logo and taglines and had even included the barcode on the back of the roll. She was convinced the costume would make her famous, at least locally, and land her on the evening news, but her father had been in a blackout that night, which meant a bunch of shit got broken, including a casserole dish, Mona's costume, and Clare's nose.

"What made you go to rehab after all this time?" Mona asked.

"Frank found out," Clare said. "You know, he never set foot in my apartment, never once in eleven years? And then one day he did, and he turned the place upside down."

Mona had spent nine years in Massachusetts. Clare visited twice: once when Mona was released from the loony bin, and then again for Mona's high school graduation. The loony-bin visit was a disaster. First, it was January, and Clare had only seen snow in photographs. Second, Mona's shrink had wanted to meet with Clare—alone, behind closed doors.

Mona had paced the hallway outside as if Clare were undergoing risky surgery. Twenty minutes later, Clare emerged in tears. Clearly, the shrink had told Clare about the fucking rowboat, the not-very-complimentary analogy Mona had expressed in therapy. Clare was safe inside a rowboat while Mona and Frank were awash in the deep dark ocean, except Mona was actually drowning while Frank was merely waving his arms, but take a wild guess who Clare saved. "They're blaming *me*," Clare said in disbelief. "They're acting like *I* was the one cutting you."

Clare was shell-shocked and incredulous for the rest of the weekend, but Mona dragged her to Cambridge. Clare didn't care for Harvard Square, but she took Mona shopping and bought her a bunch of clothes, including a good winter coat. She also bought a very expensive pinkie ring for Frank. The ring cost six hundred dollars. Clare lost the ring within hours. They spent the afternoon retracing their steps, but it was long gone. When Clare got back to Los Angeles, she checked herself into a mental hospital.

"Listen, letting you go wasn't a selfish act," Clare said. "I was afraid you'd end up pregnant and on drugs. You were already sniffing glue, and you were almost raped. I told myself you were better off in New England. It hurt to admit that, you know. It's partly why I did drugs for so many years. But I'm awake now. Wide awake." She belched softly. "It sucks being awake."

"Tell me about it," Mona said.

"I should have visited you more," she said.

"Spoon and Fork," Mona said. "What about them?"

Clare sighed. "First of all, excuse me, but those dogs were a fucking nightmare, okay? Forky's breath was so terrible it could melt your eyebrows, and Spoon was a complete psychopath. He terrorized the whole neighborhood. He killed Mittens or Buckles or whatever that cat's name was."

"Peaches," Mona said. "The cat's name was Peaches."

"There he is," Clare said suddenly, and nodded toward the front desk. Frank was standing there, squinting at a piece of paper on the counter. Clare stood up and hurried toward him, clutching her purse to her stomach.

Mona stayed seated for a minute. She watched them embrace. They loved each other more than they loved her—was that such a crime?

"Mr. Disgusting loved you more than your own parents," Terry said out of nowhere.

"I'm okay with that," Mona told Terry.

Clare and Frank were kissing. Mona approached them after they were done.

"Panic attack," Frank announced to Mona. "Not heart attack." He flashed an embarrassed smile.

Panic at El Pollo Loco, Mona thought. A new song by Frank Torres.

Frank and Clare walked hand in hand toward the exit. As usual, Mona followed four or five paces behind, staring at their backsides. Then, at the automatic doors, Frank stopped and looked back at her. She figured he'd forgotten something—his jacket, maybe—but he was looking at her face.

"Yes?" she said.

"Just waiting for you to catch up," he said.

CLARE STOPPED BY ON HER WAY TO WORK THE NEXT MORNING. Frank had called in sick, she said, which he'd never done before, and was behaving strangely.

"Strange, how?" Mona asked.

"Like he's about to die," Clare said. "He's calling everyone he knows, people he's been avoiding for years, just to 'check in.' And he's also throwing a bunch of stuff away. Stuff he loves." Clare sat on the bed next to Mona's open suitcase. "Why are you packing?"

"I'm leaving after your ceremony," Mona said.

"You know you can stay here as long as you want, right?" Clare asked.

"I thought you were getting rid of the place."

"You could take over the lease," she said. "It's not too late. We could be neighbors. I'd love that."

Mona shrugged. "Thanks, Mom."

"Let me ask you something. Why haven't you been to the beach? It's like, *right there.*"

"I find the ocean depressing," Mona said. "I don't like the sound of pounding surf. I like lakes. Placid lakes. I like the sound of water slapping a boat—"

"I'm happy you're here," Clare interrupted. She scratched her ear and looked at Mona. "Why do you look surprised?"

"Because you seem to have trouble spending more than twenty minutes alone with me."

"Not true," she said, and looked at her watch. "I've been sitting here for thirty minutes. I'm late for work, honey. Would you mind checking on Frank later? If you see him throwing away something important, stop him."

"What am I supposed to do—wrestle it out of his hands?"

"I love you," she said, and kissed Mona on the mouth. "Just call me."

FRANK WAS CERTAINLY BEHAVING AS IF HE'D HAD A HEART AT-tack. She sat on the couch and watched him wander around with a large black garbage bag, snatching various items off shelves and dropping them in. Wahkan cooed like a pigeon from his shoulder. Takoda was stuck in his cage, weeping quietly.

"He cries like Clare," Mona commented.

"Who's Clare?" Frank said.

"My mother," she said. "Why are you throwing your stuff away?"

"I feel like a giant fat man is sitting on my chest," he said. "The fat man is pigging out and can't feel me squirming, but, so. That's the image that came to me in the ambulance."

"What's the fat man eating?" Mona asked.

"A tub of fried chicken," Frank said.

As far as she knew, he'd never talked about his feelings before. Nor had she ever been alone with him as an adult, she realized now. It was just as uncomfortable as she'd always imagined.

He was asking her what she wanted. She looked around nervously, at a loss. Takoda stopped crying and loudly blew his nose.

"Hold on," Frank said, and disappeared into the bedroom. He came out a few seconds later with a small oil painting. "Check this out."

At first glance it looked like a Christian cross in flames. Then she saw that it wasn't a cross, but rather an eagle with its wings spread. But wait a minute, the eagle's face was also a Native American guy with wings, and the wings had eyes in them, and the eyes were staring at her.

"Wow," she said.

"Take it," he said happily. "It's yours, so."

"Wow," she said again. "Thanks, Frank."

"What else you want?" He walked over to a shelf and picked up a small cone-shaped basket with a bunch of feathers and bells hanging off it. "How about this?"

"Oh no," she said. "That's okay. I'm not really in the market for baskets."

"Yeah, but this is special, Mona. What they call a *burden* basket. It's made from willow fibers. And so in the old days, the Apaches used these baskets to carry food and firewood and stuff like that, so, but. Now they hang 'em on people's front doors, and visitors are supposed to place their burdens in the basket before entering, so. You know that expression, 'Leave your burdens at the door'? Well, that's where it comes from."

"My soul is a burden basket," Mona said.

Frank looked nervous.

"What else you want?" he asked. "Pick something. Anything."

She looked at the kachina dolls lined up on a shelf. Some of them were carrying burden baskets. She remembered focusing on one of the morning singers on the night with Chaz. The doll had aged considerably since then. Her hair and clothes were soiled. Originally the singer held a miniature spruce tree, but it was gone now, disappeared.

"Your vacuum," Mona said.

"Done," he said without hesitation.

"Really?"

"Get the vacuum and follow me," Frank said.

She carried the vacuum to the parking lot out back, where Frank kept his Mustang and other vintage cars. He had three. They all looked alike to her, except for the biggest one, a Ford something. She watched him caress the hood of the Mustang.

"Isn't she a beauty?" Frank asked.

"Sure is," Mona said.

Wahkan took a shit on his shoulder. "Good night, sweetheart," the bird said in a heavy lisp.

"So what're you driving out there in New Mexico?" Frank asked.

"Toyota pickup," she said. "I ran out of oil once and was still able to drive six hours."

"How many miles?"

"A lot," she said. "Over two hundred thousand."

He nodded. "You prefer the Ford, I can tell." He walked over to it, ran a clean finger over the hood and held it up for her to see.

"Time for a bath," she said.

"She's a Fairlane." He wiped his finger on his Wranglers. "Nineteen sixty-four."

She nodded and said nothing, but he seemed to want more of a response. "Wow," she said again. "Pretty old."

"Four-door sedan, which makes her less valuable," he said. "But she's in great shape. Engine's completely rebuilt, so. Want a peek under the hood?"

Mona shrugged. "No, thanks."

"Well, what the hell," he said, rubbing his chin. "She's yours."

She blinked at him, and so did Wahkan, who had delicate, kind of adorable eyelids, she noticed for the first time.

"You can have her." He fished his keys out of his pocket and removed two. "I only have one set, so don't lose them. One's for the trunk. Put the vacuum in there now so you don't forget it."

"What?"

"I also have some tomahawks you might like, and. They weigh a ton but they look really cool—" He stopped talking and studied her face. "What's the matter?"

"Who are you?"

Did a car qualify as "important"? Should she call Clare? Why was he smiling at her? Why was he holding out his hand like that? He wanted her to shake on it, apparently. When she finally did, he pulled her in and gave her a noogie.

THE VACUUM SHE CHRISTENED ESME; THE CAR, MAXINE. ESME made her giddy but that was no surprise. Maxine was something else. She'd never given a crap about cars, but her bond to Maxine was instant, deep-seated, unshakable. Her body was charcoal gray with an electric-blue pinstripe. Back in the eighties, Frank had reupholstered her seats in matching blue velvet. It was a mystery to her, but when she looked at Maxine's grille, her decorative trim, her pie-plate taillights, she felt . . . well, *happy*.

"Let's take her for a spin," Frank said, after putting the bird away. "She has a couple quirks you need to know about."

He told her to pump the gas exactly twice before starting her up. "Okay, now rev the engine a little, but not too much," he said. "Hear that? Hear how throaty she sounds?"

"Yeah," Mona said.

"Dual exhaust," Frank explained. "Gives her more horsepower, so.

Plus, it sounds cooler, obviously. Now just tap the gas when you pull out of here. Otherwise, you'll flood the engine."

"It's like driving a boat," she said.

"There's more play in the steering than you're probably used to, but. Take a left up here. We'll cruise along the ocean a few blocks."

At traffic lights Mona found herself looking at the car next to her, making eye contact with the driver and smiling. She wished someone would photograph her.

"How do you feel?" Frank asked.

"Like a winner," she said seriously.

He cleared his throat. "Yeah, well, she's a big hunk of metal, so." More throat-clearing. "We'll have to get you some fuzzy dice for the rearview."

"That's where the burden basket's going," she said.

She pulled into the driveway but didn't turn off the engine. She didn't want to leave Maxine. Frank opened the glove compartment, pulled out an old *Thomas Guide* and a pen, and signed the title over to her.

"Don't forget to get her registered."

"I guess I'll be driving back to the desert," she said. "After the ceremony."

He looked toward his apartment with a wistful expression. "It's so beautiful there, especially Taos. You're lucky to be out of the rat race, so."

"You and Mom should move there and open a gift shop," she said. "You already have the inventory."

He smiled. "It'll take you two days to get home. You should stop in Flagstaff and spend the night, but. Be careful—I have a friend whose sister was picked up hitchhiking in New Mexico and when they found her body, she'd been raped, so."

"So . . . don't rape any hitchhikers?" Mona said.

He leaned over and kissed her cheek. "It's cute when you try and act tough."

"It's not an act," Mona said. "I'm actually made of Teflon."

Except, as soon as she said "Teflon," she felt the corners of her mouth pulling down. Her eyes filled up quickly and then the tears started rolling, two big fat ones. She turned away and covered her face in her hand.

"Hey," he said, and touched her shoulder. "You're my only kid, okay? I know we're not blood, and you've always been weird, and we're nothing alike. But. So. What the hell. I accept that now." He pulled a bandana out of his pocket. "Here."

Strange, she thought, how affected you are by malice when you're a kid, how a mean word or look can unravel you, how devastating cruelty feels when you're too young to protect yourself. But eventually, after all those defense mechanisms are firmly in place, it's the so-called positive shit—mercy, not malice—that brings you to tears.

SHE WENT TO BED EARLY THAT NIGHT. AT THREE IN THE MORN-ing, she woke with a start and transcribed the Indian man's recording. Then she practiced delivering the speech to the drapes at the bedroom window. Her voice shook but she got through it. The drapes responded by vibrating. She felt the mattress shift slightly, as if a large dog had jumped onto the bed. But there was no dog. Now the bed was vibrating, too. A deep grumbling noise rose from the floor. She got the sense she was being visited by an evil spirit—the boss, Satan. The bed shook and slid away from the wall, which was cracking. Now the whole room was rocking—up and down and side to side. She stumbled to the doorway and braced herself against the jamb. She could hear someone screaming.

A man appeared and took her by the arm. He dragged her outside, down the stairs to the courtyard. As they ran through the courtyard, the bottom of the swimming pool heaved, leaving the water suspended midair for a second before splashing the building, drenching them from the waist down.

It was over by the time they reached the street, where the rest of the tenants were huddled together. They all stood in silence, gazing at the building's façade. There was no damage to the exterior that she could see, and yet the building looked different. Its pink stucco suddenly struck her as pathetic, its arched windows weak and inferior. Some of the ivy on the walls had fallen, exposing a deeper pink underneath. Mona looked toward Maxine, parked under a nearby tree. Unscathed.

That's my car, she wanted to tell her rescuer.

He'd been holding her hand absentmindedly and let it drop. Everyone was pretty much naked. She was the only woman, and the only one wearing a shirt. The rest of the tenants were in boxer shorts, except for her guy, who wore leopard-print briefs. His hands hovered over his crotch. He was refreshingly free of tattoos and piercings.

"Nice undies," she said.

"Same," he said.

Her eyes dropped. Nylon, flesh-colored, enormous. Period underwear. Except she wasn't bleeding. She folded her hands and casually rested them over her plainly visible pubic hair.

"We haven't met," he said. "I'm Kurt."

"Mona," she said.

They didn't shake hands.

We met during an earthquake, she imagined telling someone.

"Which unit do you live in?" she asked.

"Right above you," he said.

I had read his diary and knew he'd had his balls in a French woman's mouth in Cambodia. It's something we joke about now.

"How'd you know I was home?" she asked.

"I could hear you screaming," he said.

She shook her head. "Wasn't me."

He laughed. "Who was it then?" he said, looking around.

She felt her face redden. "That guy, probably," she whispered, pointing at one of the other tenants, a mixed-martial-arts type with a terrible tribal tattoo.

"You don't have to be embarrassed for screaming," he said.

She shrugged.

"You shouldn't leave your door unlocked," he added.

Neither should you, she thought.

She hung back as the men started shuffling into the building. She didn't want them looking at her ass. Unfortunately, Kurt hung back, too, as if waiting for her to lead the way. He was carrying himself stiffly, as though he had whiplash. He walked beside her through the lobby and their shoulders touched as they climbed the stairs. He paused outside her open door, poking his head in to inspect the living room. A bookcase lurched to one side and the carpet was covered in glitter, which had apparently fallen from the textured ceiling. She crossed the living room tentatively, as though it were a crime scene, and then looked back at Kurt, who stood awkwardly in the doorway.

"Come in," she said. "I'll make toast."

It was 5:03 A.M.

"Okay," he said. "But let me run upstairs quick and put some clothes on. Be right back."

She pulled on a pair of pants, brushed her teeth, applied eyeliner. Meanwhile, Clare called, wanting to know if she was alive. Mona said she was trapped under some rubble and couldn't feel her legs. Clare didn't think that was funny. Mona described how the pool had puked on her while she was being rescued by the guy upstairs. She left out the part about inviting him in for toast. Clare said that Frank and the birds were fine, but the freeways were a mess, reportedly, and so they planned to call off the ceremony. She heard Kurt knocking and got off the phone.

He'd gotten rid of the Tarzan look and was more sensibly dressed in a plain white T-shirt and jeans. He seemed shorter with his clothes on. She realized he was conventionally handsome, which was why she'd never have looked twice at him on the street. Perhaps he was a struggling actor. There was blood on his chin.

"Did you just shave?" she asked.

"Yeah," he said, and sat on the couch.

"I lied about the toast," she said. "I don't have bread. Or a toaster."

He smiled. "That's okay."

"Are you an actor?" she asked.

"Me? Hah, no. I'm in between gigs right now but I worked for Doctors Without Borders for twelve years."

"So, you're a doctor," she said. "Wow."

"I'm a logistics guy," he said. "But I burned out on all the traveling."

She sat across from him in the armchair. He had two different eyes, she noticed now, both brown, but there was a small white cloud in the iris of the right one. She remembered what the French woman had said in his diary and felt a quick impulse to quote her. *Your eye reminds me of a Magritte painting.* Then her stomach felt suddenly and acutely empty, a feeling she often mistook for hunger. It was shame.

"How long have you lived here?" he asked.

"I'm just visiting," she said. "It's my mother's place."

She watched him look around. He picked up a photograph on the floor and squinted at it.

"That's Spoon and Fork," she said. "The dogs I grew up with."

"Strange," he said. "The cats I grew up with were called Napkin and Placemat."

Between the two of them, almost an entire place setting. She took this as a sign to sit next to him. He tossed the photograph on the coffee table and turned toward her, leaning back slightly against the arm of the couch. She stared at the cloud in his eye. The cloud spoke to her. *I like you,* it said.

"Where are you visiting from?" he asked.

"Taos," she said. "New Mexico."

The cloud brightened. "I used to live there," he said, "with a bunch of weirdos out on the mesa. We lived off the grid in these crazy tire houses."

Earthships, they were called. The weirdos called themselves the Greater World. He talked about it for a few minutes, raising his arms at one point to describe the architecture. She caught a whiff of his deodorant. Old Spice. She placed him in his forties.

"I miss that landscape," he was saying. "I often wonder what the fuck I'm doing in L.A. It's like, why?"

"The beautiful people," she said.

He frowned.

"I'm kidding," she said. "I have a love/hate thing with the desert. You know those park benches with the weird armrests in the middle that prevent you from lying down? They're everywhere now. The desert reminds me of those benches. It's a giant bench with a beautiful view and it's saying, 'Look at me, allow me to enchant you, but don't get too comfortable—' "

"I like your eyes," he said suddenly.

She blinked at him. "Yours, too," she said. "Especially the right one."

The cloud said, *I'm extremely attracted to you.*

"I'm blind in this eye," he said after a pause. "That's why I had to swivel my head around when you sat next to me."

And here she'd thought the cloud had been hitting on her. If it had spoken to her at all, it had probably only said, *I can't see you.*

"There's a phony on every corner here," he said. "The rest are headcases and flakes. But you seem like a real person."

"I'm a cleaning lady," she said, and coughed. "About as real as it gets."

Now what?

"I can't swim in a straight line," he said. "I hope that doesn't bother you."

She smiled. "What else can't you do?"

"When I'm on a bicycle, sometimes I have to circle left to make a right turn," he said. "Makes me seem dumb. Or just really drunk."

"What happened to you?"

"I stabbed myself in the eye with a hunting knife," he said. "By accident. When I was seven. I was trying to cut a piece of rope. The knife wasn't lodged into my brain or anything—it was more of a poke. But there was a lot of blood—like, a heavy curtain around my face. My mother was hanging laundry and fainted when I stumbled into the yard. I had to have a bunch of surgeries, and for many years I was cross-eyed."

She leaned over and kissed him. It took him by surprise, but he kissed her back, and then stopped.

"How old are you?" he asked.

"I'll tell you later," she said. "What kind of vacuum do you have?"

He paused. "Why do you want to know?"

"Acid test," she said.

"Electrolux," he said.

"Upright or canister?"

"Canister," he said. "It's twenty years old."

She couldn't have hoped for a better answer.

"What's your last name?" she asked.

"Felt," he said.

Kurt Felt—interesting. Mona Felt—she liked that, too.

They messed around on the couch. She was ready to give it up, but he said he'd rather get to know her first, which of course startled her.

"Herpes?" she asked.

"Nope," he said.

"Ah," she said. "Something more serious."

"Nope," he said again.

His penis is tiny, she thought. Are you okay with that?

"There's nothing wrong with my dick," he said, reading her mind. "I'd really just rather get to know you better." He shrugged.

Fair enough, she supposed. He asked her some questions about her childhood and she told him a couple sob stories and then fell asleep. He left a note on the table, which she decided to save, even though it was nothing special:

> *Dear Mona,*
> > *I'm out foraging for food.*
> > *Hope you eat meat.*
> > *—Curt*

His handwriting was masculine enough, but she was a little thrown off by the C. When he returned from the outside world, she asked him if he wouldn't mind if she spelled his name with a K.

"Why?" he asked.

"Because a K has a spine," she said. "Plus, I rarely call people by their actual names."

He smiled and passed her a roast beef sandwich. "Is it okay if I call you Lum Lums?"

THEIR FIRST DATE LASTED THREE DAYS. DAY ONE: GOOD WEED, roasted lemon chicken, an old De La Soul record, *Five Easy Pieces*, kissing but no fucking. He held her hand during the aftershocks. Day two: burritos, spiked horchata, a blanket on an empty beach, more hand-holding. He told her she looked good in Clare's ridiculous snakeskin bikini from the eighties. She told him she hadn't set foot in the ocean for a dozen years.

"What?" he said. "Why?"

"Too big," she said. "Too wet."

He asked her to stand up and close her eyes.

"Focus on your nose," he said from behind her. "Focus on your elbows. Focus on your knees. Focus on your toes."

"Are you trying to guru me?" she asked.

"Shut up," he said. "Focus on your nose."

"He's trying to rom-com you," Terry murmured. "L.A. style."

"Yeah, well, guess what? I think I might be ready for this shit," Mona told Terry.

Terry clapped her hands. Mona focused on her nose.

"Focus on your throat," Kurt said. "Focus on your wrists. Focus on your ankles."

While she was busy focusing, he picked her up and carried her into the water. He didn't drop her in, but continued carrying her through the surf.

"Still too wet?" he asked.

"Wetter than I remember," she said.

That night she slept clinging to him like he was a rope, like he was her first girlfriend-slash-blanket, Brenda. In the morning, she offered to kiss his cock, but he wouldn't let her anywhere near it. They got dressed. They smoked a joint and rolled down some hills at a nearby park. They swapped stories. She told him about the time she found poop in a house she was cleaning, and he suggested she write a detective novel.

"You can write it in the motel I've just inherited," Kurt said. "Like Raymond Chandler."

"Raymond Chandler wrote in a motel?"

"Probably," Kurt said.

"Where is this motel?"

"Bakersfield," he said.

Mona tried to summon an image of Bakersfield. All she saw was brown.

"It's really brown there, right?" she asked.

"And green," Kurt said. "Think *The Grapes of Wrath*."

"Which reminds me," she said. "We're out of wine. Will you carry me to the liquor store?"

He nodded. "Also, I'd like to sleep next to you again tonight," he said. "If that's okay."

"Naked," she said.

He shook his head. "I'll be wearing two pairs of pants," he said. "One of them will be backward."

She laughed.

He waited until the following morning to make a move. The sex was sweaty and mediocre, but she felt an immediate, easy intimacy, as if, in addition to saliva and come, they'd exchanged several pints of blood.

LITTLE SWEDEN

THEY WERE LIVING IN BAKERSFIELD, IN THE MOTEL KURT IN-
herited from his parents. The place was surrounded by fruit farms on a
forgotten highway on the edge of nowhere. Kurt's father had bought it off
a Swedish immigrant who'd named it Little Sweden, but unless Swedes
had a secret love for drab, mud-colored rooms overrun with carpet bee-
tles, nothing about the place brought Sweden to mind.

To spruce up, they'd repainted the doors Easter colors and commissioned a blinking red and blue neon windmill—her idea, even though
she knew Sweden was not known for its windmills. They hired an exter-
minator and became pet-friendly, which gave them a competitive edge.
The change in ownership went unnoticed and the motel continued to
serve the needs of its regulars: truckers, hookers, fruit pickers, speed
freaks, and "nooners"—couples from town who arrived in separate cars
and rented a room on their lunch hour.

They'd arrived in winter, when the tule fog settled thickly in the valley and you couldn't see your hand in front of your face. In bed, they'd
listened to cars crash on the shrouded highway. One of those cars had
contained Connie, the middle-aged cleaning lady who'd come with the

motel. She'd sped through the fog into a ditch and could no longer work. Mona had offered to step in for her, just until they found someone else. Almost two years later, she was still cleaning the twenty-two rooms as well as their apartment, a tidy two-bed above the office.

Right now, she was sweating her ass off in the windowless laundry room. Only noon and already 105 degrees. She transferred a load of towels and bundled sheets into the washer. Bleach burned her nose and throat, tainting anything she put in her mouth. For lunch, bleach tacos. For dinner, pork chops and bleach sauce.

"What about dessert?" Terry asked sweetly.

"Bleach cobbler," Mona said.

"Mmm," Terry said. "And where are you on the Sui-Scale today?"

"Dude," Mona said. "Way to kill my buzz."

"Well," Terry said, "you haven't mentioned it lately, and I'm wondering if you're still keeping track."

When she'd first arrived in Bakersfield, she'd almost broken the scale. She could barely get out of bed. You seem down, Kurt had said. He'd whispered soothing nonsense into her ear and then read to her in a deep, calm voice. She preferred dry material, the drier the better, such as the instruction manual for their rice cooker.

"I would say I'm three point four presently," Mona told Terry.

"Not too shabby," Terry said.

"We hired a new laundry person—she starts next week—and this Cat Piss certainly doesn't hurt."

Last year, Kurt had converted the old fallout shelter into a grow room to indulge his interest in high-grade weed. The strains had names like Green Crack, Cheese, Panty Sweat, and Cat Piss, and had become a necessary component to Mona's happiness. Sober, she felt trapped in a boring passage of a Steinbeck novel. Stoned on Panty Sweat, the place seemed a lot less grim. Either way, she'd never been a fan of hicks, rednecks, God and Country, and no amount of pot would ever change that.

She smoked half a joint before cleaning Room 18 and very distinctly remembered being a bee in a past life. Weak limbed, bottom heavy, hyper-aware of the hairs on her arms and legs. For a few seconds, she was fully conscious of every hair on her body, including the individual strands on her head.

"Did you know that bees have no idea they're small?" she asked Terry.

"I don't like talking when you're stoned," Terry reminded her.

Mona squeezed Terry's shoulder. "Yes, Terry, I know. I'm sorry."

Terry had become more than just a voice in her head. Now Mona conjured Terry's physical being: her face, arms, hands—even her toes. Terry's toes, she imagined, were long, elegant, and unpainted.

Mona liked to envision herself hanging out with Terry at WHYY. In the studio fantasies, she and Terry weren't in separate booths, or even sitting across a table from each other, or on opposite sides of a console. Rather, Mona was sitting on Terry's lap with her arm around Terry's shoulders, and they were sharing a microphone.

"Be a bee," Terry said, and rubbed Mona's lower back. "Talk to me later when you're back in your body."

Terry didn't get it, obviously. Mona couldn't just "be a bee" whenever she wanted. It didn't work like that!

A man and two hookers had romped in Room 14 the previous night. She yanked the spread and surveyed the mattress: a romance cocktail of menstrual blood, come, and blue mascara. They'd used the nightstand drawer as an ashtray. She stripped the bed and sprayed it with Fantastik. After cleaning everything, she turned off the lights, closed the heavy curtains, and switched on the Eureka. She loved to vacuum in the dark, with only the warm, golden beam of the Eureka's headlight to guide her.

Room 16 had been used as a makeshift tinker space. Two tweakers had spent several days assembling and reassembling radios, lamps, a bicycle, and other crap. They'd left soot marks on the soiled, smelly sheets—apparently, they'd snuggled under the covers clutching their crack pipes. Since they hadn't showered, the bathroom was a breeze, but they'd stolen all the toilet paper and two of the towels.

The phone rang while she was wiping the TV screen. It was Kurt, as usual, calling from the front desk. He had a sixth sense and usually knew which room she was in at any given time.

"My luscious Lum Lums," he said when she picked up.

"Nasty period sex in fourteen last night," she said.

"Just ordered new linens," he said.

"No more speed freaks," Mona said. "And no more nooners. If they arrive in separate cars—"

"We need the nooners," he said.

"Can we get rid of hookers on the rag?" she asked.

"Hookers love us," Kurt said.

This was true. They actually rated Little Sweden online. Three stars. Everyone else gave the place two.

"Let's run away to Cambodia," Mona said. "I'll pretend I'm French and take your balls in my mouth."

"Mama," Kurt said.

"Please don't call me that," she said.

He'd been talking like a hick for months, especially in the bedroom. The novelty had charmed her at first. Now it made her wish for another earthquake.

"We'll run away someday," Kurt said. "Just not yet."

He meant never, she was beginning to realize. She'd asked to read his travel diaries, even though she'd read them already without his knowledge—twice. He'd traveled to places like Tasmania, Estonia, and Uruguay. On the page, he was edgy, adventurous. In person, he was lumpy oatmeal. Reconciling the two Kurts was difficult because the contrast was so extreme. "Like night and day," she'd told him. He had only blinked and said, "But night and day are part of the same twenty-four hours."

Kurt cleared his throat. "You don't have to do this, you know."

"What?" she sniffed.

"We can hire a cleaning lady really easily," he said.

They could, but what would she do? What else could she *be*? She supposed she could be a . . . *writer*. Waiter. *Writer*. Waiter. Both? In any case, Kurt paid her double the going rate, so for the first time in her life she'd built a savings account. Thirteen grand. Enough to start over somewhere.

There was rustling on his end. She looked across the parking lot to the office window. She could see the top of his newly balding head above the desk.

"I want to get away, too, but I'm worried," he said. "I'm worried about this place. The plumbing's bad, the water's rusty, the roof's a piece of crap."

"You'll fix it," she said.

"I feel like a failure," he said. "I'm forty-four. I don't want to get old and have nothing."

They had their most intimate conversations on the motel line. The problem was, while he was sharing, expressing, confessing, and sometimes crying, she couldn't stop yawning. Once she let one loose, they kept coming, one after the next after the next, like waves crashing. They often came in sets of three. Then, a little break. Then another set arrived. They seemed to be generated by something deep inside her, deeper than boredom, some force she didn't understand. Perhaps if she yawned openly and loudly, she wouldn't have this problem. Instead, she yawned silently, out of politeness.

"Maybe you should try slapping yourself," Terry suggested.

"Are you there?" he asked.

"You don't have nothing." She held the phone away and yawned with her entire face. Her left eye always leaked more than the right. "You have me."

"You know what's wrong with you, Mona?" he asked.

"What?" she said.

"Absolutely nothing," he said.

Soul juice. This was why she was here. And why she stayed. Right, Terry?

She felt another one coming. A tidal wave. This one was impossible to contain. She made some weird noises toward the end of it, and then finished with, "Oh, God."

He cleared his throat. "Hey, I need your keys. I can't find mine. Also, Hugh called—he needs fresh towels."

"Give me fifteen minutes," she said, and hung up.

FOUR OF THE ROOMS WERE EFFICIENCIES RENTED BY THE MONTH. Hugh, an off-the-boat Irishman and former drunk, rented the end unit. He always answered the door in his bathrobe. What had brought him here, of all places, she never knew and never asked, but she suspected it was a tragic story. She called him Mr. Terrible News.

"How are you, Hugh?" she asked when he opened the door.

"I used to work so that I could drink," he said. "Now, what's the point?"

"What's the point" was Hugh's favorite phrase. Except, in his brogue, it came out as, "What's the pint? What's the fecken pint?"

"I got fresh towels for you, Hugh." She noticed his cat curled up on the bed. "Hello, Ingrid."

"She hates me," Hugh said.

Mona frowned and handed him the towels. "Who was that lady visiting last week?"

"My mother," he said. "She hates me, too."

Poor beast in the rain, she thought. It was another of Hugh's favorite phrases, one she repeated many times a day. If Hugh weren't prone to paranoia and sober, she'd have offered him some Master Kush to take the edge off.

"The stupid post office lost a package," he said. "I broke my glasses, so I can't read the paper. Now my sciatica is acting up."

"Poor beast," Mona said, and smiled.

"Fair play to you," Hugh said.

ACROSS THE LOT, KURT WAS EATING A MICROWAVED SOFT PRET-zel. She hated what he was wearing—a pair of too-tight cut-off jeans trimmed too short, a too-big rumpled plaid shirt, and too-girly yellow flip-flops. He wrapped her up and kissed her wetly on the mouth. She kept her eyes open and stared at his eyelids fluttering behind his glasses. He was wearing his emergency pair, which looked like they'd been is-sued by the military. Birth control glasses, he called them.

"How's Mr. Terrible News?" he asked.

"Fresh and clean as a whistle, cool like an Irish spring," Mona said, faking a brogue.

"It's slow today," he said. "How about a siesta later?"

"We'll see, mister," she said. She stepped into his blind spot. The cloud in his eye was a favorite hiding place. "I want to work on my paint-ing for a bit."

She was doing a landscape of the view outside their bedroom win-dow. It was the most uninspired view she'd ever attempted to render, but lately it offered her a convenient out. Kurt had gained weight, even in his nipples, and had stopped cutting his hair. He was becoming his own country. Kurtfoundland. Kurtganistan. Kurtvania.

"Maybe you can squeeze me in," he said, touching her on the shoul-der. "It might help you . . . relax."

Impatiently, she watched him finish his pretzel. He chewed each bite twenty-five times—she counted. They hadn't had sex since his birthday last month. She remembered lying there like a starfish, gazing at the lampshade.

"Mind bringing my cart to the office?" she asked. "I need to restock."

She missed the days when all her supplies fit into a bucket. Kurt pushed the heavy cart toward the office, one-handed.

"Like walking a fat girl home," he said.

She smiled. Sometimes she wondered if Kurt wanted her to expand and soften, to lose all her edges. He did the cooking. And the cocktails. He'd been plumping her with extra cheese and guacamole and basting her with mojitos. If she became hugely, disgustingly fat, perhaps they'd live happily ever after.

"Where're you taking Maxine?" she asked.

"Oil change."

She handed him the keys and watched him climb into their car, which she still thought of as *her* car. Maxine stalled as he backed out.

"Just tap the gas!" Mona yelled.

"Tap my ass!" he yelled back.

He peeled out, and she stood there briefly, admiring Maxine's rear end.

AS SHE CROSSED THE LOT, A BLACKBIRD SWOOPED DOWN AND clawed at her. She shrieked and ran under the awning near Room 5. She looked around. Any witnesses? A tall, lanky guy wearing a cowboy hat and mirrored sunglasses stood in the doorway to Room 8.

"You saw that?" she called out.

She could still hear the noise she'd made.

"Likely an omen of some kind," he said solemnly.

"I think they're protecting their nests," she said. "It's hatching season."

He sauntered out to her abandoned cart and pushed it toward her. He was dressed like a mechanic. "Leonard" was stitched onto his jacket and the knees of his trousers were dirty.

"Maybe the omen is me," he said, leaving the cart at her side.

Who was this joker?

"Your apron matches the door to my room," he said. "Is that on purpose?"

One look at his hands and her mouth went dry. Her surprise must have shown, because he quickly removed his sunglasses and hooked them onto his T-shirt, and then he took off his hat and held it in his MORE hand.

"How did you find me?" she asked.

He looked handsomer than she remembered.

"Your name is attached to this place," Dark said. "On the Internet."

She scanned the mostly empty parking lot. Where had he come from? Was he an actual guest, or was he trespassing? Kurt must have checked him in and forgotten to tell her. She tried to picture Dark filling out the form at the front desk and making chitchat with Kurt. He must have used a fake address—Kurt would've mentioned someone visiting from Taos.

"How did you get here?" she asked.

"I drove," he said. "But I broke down a few miles outside of town. Car's in the shop, so it looks like I'm here for a day or two." He smiled.

A day or two. It was Monday. He would be gone by Wednesday, so she had until then to . . . what?

"I want to talk about what happened between us," he said.

"It's all water under the et cetera," she said.

"What?"

She waved her hand dismissively and knocked a couple of shampoo bottles off the cart. They rolled to his feet. He crouched down and picked them up with his LOVE hand. She remembered him on his knees with his head under her apron. He used to pet her with one finger before putting his mouth on her. He was looking up at her now, holding the shampoo bottles in his outstretched hand. There it was, his goddamn pencil smell, freshly sharpened, erasing everything.

"You keep those," she said.

She wheeled her cart a few doors down, shoes squeaking on the cement. When she looked back he was still crouched there, staring at her. She dragged the Eureka into Room 3 and shut the door. The room was already clean, but you couldn't vacuum these floors too often. She went over the carpet three times and then fixed her hair in the mirror. Maybe she could get away with sniffing his armpit and nothing else. Maybe she was a dog trapped in a woman's—

"Don't," Terry snapped. "Don't do this. Kurt lights your cigarettes and he doesn't even smoke. He cuts the calluses off your feet. He brings you coffee in bed, and he bakes scones on Sundays. From scratch."

Mona didn't say anything.

"The man bakes scones," Terry repeated. "With teeny golden raisins."

She had a point. Kurt was oatmeal and he gave her the hard-core yawns, but he was warm—always. And kind.

"He kisses like a guppy," Mona said.

"Only when he's drunk," Terry reminded her.

She decided to seek a second opinion. Who would she call? Clare and Frank were vacationing in Hawaii. She pulled out her phone and dialed Yoko and Yoko. They sent each other handwritten notes every couple of months, but they rarely talked on the phone. To her surprise, Nigel answered on the first ring.

"Are you taking care of yourself?" he asked.

She asked him if he remembered Dark, the blind lady's husband, the one she used to have loud sex with three nights a week.

"Well, he's *here*," Mona said. "In Bakersfield. In my motel. Room Eight. I didn't recognize him at first, but when I did, it all came rushing back. It felt like licking a nine-volt battery."

"Was he wearing a disguise?" Nigel mysteriously asked.

"Sort of," she said. "He looked like a gas station cowboy."

"When Odysseus returns home after twenty years—"

"Oh God," Mona said. "No Homer, Nigel. Not now."

"It's relevant," Nigel assured her. "When Odysseus returns home—at long last, two decades later—he disguises himself as a beggar, and the only person who recognizes him is Eurycleia, his former maid—"

"Don't forget the dog," Shiori said.

"I'm on speaker?" Mona asked.

"The dog recognizes him and dies of excitement," Nigel continued. "But Eurycleia is a maid, like you, and she was also Odysseus's wet nurse, and so she knows him better than anyone. She washes his feet and recognizes the scar on his leg."

"I recognized his knuckle tattoos," Mona said. "Should I go wash his feet, or what?"

"Odysseus puts his hand around Eurycleia's throat and threatens to kill her if she tells anyone," Nigel said.

"So that's a no?" Mona asked.

"Yes," Nigel said.

"Don't wash his feet?" Mona asked.

"Absolutely not," Nigel said. "Do nothing of the kind."

"What do you think, Shiori?" Mona said.

"Do you feel him in your body?" Shiori asked.

"He's in my spine," Mona said.

"Near your tailbone?" Shiori asked.

"The whole thing," Mona said.

"Don't do anything silly," Nigel said. "You can't afford the karma."

"Or the heartache," Shiori said softly.

Yoko and Yoko had a hard-on for Kurt. They'd only met him once, when Kurt helped her move from Taos, and they'd all spent an evening together. Kurt made an elaborate vegan meal. During dinner, Kurt claimed to have manifested the earthquake that brought him and Mona together, so that they could help each other "confront the wreckage of their pasts." Yoko and Yoko swooned and practically creamed their pajamas.

KURT WAS BACK, TINKERING UNDER MAXINE'S HOOD, SO SHE felt safe to leave Room 3. She checked for birds overhead and trotted toward him. She put her arms around him, consciously turning her back toward Room 8. He let her squeeze him. She hoped Dark was watching.

"You haven't hugged me like this in a long time," he said.

"I was attacked by a bird earlier," she said.

He turned around to face her. "Where?"

"My scalp," she said. "I have a feeling it was personal."

"You and your bird trauma," he said, and kissed the part in her hair.

In their apartment upstairs, Kurt took off his shirt, opened a bottle of red, and warmed leftover lasagna. They ate at the kitchen table. He rattled on, for a solid twenty-three minutes, about the Bakersfield earthquake of 1952, how it had twisted cotton fields into U shapes and slid a shoulder of the Tehachapi Mountains across four lanes of highway, and then he blathered on about pH balances, fertilizers, the current drought, how much water almond trees require, and also the honeybee problem. She focused on the beautiful white cloud in his eye, which still aroused her now and then, or, at a minimum, kept her awake. Was she aroused by the cloud itself, or the hunting knife that had made it? She longed for sharpness, a honed edge with which to cut herself. She often avoided his eye that could see, especially when he was on top of her, because she couldn't bear all the love in it. Too much mush.

She supposed Dark had looked at her that way, too, but she had been disarmed by his earthy smell and the tattoo on his chest, *A Steady Diet of Nothing*. Kurt's tattoo would have said *A Heaping Helping of Hugs*. Two years together and she couldn't clearly describe Kurt's smell. He showered twice a day and slathered on deodorant. He'd have douched his balls, if possible. Dark's balls, on the other hand—

"Dark's balls?" Terry asked. "Really? What about faithful *Kurt*, the man *living with you*, the man *right in front of you*, who wants to *marry you*, the man who carried you out of Los Angeles, away from the vampires— how about that?"

"Kurt's knuckle tattoos would read, 'MORE FOOD,'" Mona told Terry.

"He's not obese," Terry said. "He's slightly chubby. When did you become so shallow?"

"If you're so in love with him, Terr," Mona said, "why don't you marry him?"

It seemed everyone had a hard-on for Kurt. Everyone except Mona. Was she a shithead?

"I never called you a shithead," Terry said.

"Mona?" Kurt put down his fork. "Where are you?"

"Sorry," Mona said, startled.

The motel line rang, forwarded from the office downstairs. Kurt got up.

"Front desk," she heard him say.

She finished her wine. As she stared absently at the portrait of Rose she'd stolen years ago, the letter R suddenly appeared, floating on its back like Rose. She stood for a closer look. An upside-down G floated near Rose's feet, and an E with one too many teeth. She found the A, also inverse and wearing a halo. Where was the C? Not in the water. Not in the trees. There it was, near Rose's crotch. She laughed out loud, delighted.

"What's funny?" Kurt said after hanging up.

"I finally found the Grace stain," she said. "Only took me two and a half years." She pointed out each letter. "See? Now that I see it, I can't seem to *unsee* it."

He smiled. "Maybe it's a sign."

They both sat again and she watched him finish her lasagna.

"This morning I remembered being a bee in a past life. I was pretty happy. It felt good to have such a clear purpose."

Kurt looked at her adoringly. "I like the way your brain works."

"Who called—Mr. Terrible News?"

"No, the guy in Room Eight," Kurt said. "He wanted to know if we had room service."

Mona snorted and poured herself more wine.

"His car's in the shop so he's stranded in Bako," Kurt said.

Bako. Barf.

"The guy seems lost," Kurt said. "He checked in late, after you'd gone to bed."

"Did he say where he was coming from?" she asked.

"Alaska," he said. "Or Nebraska? One of those. The guy smells like a goat. It's enough to knock you over."

AFTER DINNER, SHE CARRIED A PLATE OF LASAGNA DOWN-stairs for Room 8. Kurt's idea, of course. He fed anyone who looked vaguely hungry: travelers, migrant workers, hookers, even smelly goat men. Kurt was in the shower now, so she figured she had fifteen minutes with Dark. As she descended the stairs she blindly applied lipstick.

"Too red," Terry said. "Too obvious."

She blotted her lips and tightened the belt on her thrift store dress, a checkered tangerine-and-cream thing with black piping.

His door was ajar. She pushed it open with her foot.

"Room service," she announced.

He was sitting on the bed, shirtless, with the phone in his lap, a look of mild surprise on his face. She placed the food on the little table next to the window. Lasagna, she said, still warm.

"It has hard-boiled eggs in it," she warned him. "And you'll have to eat with your hands because I forgot a fork."

"I was just trying to think of an excuse to call the front desk again," he said. "But I was worried your husband would answer."

"We're not married," she said. "We met during an earthquake."

He put the phone back and patted the space next to him, inviting her to sit. If she sat anywhere near his armpit, she was a goner. She sat in the nearest chair.

"How's Rose?"

"We split up," he said. "I went back to school and then moved to Anchorage."

"You drove here from Alaska?"

"Nebraska," he said. "I just finished my last year with the Lakota."

Right. Sun Dance. The tree, the hooks, the incredible thirst.

"I was hallucinating pretty hard near the end and you were in my visions. You were here in this exact place, except you had a dog."

She looked at his chest. She remembered the wounds being closer to his nipples. His brown nipples on his brown, muscular chest. Her fingers vibrated with the urge to touch him. She sat on her hands, hoping it would pass.

"Still writing?" he asked. "And taking pictures?"

"No," she said. "I put a portfolio together but I buried it back in Taos."

"Let's go dig it up," he said.

She laughed. "Why?"

"You don't belong here," he said.

They stared at each other quietly for a minute. His eyes slipped down the front of her dress and landed on her legs.

"I'm comfortable," she said.

"You're comfortable sitting on your hands?" he asked.

She brought her hands to her lap. "What did you do in Alaska?"

"I drove a cab," he said. "Then I worked in a halfway house for newly released prisoners. Long-timers. I lived there, helping them readjust, but mostly I drove them around in a van. I slept with a knife under my pillow."

"Wow," she said.

"You changed your hair," he said.

Kurt had convinced her to grow out her bangs so that he could see her "beautiful face."

"If I were your boyfriend," he said, "I'd be torturing your box right now and you'd be coming all over the place."

Jesus, that was sudden. Kurt would never in a million years call it a box. Even if he did, he would only cuddle and kiss it tenderly. She missed how dirty Dark was, how rough and raunchy and out there, how willingly he turned his insides out for her to see.

"Have you learned any Spanish?" he asked.

"*Caras vemos, corazones no sabemos*," she said. " 'Faces we see, hearts we do not know.' "

A phrase from a postcard left by a fruit picker.

"You know my heart," he said.

"I should get going," she said, and stood up. "He's waiting for me."

WALKING BACK, SHE DECIDED NOT TO SHOWER. KURT WOULDN'T touch her unless she was squeaky clean. She found him playing video games. Off the hook, apparently. She kissed his retreating hairline and disappeared into the bedroom. She felt numb. She painted through a cheerless hour. Then she smoked and fell asleep.

In the morning, Kurt asked if she could clean Rooms 17 and 21, and also change the sheets in Room 8. Dark's room.

"But not until one o'clock," Kurt said. "He'll be out running errands after one. He spilled booze on the bed, or something."

Bullshit. His sheets were clean—he just wanted to see her twisted up in them. He would be waiting for her. She showered and retrieved his favorite underwear from a box in her closet, where she hid his love notes. They still fit.

She cleaned all morning. Kurt left for the hardware store. Now it was 1:08. Time to change Dark's sheets. She knocked and imagined shutting the curtains, falling face-first onto the bed. He pulled up her skirt, placed his hands on her ass, and then licked the backs of her knees—

No answer. She let herself in, hoping he was in the bathroom. He wasn't anywhere. She even checked under the bed, but all she found was a limp ten-dollar bill and a grocery bag containing a box of black hair dye and a pair of stockings. And he had in fact spilled booze on the sheets—a whole glass of bourbon, it looked like, near the headboard. She felt as though she were being watched. She looked out the window and then opened the closet—no one there, of course.

She rifled through his open suitcase. Dirty clothes and crusty socks, but no papers or rubbers or anything interesting. Then she saw a brown leather satchel stuffed in the lining. She felt the old excitement as she opened it.

The photographs were zipped into a pocket. A loose handful, some with torn edges. Her hands shook as she shuffled through them. The first four featured a highly unattractive peroxide blonde in her early forties, fully clothed in a skirt and with a run in her stocking, obviously wasted, passed out on a bed with a tacky mirrored headboard. Long shots from every angle, then close-ups of her semi-hairy legs. In the next few, another woman, passed out and fully dressed, this time clutching a handbag. It looked as though she'd been ready to go somewhere but never made it out the door. A man's hand held up her skirt. In the next set, a woman out cold in an empty bathtub, razor burn on her foreshortened legs, what looked like a painful bunion on her left toe. The fourth batch featured a buxom woman around Mona's age. In the first shot she was wide awake and topless and giving two thumbs up; in the rest, she was passed out on a twin bed with only her legs exposed.

Clearly, Dark was a little darker than she'd realized. As she shuffled through, she found herself coveting the photos. They had a certain snapshot aesthetic she admired. They looked like Nan Goldin prints, except not quite as artistic or hip. They were the sort of fucked-up photographs you'd find in the trash.

"You know, Terry," Mona said, "most women would run for the hills right now, or run back to the comforts of Kurtfoundland, but these photos don't creep me out in the slightest. It feels utterly familiar. I feel like I've known this guy all my life."

"Well, that's because you *have*," Terry said slowly. "He's your father. He's your grandfather. He's every man you've ever been close to."

Except Kurt.

"But don't the photographs remind you of something else?" Terry asked.

"Vaguely," Mona said. "I guess they look like pictures my dad would've taken."

"They look like pictures *you* would've taken," Terry said. "Of yourself. Pretending to be dead. In your clients' houses. Remember?"

"Huh," Mona said.

"Steal them," Terry said. "Figure out a way to use them in your own work—"

"Shhh," Mona said.

Outside, a car door slammed. She rushed to the window. It was only Mr. Terrible News pulling a bag of kitty litter out of his hatchback. She hid the photographs in her cleaning cart.

Dark's note she found in his dirty sheets.

Mona,

I feel you in my guts, an aching column down the center of my body. You are a want that stretches from my first hope as a child to my first full want as a man. I've been in love with you since we met. I believe we belong together. Like you, I have had a death wish forever, and yet you make me want to live twice.

I'm leaving tonight. Will you take a ride with me to L.A.? Palm trees. Wild parrots. A warm breeze. A vivid swim in the sea. Could you get away for a night or two? I'm picking up my car at the shop right now. It's an old black sedan, which I'll park out back. I'll be leaving around four o'clock. If this is too crazy and you can't come with me, I hope you'll at least say goodbye.

KURT WAS ON TOP OF HER AN HOUR LATER. HE'D STOPPED AT Guthrie's on his way back from the hardware store, had a few "road sodas," and now he was taking too long to come. She turned her head to avoid his beery breath and looked at the clock—2:53. She wished she'd done laundry. Flies triangulated the room lazily. Kurt pressed her legs to his shoulders. She gazed at her knees briefly and then closed her eyes. She was the unconscious blonde with a run in her stocking, and Dark was beside the bed, holding a camera and touching himself—

Kurt finished before she got any further.

"You're miles away," he huffed, catching his breath. "Again."

"Am I?"

It was 3:13. She studied her painting—the composition lacked interest and a focal point. Some grape pickers in the field, maybe, or a farmer on a tractor, or Kurt fixing the roof.

"I went ahead and got a 'For Sale' sign at the hardware store," Kurt said.

"You're selling the motel?"

He laughed. "No," he said. "It's for Maxine. I think we should sell her and get a truck."

"Well, think again."

"She's got rust on her belly," he said.

"And?"

"It's like cancer. She'll be rusted out in six months. We should sell her now while we can."

"Nope," she said.

She turned back to the canvas. The painting didn't need people in it. People were stupid.

Kurt sat up and looked at her. "I'm sick of making love to a corpse," he said suddenly.

"You mean me," she said.

"Who else."

She cupped both of her hands over her ears. "I'm sick of living with you in this hellhole," she said. Her voice sounded steadier and more sonorous with her ears blocked.

He blinked at her.

"You bore the fuck out of me," she said, too loudly.

His lips were moving. She loosened her hands and heard him say, "—so if that's what you're saying—," then clamped down again, firmer this time. He stopped and sat there, frowning. She lowered her hands. He got up to open a window, forgetting they were painted shut. He slammed the heel of his hand up against the frame a couple of times, swung around in frustration, and knocked the canvas to the floor. She watched him set it back on the easel.

"I'm sorry," she said.

"Damage is done," he said. "I shouldn't have called you a corpse."

"Okay," she said. "I shouldn't have called you boring."

He gave her a patient smile. "I still think we should sell Maxine."

"I think you need a nap," she said.

HE WAS SNORING FIFTEEN MINUTES LATER. SHE RECALLED HER morning: sweaty tits by ten A.M., wheeling her cleaning cart across the parking lot, folding laundry, the blackbirds eyeing her from the rain gutter. She pictured her future here.

She grabbed a brush. Inspired, she worked quickly, covering the canvas with ugly vertical strokes. Prison bars.

She packed a duffel bag. In the kitchen, she left Kurt a note saying she was taking the bus to visit her mother in L.A. and would be back in two nights. He seemed to like her trips away. It gave him the opportunity for a bender—booze, porn, video games—and to miss her. They were always sweet to each other when she got back.

She made sure the motel calls forwarded upstairs before stepping out. The sky, stiff and pale all morning, was now a wide, cheerful blue. She found Dark around back, idling in a black, late-eighties Crown Vic. She leaned into the open passenger-side window. He'd trimmed his beard and was wearing a clean white shirt.

"You found my note," he said. "Are you saying goodbye or coming with me?"

"I'm coming."

He smiled. "Mind riding in the back? The front seat's broken."

Yellow foam poked through the leather, along with a metal spring. It looked like it had been clawed by a bear or a mad slasher.

"It's a retired cop car," he said, as if that explained it.

She climbed into the backseat. The car smelled strongly of motel soap. He turned toward her, put his arm over the seat, and touched her knee with his MORE hand. His LOVE hand rested on the steering wheel.

"I didn't think you'd actually come," he said.

"Yes, you did," she said.

He started driving. Once on the highway he sat bolt upright and kept his hands at ten and two on the steering wheel. She realized she hadn't driven around with him much in Taos.

"I looked through your things," she said.

"What'd you find?" he asked.

"Pictures," she said.

He was silent for a while, but it didn't bother her.

"Are you okay?" he asked. "You seem tired."

"I clean motel rooms." She stretched her legs out on the seat. "If I pass out, are you going to take pictures of my legs?"

"Would you like that?" he asked.

"I don't know," she said truthfully.

"They're not my pictures," he said. "They belonged to an ex-con at the halfway house. His name was Clifford. He had a fetish for unconscious women."

"Did he have sex with them?"

"He told me he only touched their legs."

"With his penis," she said.

He laughed. "No, with his hands. But he touched his own penis. He asked me to throw them away. For some reason, I never did."

"Thinking of you photographing me passed out turns me on." She watched his neck redden. "Are you blushing?" she asked.

He smiled and rubbed his neck with his MORE hand.

"Anyway, I stole the pictures," she said.

"Why?" he asked.

"Terry Gross made me do it," she said.

He laughed. "You're still in touch with her?"

"Of course," she said. "Who else am I going to talk to?"

"Me," Dark said. "I'm here now."

THEY STOPPED FOR GAS. DARK LET HER OUT OF THE BACK-seat—there were no door handles inside the back—to use the restroom. Dark disappeared for smokes and water. Back at the car, she opened the door and a dog jumped in. A small black-and-white terrier wearing a scruffy goatee and a dusty coat looked from her face to the windshield. His expression said, "What're you waiting for? Drive, bitch! Get me out of here!"

She laughed. "Let's go," she said, motioning for him to climb out. "This way."

He ignored her. He had no collar.

"You," she said. "Come here."

He shifted his weight between his front paws and scratched behind his ear with a hind leg. She heard a sharp whistle and watched his body go rigid midscratch. He jumped out and trotted behind the convenience store building. She followed him to an empty lot beside a moldy stucco house. An elderly Spanish man sat in a camp chair next to a card table, reading a paperback. Despite the heat, he was wearing a hat, a flannel shirt, jeans, and boots. The dog lay down under the table and closed his eyes.

The man looked up at her. "Do you need help?"

"Your dog," she said. "He, uh, jumped in my car."

He smiled. "He does that."

"He was acting like we'd just robbed a bank together."

The man nodded. "He likes to ride in cars."

On the table, clear baggies filled with what looked like yellowed baby teeth.

"What are you selling?" she asked.

"Piñons," he said. "Pine nuts. Here, help yourself."

She plucked a bag off the table and put it in her pocket. "Thank you. What's your dog's name?"

"Piñon," he said. "He's a nut, too."

She smiled at the dog.

"His owner died," he said. "I'm on my way out. You want him? He has all his shots. No fleas. Still has his balls, though."

She shuffled her feet. Was there a way to get a look at the dog's butthole? It couldn't be too big or too visible or the wrong color. She craned her neck to look under the table.

"Piñon," the man said, and snapped his fingers. "Let this lady have a look at you."

She scratched his lower back. His butthole looked classy and distinguished. He sat on Mona's left foot and gazed at the horizon. *Check out my profile*, he seemed to say. *Notice my eyebrows*. She tapped her foot and he stood up. He did a little dance, looking up at her. A box step. She realized his feet were burning on the pavement.

"Mind if I pick him up?" she asked.

"Sure," the man said. "He loves to be carried. He also loves water of any kind, even bathwater."

He weighed about twenty pounds, she guessed. Grateful to be off the ground, he licked her cheek and earlobe. His tongue was pleasantly dry. He seemed like an intense little dude. She decided she couldn't leave without him.

The man patted the dog and said goodbye, and Mona carried him to the car. Dark was nervously drumming the roof with his fingers next to the open back door.

"Jesus, Mona," he said. "You scared me. I thought you took off."

"I have a dog now," she said. "His name is Piñon."

Dark peered at Piñon's face. "I know this dog," he said. "He's the dog you were with in my vision."

Piñon's stomach growled. "He might be hungry," she said.

Dark ducked back into the store for dog food. Mona hosed down Piñon in the service area. As soon as the water hit him, his nose wrinkled and he moaned with pleasure. She'd never heard a dog make that noise before. He was shaking himself dry when Dark came back.

"Here," Dark said. "He was wearing this in my vision."

An orange bandana. She tied it around his neck and they hit the road. Piñon hung his head out the window and then curled up next to her and dozed off. She couldn't stop staring at his paws and the tufts of hair between his toes. His feet smelled like Fritos.

She wondered if Kurt had found her note. In the storytelling phase of their relationship, he'd told her he'd followed his dog for miles when he was only five. His dog had dug a hole under the fence and Kurt followed. They went missing all day. It made the local paper. Kurt said he would have followed that dog to the end of the earth. Would he follow her?

"Are you hungry?" Dark asked.

"Famished," she said.

They stopped at a crowded steakhouse and ordered sirloins. She made sure to get a seat near the window so that they could keep an eye on Piñon. Dark drank coffee; Mona drank something fruity with vodka. She grilled him about his cab-driving days in Anchorage. He told her that most of his fares had been strippers, and she asked if he'd gotten any lap dances. He said no, but one of the strippers had offered blow jobs as payment.

"Did you accept?" she asked.

"A few times," he said. "It sounds terrible, but when you drive a cab from dusk to dawn, a blow job begins to feel like a blessing, like someone's watching over you."

"Speaking of strippers," Mona said, and cleared her throat. "I modeled nude dressed as a stripper for an artist in Taos—an old Hungarian guy. It was a weird scene. Flash forward two years, I find a *Penthouse* in a room at the motel. Flipping through, I see a feature on erotic art by living artists. And then there's a nude painting of me. Full page. I'm bent over, touching my toes, legs and ass spread to the viewer. The motherfucker painted a smile on my face."

Dark laughed. "Which issue?"

"I'll never tell you," she said. "You wouldn't know it was me, anyway."

"I know your pussy like the inside of my eyelid," he said.

His LOVE hand moved across the table. It knocked over the salt and pepper. It touched her wrist, grabbed on to her fingers. It seemed hungry.

"I don't usually do this," he said.

"Abscond with the cleaning lady?"

"Hold hands across the table in a steakhouse."

Under the table, his MORE hand touched her knee. She uncrossed her legs.

"I bought you something today," he said suddenly.

His hand disappeared into his jacket pocket. Out came a small wooden box. He slid it toward her across the table. Jewelry, she figured, but it was too heavy. She opened the box to find . . . what was it? A metal cube?

Rare earth magnets, he explained. Two of them stuck together. Impossible to pull apart without hurting yourself.

"Like you and me," he said.

She closed the box and placed it in her purse. "I have to go back, you know," she said. "I can't run away with you—not now."

"Of course you can," he said confidently. "You don't know this yet, but we're going to be together for a long time."

She checked his face to see if he was fucking with her. He wasn't. She chugged her drink and ordered another. Their food arrived. She ate a bit of the meat, finished her drink, and then excused herself to go to the ladies'. While she was peeing, she waited for Terry to say something.

"Are you there, Terry? It's me, Mona."

No answer. She washed her hands at the sink.

"My face looks fucked up," she told Terry. "Right?"

"You don't need me anymore," Terry said, and patted Mona's thigh. "You have Piñon now. In fact, go check on him. And be careful—your vision is blurring at the edges."

Back at the table, Dark was gone, and so was her purse. He'd paid their tab. She went out to the parking lot and found Dark leaning into the backseat. From behind him, she caught a glimpse of Piñon. The inside of his left ear, the white of his left eye. Dark had him pinned to the seat with both hands and was talking to him in a low voice.

"What's wrong?" she asked.

He released Piñon and closed the door. "He was barking at me and then he bit me," Dark said. "So, I let him know he can't do that."

"Bit you where?" she asked.

He held out his arm, but she didn't see anything. Piñon stood and made confident eye contact with her through the window. *It's cool*, he seemed to say. *Whatever.* A few cars down, someone was blasting Roy Orbison's "In Dreams," one of the saddest songs ever recorded, in her opinion. She and Dark lingered outside his car. He asked her to dance. She stood on the steel toes of his boots and clung to him. They swayed for a few minutes.

"Are you having visions?" she whispered.

"I'm right here," he said.

"Do you want to make a flesh offering?"

He leaned her against the car and kissed her. She kept her eyes closed and the world seemed to fall away. Everything was sliding, sliding, and he kept pausing to lift her up, to keep her stationary against the car. When he reached under her skirt, she told him she felt Spanish again.

———

SHE'D BEEN SOUND ASLEEP FOR WHAT FELT LIKE HOURS WHEN he pulled to the side of the road. Her face was sweaty and she'd been slumped against the door. Piñon stood next to her, staring at her face and wagging his tail. In the failing light, she saw a small oil field dotted with three nodding donkeys. Or thirsty birds, in this case, as they were painted to look like toucans pecking the scrubby earth. The sun was orange and low in the sky and the wind buffeted the car. Dark killed the engine and looked straight ahead.

"Where are we? Why are we stopped?"

"Cops," he said.

She turned and saw a policeman approaching the passenger side. Dark reached over, rolled down the window, and the cop asked for his license and registration. He was young, on the beefy side, and wore a green felt hat with a wide brim. Piñon didn't make a sound. While Dark rooted around in the glove compartment, the cop removed his Ray-Bans and made eye contact with Mona in the backseat. His eyes were blue and watery.

"Was I speeding?" Dark asked.

"No," the cop said.

Dark handed him his license. He studied it briefly and then asked Mona to step out of the car.

"Me?" she asked.

"Why her?" Dark asked.

"Step out of the car, please," he said impatiently.

She looked for the door handle and remembered there wasn't one. "I can't," she said. "There's no handle."

The cop seemed nervous suddenly and touched his gun.

"You have to open it from the outside," Dark explained. "It was a police interceptor."

"Keep your hands on the steering wheel," he warned Dark. Then, to Mona, "Climb over the front seat."

———

It was awkward with Piñon in her arms. The cop told Dark to remain in the vehicle and then directed Mona to stand behind their car. Putting one foot in front of the other was difficult. Piñon squirmed, so she put him down. He lifted his leg and seemed to smile at her as he pissed on Dark's back tire.

"Are you all right?" the cop asked. He touched her lightly on the elbow.

Her mouth tasted like rotten vegetables. "I have a bad taste in my mouth," she said.

He nodded quickly, as if she were speaking metaphorically. "Someone called in this license plate, suspecting you were being kidnapped."

"Really?"

"Are you being kidnapped?"

"No," she said, and picked up Piñon. "But I think I need to lie down."

"Are you intoxicated?"

"I was, earlier," she said. "How close to L.A. are we?"

"Are you on your way to Los Angeles? You're on the wrong side of the highway. You're headed east, toward the Mojave."

That's what was wrong, she realized now: no traffic.

The cop studied Dark's license. "Where are you and Mr. Booth coming from?"

"Can I see that?" she asked, pointing to the license.

He flashed it at her like a badge, as if afraid she was going to steal it. She squinted at it. There was Dark in the photograph, with a little extra weight in his face.

"What's your relation to Mr. Booth?"

"None," she said. She felt dizzy.

"He looks a little off," the cop said.

She looked back at the car. Dark was staring at her through the back window. The sadness in his eyes reminded her of a drawing she'd been asked to interpret by a shrink. The drawing featured a little girl lying in bed with her eyes closed while an older man stood over her with a pained expression on his face. She'd been instructed to say the very first thing that came to mind. She thought the little girl was pretending to be asleep to avoid getting molested by her father, who was drunk, and that's why he was upset. But she'd told the shrink that the girl was dead or dying, and the man, her father, was grieving. It had seemed like the appropriate answer. She'd lied about every one of the drawings, but it hadn't mattered. She was still committed to the loony bin.

"I need to go home," she said.

"Where's home?"

Home was buried in a trash bag in her backyard in Taos. Home was parked in the motel parking lot. Home was licking her cheek with its dry tongue. She could take Piñon to Taos. They could dig up her portfolio. But first she needed to fetch her car. She tried to explain this to the cop.

"You want to go to Sweden?" he asked. "The country?"

"Little Sweden," she said. "It's a motel. It's nothing like Sweden."

THE END

ACKNOWLEDGMENTS

Like Mona, I tend to be more productive in other people's houses. I wouldn't have finished this book without the hospitality of Rebecca Goldman, Kym Scott, Alan Grostephan and Maria Korol, Vickie and Bill Reuell, and Shane and Krista Beagin.

Thank you, Sissy Onet, for letting me live in your weird, beautiful house and for introducing me to proper bed linens, fifty thousand bees, two donkeys, and a bunch of other stuff.

Thanks to Michelle Latiolais, forever. To Binky Urban for the opening of that first email: "Who are you? Where are you?" and for taking a chance on me. To the Whiting Foundation for picking me. To Daniel Loedel for editing out the earnestness, among other things, and to Kate Lloyd and the rest of the excellent staff at Scribner.

Thanks to my mother and stepfather for all the incredible material and to Lori and Traci for being there.

Thanks to Franny Shaw for the encouragement and gifted copyedits. To Kate Barrett and our thirty-five-year friendship and correspondence. To my friends Marylynne Drexler, Nicole and John Mullen, Kat Dunn,

ACKNOWLEDGMENTS

Laeticia Hussain, Andi State, Michelle McLaughlin, Linnea Rickard, Angela G. Sullivan, and my family at Sophia's Grotto.

To Laura Dombrowski, who I should've thanked the first time. To my old friend and first love, Glen Green.

For more love (and pain), thank you, Mark Lacoy.

Thank you, Leah Ryan.

To David Netto, who essentially designed and decorated the house in Barbarians.

And of course many, many thanks to Terry Gross, for the inspiration and imaginary companionship.

ALSO BY JEN BEAGIN
PRETEND I'M DEAD

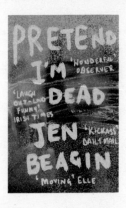

Whiting Award-winner Jen Beagin's brilliant, off-beat and deeply moving novel introduces an unforgettable character, Mona – almost twenty-four, emotionally adrift and cleaning houses to get by. Volunteering for a needle-exchange programme, she falls for a recipient she calls Mr Disgusting, who proceeds to break her heart in unimaginable ways. In search of healing, Mona decamps to Taos, New Mexico, for a fresh start. But lurking just beneath the surface are her memories of growing up in a chaotic, destructive family, and the crushing legacy of the past she left behind.

The story of Mona's journey to find her place in the world is at once fearless and wonderfully strange, true to life and boldly human, and introduces a stunning, one-of-a-kind new voice in American fiction.

'It's Mona's ballsy, kickass voice that makes this novel tick. Unreliable, sharply observant and funny.' *Daily Mail*

'One of the funniest, most twisted and freshest things I've read in a long time.'
Jess Kidd, *Observer*

© Beowulf Sheehan

Jen Beagin holds an MFA in creative writing from the University of California, Irvine. Her stories have been published in journals and literary magazines including *Juked* and *Faultline*. In 2017, she was awarded a prestigious Whiting Award for her debut novel *Pretend I'm Dead* (Oneworld 2018), which was also shortlisted for the Center for Fiction First Novel Prize. A former cleaning lady, she lives in Hudson, New York.